RACE FOR THE FRONTIER

Doggedly, she pushed on, following the line of panting men. And then, just as they were approaching the summit, she heard the thunderous echo of rotor blades and realised with a sinking heart their flight had been detected. The helicopter came out of nowhere, a grotesque shape, impossibly ugly, swaying in the air currents. They backed against the hillside, sheltering their faces from the buffeting downdraught.

Tracey wanted to run, but somehow she couldn't move. She felt her heart thumping against her ribcage. The pilot was hovering almost level with her face, struggling to keep his machine steady as his companion carefully adjusted his aim. At such close range, she realised he couldn't miss . . .

East of Everest

BOB LANGLEY

SPHERE BOOKS LIMITED

Sphere Books Limited,
27 Wrights Lane, London W8 5TZ
First published in Great Britain by
Michael Joseph Ltd 1984
Copyright © 1984 by Bob Langley
Published by Sphere Books Ltd 1987

TRADE
MARK

Set in 10/10½ pt Compugraphic Plantin

Printed and bound in Great Britain by
Cox & Wyman Ltd, Reading

CHAPTER ONE

At approximately 3.15 on the afternoon of Tuesday, 4 January, in the province of Ghyankhala in the south-west corner of Tibet, a unit of the Chinese People's Liberation Army arrived to conduct a military census and collect from the inhabitants their annual taxes of goats, yaks, butter and salt. The officer in command of this detachment was Chou Yung Yan, an ex-steelworker from the Suzhou Creek district of Shanghai who had joined the army on a special inductees' training course run by the Central Revolutionary Committee in 1981. He was small in stature, stocky in build and carried a certain brooding air often mistaken by his younger colleagues for the mark of a deep thinker. This impression was false, however, for Chou Yung Yan was not, in any sense of the word, an intelligent man; he had paid little attention to the Himalayan terrain (most of Ghyankhala's isolated valleys lay around 13,000 feet above sea level) and by pushing ahead without allowing his troops to acclimatise to the rarified atmosphere, had caused fourteen of his men to come down with altitude sickness. He had also ignored the dark clouds swirling menacingly over the Himalayan peaks, but with the clouds had come driving snow, and with the snow, savage gales which had forced Chou Yung Yan to seek refuge in the tiny scattering of yak-herders' huts cluttering the summit of Tangpoche La pass.

Ghyankhala is the most isolated province in the whole of Tibet, and the village, described on Chou Yung Yan's map as Changappo, was primitive in the extreme. The hut Chou Yung Yan had chosen as his private quarters was approximately twenty feet long and six feet wide, with a mud stove occupying its central wall. Fuel for the stove, balls of dried yak-dung, lay in an untidy heap beneath the solitary window. As in most Himalayan houses, there was no chimney. The smoke was allowed to fill the room, then seep out through cracks in the rooftiles. Despite the cold the atmosphere was suffocating, with tiny yak-butter lamps, sizzling gently on the rough-hewn table, adding to the general oppressiveness.

Chou Yung Yan was thinking of his wife, whom he had not seen for more than a year, and his two children who were attending the Fudan University in the northern sector of Shanghai, when suddenly the heavy wood door swung open, letting in spiralling spumes of wind-driven snow, and Chou Yung Yan's aide, Yang Fengying, a small heavy-jowled man from the Badain Jaran on the Yellow River, stumbled over the threshold. He bolted the door against the thundering gale and stood breathing deeply in the lamplight, his face almost obscured in the palls of black smoke which hung beneath the ceiling rafters.

'I am sorry to intrude at such a late hour,' he said, 'but we have picked up an intruder lying in the snow. A man dressed in animal skins. We found him unconscious on the outskirts of the village.'

Chou Yung Yan was amazed. The idea of anyone wandering the mountains in such outrageous weather seemed almost beyond belief. He ordered the intruder to be brought at once into his presence.

Opening the door, Fengying barked a command into the blustering storm and two soldiers stumbled into the room, clutching between them a figure completely encrusted with snow. They stopped in the centre of the floor, moisture dripping from their clothing, and Chou Yung Yan studied the newcomer intently. He was a tall man, his limbs bony and uneven, his face wolfish in appearance. He carried an elusive strength in his heavily-bearded chin, a stoic indifference to discomfort and suffering, and – more disturbing still – a faintly deranged glitter in his hard small eyes. His hair was long and tangled, and his body was clad in thick animal furs sewn haphazardly together. Around his throat was a livid weal. It appeared to have been painted there, its dull sheen reflecting the flickering glow of the butter lamps.

Chou Yung Yan stepped forward to examine the intruder more closely. The man did not flinch as the Chinaman's gaze swept over him. His eyes seemed strangely bereft of emotion.

'Has he been searched?' Chou Yung Yan demanded.

'Yes, comrade major,' one of the guards replied. 'He carried nothing. Not even a prayer wheel to convey his devotion to the gods.'

Chou Yung Yan pursed his lips. 'Who are you?' he demanded. 'Where have you come from?'

The intruder gave no answer. He seemed oblivious to his surroundings. The lamps cast ripples of light across his face and the unruly tangle of hair.

Chou Yung Yan turned on his heel, walking slowly across the floor. He was not a bright man at the best of times, and faced with such an unexpected situation, felt uncertain how to proceed. 'Bring him over to the stove,' he ordered.

The sentries pushed the man forward, steering him toward the firelight like men guiding a blind beggar.

'Warm yourself,' Chou Yung Yan told him.

The man's eyes flickered to the table. Standing beside the butter lamps was a bowl of rice Chou Yung Yan had been eating for supper. He had barely picked at it. The nausea in his stomach caused by the high altitude had killed off his appetite. Now he reached for the bowl and held it in front of the prisoner's chin. 'Is this what you want? Food? I will give you food. All you can eat. But first you must answer my questions. Who are you? Where have you come from? What are you doing here?'

The intruder gave no answer. His haggard cheeks looked like pitted hollows chiselled into the front of his skull.

Sighing, Chou Yung Yan slapped the man's face hard, jerking his head viciously to one side. The mark of the palm print left a crimson blush on the prisoner's cheek, and for the first time, Chou Yung Yan realised how dirty the man was. His hair was coarse and greasy, and a powerful odour emanated from his unwashed body.

Again, Chou Yung Yan's attention was drawn to the scar on the prisoner's throat. It ran in an unbroken circle around the entire circumference of the neck. At one point, immediately below the left earlobe, there was an angry burn-mark where the skin had crimsoned, assuming the texture of melted wax. It was, Chou Yung Yan realised, the kind of scar one might expect from an executioner's rope, and the thought brought a strange chill to his temples.

He was in a quandary what to do. Strictly speaking, all intruders in the Ghyankhala region were to be arrested and transported at once to Lhasa, but with the storm worsening by the hour, Chou Yung Yan did not see how he could spare the men as escort. On the other hand, if he left the prisoner behind

3

under guard, it meant he would have to return by this route instead of via the shorter and more direct Pilgrims' Path over the Nanjung and Trasi Danda passes. There was, he realised, a simple alternative. A quiet stroll into the driving snow. A bullet surreptitiously delivered into the prisoner's skull. The corpse would be covered within an hour, and by the time the snows melted, there would be nothing left but a heap of meaningless bones.

It was at this point Chou Yung Yan noticed for the first time a chain hanging around the captive's neck and, frowning, he tugged open the man's shirt. Nestling in the hollow of the breastbone was a silver pendant. Chou Yung Yan turned it over and studied it closely in the flickering lamplight. He could just make out an inscription engraved into the shiny metal. The words were in English, and though Chou Yung Yan understood little of the unfamiliar tongue, he was able to read haltingly: *Harold Wayne Morrill, Machusa Island University, 1977.*

The name brought an instant reaction from Chou Yung Yan. His body tensed, his features hardened, and he was about to deliver an order when suddenly he heard, above the roaring of the storm, a strange hissing sound which grew steadily louder until it was ringing in his eardrums. Chou Yung Yan had heard the sound many times before on the firing range in Jiangsu Province. It was the whine of an incoming radio-controlled rocket. He knew there were no missile launchers in his own detachment. Since there were few roads in the Ghyankhala, he had been forced to transport his equipment by yak and his men were lightly armed by necessity.

As he was thinking this, there was a thunderous eruption outside and a great ball of flame billowed past the solitary window. The door burst open and debris scattered across the threshold. Above the howl of the storm, he heard the ominous clatter of rifles opening up.

With a cry of alarm his aide, Fengying, scrambled to the doorway. For a moment, he stood outlined against the driving snow, peering into the night. Then before Chou Yung Yan's frozen gaze, Fengying's body was ripped abruptly in two by a merciless burst of machine-gun fire.

With whimpers of terror, the two guards dropped their carbines and dived under the flimsy table. Startled, Chou Yung

4

Yan turned to look at the prisoner. The man's vacant expression had vanished completely, and in its place was a murderous glitter. He had taken off the cord binding the furs at his waist and was holding it taut between his clenched fists. Silently, he moved in Chou Yung Yan's direction. Panic burst in Chou Yung Yan's chest. He is going to strangle me, he thought.

As the prisoner advanced steadily toward him, Chou Yung Yan, mesmerised with terror, backed slowly away. Where were the guards on the floor? Why didn't they come to his aid?

The intruder was smiling now, his thin lips twisting beneath the heavy beard. Chou Yung Yan's eyes focused glazedly on the taut strip of nylon cord, the intruder's features blurring in his vision. Desperately, he clawed for the pistol at his belt.

Then the man moved. In one rapid motion, he leapt forward and whipped the cord around Chou Yung Yan's neck, jerking it tight until his knuckles gleamed white through the skin. Chou Yung Yan tried to protest, but no sound issued through his flaccid lips. His eyes bulged as the coarse strand bit deep into his flesh, blocking the air from his windpipe. He felt his tongue swelling against the roof of his mouth. Frantically he tried to struggle, but the man tugged the noose tighter and Chou Yung Yan's legs folded beneath him as he slithered to the floor. He saw the ceiling rafters thick with smoke. He saw Fengying's body sprawled across the threshold, snow gathering like drifting dunes over the bloodsoaked torso. He saw men running beyond the open doorway, firing their rifles in a frenzied blur of confusion. Then the room darkened, the lamplight dimmed, and Chou Yung Yan never saw anything ever again.

Excerpt from Supplementary Fatality Report on Harold Morrill conducted by the Foreign Operations Board of the CIA, dated 7 January, 1979:

Name: Harold Wayne Morrill.   Age:22.
Height: 6′2″.   Weight: 180.
Hair: Brown.   Eyes (Color): Blue.
Special Peculiarities: None.
Date of death: December 19th, 1978.
Cause of death: Strangulation.

From CIA Files:

Date and Day – 8–1–79. Time: 1500.
Investigation disclosed that Harold Wayne Morrill (G–15782) was garrotted during the course of his duty on 19 December last year. Current location of body unknown. No announcements to be made, no proprieties observed.

Except from a letter to Head of the Foreign Operations Board, Washington DC, signed by Jerry Schonfeld, post-marked Cincinatti, 4 March, 1984.

'. . . I have not been able to get his [Harold Wayne Morrill's] death off my conscience for more than six years now, and the doctors feel only a complete change of environment will alleviate my present condition. Request permission for immediate transfer to Section 1, Department for Research and Development.'

Paris, Wednesday 19 January

Waldo Friedman was standing in the shower when the waiter brought his breakfast. He bellowed at the man to leave the tray on the bedside table and, humming softly, dried himself with the towel, pulled on his robe and wandered into the hotel bedroom.

The waiter had drawn the curtains, and beyond the balcony the Boulevard de Vauvert sparkled in the morning sunshine. Though it was still midwinter, there was a sense of approaching spring in the air which gave the day a special brilliance.

Friedman loved Paris, always had, even as a boy. His father had brought him here straight out of high school, and he had spent some of the most memorable weeks of his life wandering the narrow streets and elegant boulevards, bewitched by the magic of what he had come to regard as the world's most enchanting city.

He sat down at the breakfast table and poured his coffee, then he picked up his morning edition of the *Herald Tribune* and propped it against the flowerpot in front of him. He liked to read at breakfast, though his wife told him constantly it would ruin his digestion. Waldo missed his wife acutely. He had spent the last two months alone, negotiating a science and technology agreement with the Chinese government, on behalf of the American State Department in Washington, and the one thing he had missed during his sojourn in this delightful city had been the presence of his beloved Martha.

He had just broken off a piece of croissant and was about to dip it into his cup when the telephone rang. Reaching across, he picked up the receiver.

'Good morning, Waldo,' a voice said.

It was Jack Hirsch, Friedman's section chief in the United States. Friedman was surprised. He rarely heard from Hirsch directly unless there was some kind of emergency.

'Jack?' he muttered.

'How soon do you meet the Chinese?' Hirsch demanded briskly.

'Conference starts at ten-thirty,' Friedman said. 'What time is it over there?'

'It's two o'clock in the morning, Waldo.'

'Two o'clock in the morning? Jesus. It's barely eight a.m. here in Paris. What are you calling for?'

'Just thought I'd wish you luck. Tell you how much we're counting on you.'

Friedman blinked. 'You're not serious, are you Jack? You got up at two o'clock in the morning to tell me that?'

'Well, not exactly. The Secretary's here. We've been having a late night supper. He thought it might be a good idea if I dropped a little word in your ear.'

'You're not worrying, are you Jack?'

'Of course not, Waldo. We have the greatest confidence in you.'

'I mean, the agreement's practically in the bag. We're down to the final details. Another day, two at the outside, and it'll all be over.'

'You've done a terrific job, Waldo. I know how tough those orientals can be when it comes to the negotiating table. Nobody could have handled it better.'

'Then what are you getting so jittery about?'

'Nobody's jittery. Just thought I'd wish you luck, that's all.'

'Okay. I appreciate that. Thanks.'

'You know how important this is, Waldo. If you pull this off, the Secretary is going to be very appreciative.'

'That's nice of the Secretary.'

'I mean it, Waldo. It'll do you a great deal of good in this department. You'll call me if you have any news?'

'I promise, Jack. The minute we reach a definite conclusion, I'll be on the phone.'

'Good boy. 'Bye, Waldo.'

' 'Bye, Jack.'

Waldo was smiling as he hung up the receiver. He knew if he managed to wrap up the agreement today, it would be the highlight of his career.

Dressing quickly, he took a taxi to the Chaumont Palace. The gendarmes on duty saluted him politely and the guard at the security desk smiled as he paused to sign his name in the Visitors' Book.

'Lovely morning, M'sieur Friedman,' the guard said.

'Beautiful morning, Georges. The air is like chilled wine. Pity you can't bottle it. You'd make a fortune in New York.'

The security guard laughed. 'M'sieur Le Gras asked if you would pop into his office on your way to the conference room,' he said.

Friedman was surprised. Le Gras was the Palace supervisor, and as a rule kept himself scrupulously in the background.

Friedman took the elevator upstairs, tapped lightly on Le Gras' office door and stepped inside. Le Gras was standing in front of the window, sifting through a cardboard file. He glanced up as Friedman entered. 'Thank God you've come, Waldo,' he exclaimed, his French accent almost indiscernible beneath his perfectly modulated English. 'I tried to get you at your hotel but you'd already left.'

'What's wrong, Emile?'

Le Gras' features tightened as he moved behind his desk. 'Waldo, there's no point in you going to the conference room this morning. Nobody's there.'

Friedman blinked. 'What are you talking about? I was chatting to the Chinese only last night.'

Le Gras shook his head wearily. 'I'm sorry Waldo, it's all over. The Chinese delegation has been ordered by its government to return at once to Peking. A formal complaint has already been dispatched to your president in Washington. I'm afraid the science and technology talks have broken down.'

Excerpt from *Washington Post* dated Monday 24 January:

A State Department spokesman poured scorn today on Chinese allegations that American infiltrators have been carrying out terrorist raids within China's borders. The claim followed last week's dramatic boycotting of the science and technology talks in Paris, when the Chinese damned US military interference in the Autonomous Region of Tibet. The State Department spokesman condemned the accusations as absurd, and added that the man Peking claim to be leading the raids has been dead since 1978.

Washington DC, Monday 24 January

'Jack, I want to know what the hell is going on,' the Secretary of State said.

In the spacious office overlooking the west lawn of the White House, Jack Hirsch settled himself in the armchair and casually crossed his legs. He always affected an air of nonchalance at moments he felt tense; it was part of a reflex action stemming from the deeply-ingrained belief that the quickest way out of any tight spot was never to let others know what you were thinking. Under the surface however, he was feeling far from nonchalant, for he could see the Secretary of State was agitated and upset, and when the Secretary became upset it usually resulted in considerable upheaval for Jack Hirsch's department.

'If I knew that, Mr Secretary,' Hirsch declared, 'I'd tell you. Unfortunately, I'm still pretty much in the dark myself.'

The Secretary of State leaned back in this chair, drumming lightly on the desktop with his fingertips. He was a chunky man, solid without being plump, but the shortness of his frame and the roundness of his girth conveyed the misleading impression of obesity.

'Two months at the negotiating table,' he muttered. 'By now that agreement should have been wrapped up and safely in the can.'

'I know that, Sir.'

'Understand me, Jack, it's not the science and technology side I'm worried about, it's the American monitoring station we hoped to build on the Chinese mainland. That station would have given us the opportunity to track Soviet movements in the Sakhalin and Kuril islands off the Japanese coastline.'

'Yes, sir. I'm aware of that, Mr Secretary.'

'Are you, Jack? Are you really aware of the true strategic significance of those islands? The Russians see them as a natural defensive barrier to their eastern seaboard. From there, they can guard their submarines and destroyers sailing out of the building yards at Khabarovsk and Komsomolsk and even, if they need to, use them as a base to strike deep into the United States itself. That's why this agreement is so important. That station could be our most vital link in the Far East Theater.'

Hirsch hesitated. He hated being put on the spot like this, liked always to work out his propositions beforehand, but there was no time for niceties; he had to think on his feet.

'The fact is,' he grunted, 'the Chinese say they can no longer carry on negotiations with a country conducting armed aggression within their frontiers. They claim the CIA is leading guerrilla attacks in the Ghyankhala region of Tibet, up near the Nepalese border. They've dug up a name they can point to. A man called Morrill. Harold Wayne Morrill.'

The Secretary of State looked at him. 'Jack, are you telling me that while the State Department has been working its butt off trying to improve US relations with Communist China, the damned CIA has been jeopardising the entire project by conducting clandestine operations inside the Tibetan border?'

'No sir. The Chinese are mistaken. I talked to the CIA this morning. Harold Wayne Morrill died back in 1978.'

'You're sure?'

'He was strangled.'

'Strangled?'

'Yes. A rather unpleasant incident, I understand. I'm not fully aware of the details.'

The Secretary of State pursed his lips and leaned forward, resting his arms on the front of the desk; his face, round and solid, with thin strands of hair straddling the dome of his skull, glistened beneath the fluorescent light.

'Jack, this story gets more bizarre by the minute. A man killed in 1978 disrupts important technology talks because the Chinese believe he's leading terrorist attacks along their Tibetan border? It's nonsense, Jack. It defies credulity. We've got to thrash this out. I want the Director of the CIA in this

10

office right away. One way or another, I intend to discover the truth.'

Dharmsala, India, Monday 24 January

Losang Gyatso stood alone on the palace terrace, staring at the stars. He could see only the faint outline of the nearby mountains, their contours blurred into variable textures of grey, their snowcapped tips curiously remote against the luminous sprawl of the night sky. Before him, the land receded into the level flatness of the open plain. Lights twinkled in the village below. They looked like fairy lamps scattered across the hillside, and as Losang watched, he saw the beam of a motor car leave the village periphery and carve a slowly-moving arc across the valley beyond.

Dharmsala was divided into two sections, Lower Dharmsala, the headquarters of Kangra District which stood at 4,500 feet above sea level, and Upper Dharmsala, 2,000 feet higher, which formed the last redoubt for the Tibetan Government-in-exile and the home of His Holiness, the Dalai Lama.

Losang Gyatso was a slim man, medium-sized and narrow-cheeked, who had acquired during his years as a refugee many western habits. He did not dress in the customary orange robes of his calling but had taken to wearing American business suits, and might at first glance have been mistaken for a successful lawyer or surgeon, except for his scrupulously shaved skull. During his childhood in the city of Lhasa, Losang Gyatso had been groomed as a monk of the Tsedrung foundation, the most powerful of all the secular orders of Tibet and one which formed the immediate entourage of the god king himself.

When in 1959, the Dalai Lama had fled the Chinese occupation, Losang, then little more than a boy, had travelled with him. He had spent the formative years of his life subjected to the pressures and influences of an alien society, but in all matters other than the most external and trivial, he was a devout patriot and a man of deep religious faith. He never, for instance, touched food from which life had been taken. He taught the doctrines of Buddha and his apostles to the children in the local nursery school. He treated the sick with urine taken from their most saintly lamas. And when the occasion demanded it, he assumed the function of the State Oracle. The Tibetan Government-in-Exile seldom took any important decision without first consulting the Oracle, and on such days, Losang would throw himself into a trance to enable the god of the temple to speak through his lips. Whatever advice Losang imparted during these sessions, the Tibetans accepted and followed implicitly.

Losang was staring at the stars, and did not hear the door open as Wangdui Phinto entered the terrace behind him. When the young monk coughed politely, Losang gave an involuntary jump.

'I am sorry,' Wangdui said, 'I did not mean to startle you.'

Though he dressed in the traditional robes of the Tsedrung, Wangdui wore a pair of wire-framed spectacles with reinforced lenses which gave him a curiously eccentric air.

Losang studied him silently, his eyes glittering in the starlight. 'Have you reached a decision?' he asked.

'He is ready,' Wangdui said, inclining his head.

'You are sure? There must be no mistake.'

Wangdui nodded. 'Everyone is agreed. He has passed all the tests. There can be no further doubt.'

'Very well. Tell the others we begin our journey in three days' time. Only the strongest will be chosen. They must prepare for great hardship and physical danger.'

'They expect nothing else,' Wangdui said.

'Good.'

Losang's face was sombre but there was a strange light in his eyes, a glimmer of hidden excitement. 'The time has come then,' he whispered. 'The re-awakening.'

Wangdui nodded again. His features looked grave. 'In such circumstances, is it right to keep our secret any longer?' he asked.

Losang considered this for a moment, then without a word he turned on his heel and walked slowly down the stone staircase, Wangdui following. Taking out a key, Losang unlocked a door facing the wide garden. The room was in darkness as he entered, but starlight drifting through the barred windows cast an eerie sheen across the cobwebbed rafters. The air hung heavy with the odour of embalming liquid. In the centre of the floor, stretched out on a raised dais and completely encased in a crystal coffin, lay the body of a man. His cheeks had been carefully rouged to create the impression he was merely sleeping, but the texture of the skin, the deep craters below the

12

cheekbones, and the gossamer quality of the eyelids indicated that the corpse had been dead for a very long time.

Though the outer casing of flesh had settled against the front of the skull, creating an uncomfortable impression of the bone structure beneath, the face was that of a man in early middle age, full but not plump, and carrying a curious gracefulness which seemed out of place in the rigidity of death. The hair had been cropped close to the skull, but streaks of grey showed above the temples and the upper part of the crown.

Losang stood in silence for a moment, staring down at the waxlike features. Then slowly he bowed his head. 'Tomorrow,' he said, 'we will tell the world that the Dalai Lama is dead.'

CHAPTER TWO

Washington DC, Monday 24 January
Schonfeld was sitting in the conservatory, wrapped in heavy wool blankets. Through the window, he could see the flat, snow-covered lawns and the plane trees lining the cindered footpaths. A helicopter droned by, following its flight route along the Potomac River.

He heard the fat nurse approaching, her thighs swishing beneath her starched white skirt. In his mind, he had labelled the fat nurse 'Arbuckle'. She had heavy jowls and a thin moustache which never failed to repel him.

When she bent over his chest, she smelled of lysol and deodorant. 'And how are we feeling today, Mr Schonfeld?' she asked brightly.

'Lousy,' Schonfeld told her, resisting the temptation to add an obscene expletive. The fat nurse was unshockable, he had discovered. Unreachable even, since she parried every remark with the same brittle professional tone which irritated Schonfeld beyond reason.

She was using it now as she put down her tray and gently straightened his blankets. 'How you love to exaggerate, Mr Schonfeld.'

He watched her massive buttocks wobble as she bent over and picked up a glass from her tray. 'Time for your medication.'

'Miss Aitken, why don't you stick my medication where it'll do the most good?' he growled.

'My, my, aren't we aggressive this evening?'

She pushed the glass into his hand and with the same tight smile picked up his wrist and began to check his pulse rate. Schonfeld stared at her dully. He hated that smile. 'Miss Aitken, can I ask you something? Have you ever been laid?'

The nurse's expression scarcely faltered. As if he had never spoken, she said in the same bright voice: 'Straight down the hatch now. No sipping.'

'Don't try to evade the question. Tell me the truth. Have you?'

She tilted her head, eyeing him reproachfully. 'That's a secret between me and my conscience, Mr Schonfeld. I've told you before, you are wasting your time attempting to disgust me. I have been worked on by experts. Now finish your medication. There's someone waiting to see you in the Director's office.'

Schonfeld looked at her with surprise. 'For me? Who?'

'I really couldn't say. The gentleman didn't give his name.'

Schonfeld felt intrigued. In the six months he had been at the hospital, no one had visited him apart from his wife who, because she worked in a Georgetown delicatessen, only managed to get in on Sunday afternoons. Any change in routine was a welcome respite from boredom, he thought, and he felt his spirits rising as he drained the glass, tossed his blankets into a nearby chair and made his way along the thickly-carpeted corridors towards the Director's office. There was an air of carefully-ordered serenity about the place which got on Schonfeld's nerves. Nobody rushed. Everything was done at a leisurely, unhurried pace enhanced and encouraged by soothing music humming relentlessly over the loudspeaker system. Schonfeld was often filled with a desire to leap on the tables and bellow at the top of his voice, but had never done so. He knew such unorthodox behaviour would merely result in an unpleasant sojourn among the padded cells on the floor below.

When he reached the Director's office, he found a slender young man with rugged features sitting in the reception room.

The young man rose as Schonfeld entered. 'Mr Schonfeld?' he said.

For some reason, Schonfeld felt unaccountably nervous. I've been in here too long, he thought. 'Who are you?' he demanded.

'Simon Grant. Foreign Operations Board.'

'You work for the Company?'

'That's right. I've come to take you out of here.'

Schonfeld hesitated. He hadn't considered that possibility. The prospect of leaving his meticulously-ordered sanctuary suddenly frightened him. 'Can you do that?' he asked.

'Well, only for an hour or two. The Secretary of State wants to see you right away.'

'The Secretary of State?'

'Yes, sir.'

'Is this some kind of joke?'

'No joke, Mr Schonfeld. It's an emergency.'

Jesus, Schonfeld thought, the nearest he had been to the Secretary of State had been a fleeting glimpse in a crowded Georgetown restaurant during a political rally the previous spring. Apart from that, as far as Schonfeld could remember, he'd seen the man only on TV.

In a daze, he watched Simon Grant sign him out at the hospital registry and lead him down the steps to a shiny limousine parked on the cindered forecourt. As they drove slowly along the drive, Grant peered through the windshield at the long lines of plane trees flanking the snow-covered lawns. 'How long have you been in this place?' he asked conversationally.

'Six months,' Schonfeld told him. 'Nearly seven.'

'What's the problem?'

'I had a breakdown. I'm practically cured now though.'

Grant glanced in the driving mirror as they cruised gently through the hospital gates. 'I don't know how you stand it, all that order and uniformity. It would drive me crazy.'

Schonfeld laughed. 'You'll get used to it,' he promised. 'Don't worry, we all end up here sooner or later.'

It felt strange driving through the Washington streets again. Schonfeld had forgotten how chaotic the city could be. Traffic nipped by dizzily in all directions. A gritting truck scattered shale-chips across the highway's icy surface. The streets looked cold and cheerless.

'Where are we going?' he asked in a low voice.

'The White House,' Grant told him.

The White House. Jesus. What if they ran into the president, for Christ's sake?

At the security gate, the guards asked Schonfeld to get out of the car and stand in front of the checkpoint office. When he did so, a little red light flashed on the armoured rooftop.

'You packing heat, sir?' the sergeant asked him brightly.

For a moment, Schonfeld was puzzled, then he suddenly remembered his cigarette case. He took it out, handed it to the sergeant who slipped it into a small compartment on the office wall and closed the hatch. Instantly, the red light went out. The sergeant removed the cigarette case and handed it back to Schonfeld, smiling thinly. 'Can't be too careful,' he said.

They entered the White House by the west door and for the second time they were stopped at a security desk and carefully screened. Then a uniformed usher led Schonfeld along a maze of plushly-carpeted corridors lined with ship-prints and early sepia photographs.

The usher stopped at a door marked 'Secretary of State', tapped lightly and waved Schonfeld inside. The Secretary's personal assistant, Miles Brompton, was waiting in the reception room. He glanced at his watch, smiling. 'Good timing, Mr Schonfeld. We figured you'd be another thirty minutes yet. The Secretary is waiting for you. I'll tell him you're here.'

He popped his head into the inner office, then nodded to Schonfeld to enter. Schonfeld's heart was pounding as he walked in and heard the door softly close behind him.

The Secretary was sitting at his desk in front of the floodlit window. Facing him was Schonfeld's boss, the Director of the Central Intelligence Agency, Culver C. Zahl, and a man Schonfeld had never seen before. The man was about forty-six years old, solidly built, with a muscular neck and a heavy pugnacious jaw. He glanced up briefly as Schonfeld entered.

'Come in, Jerry,' the Secretary said, speaking as if they'd known each other for years. 'You know Mr Zahl, of course, your agency chief. This is Jack Hirsch of the State Department.'

Schonfeld nodded to the stranger then, at a gesture from the Secretary, drew up a chair and sat himself down. The Secretary studied him gravely for a moment. 'How's the treatment going?'

'Pretty good, sir,' Schonfeld said uncertainly.

'Some kind of nervous disorder, wasn't it?'

'Breakdown, sir.'

'Feeling better?'

'I'll be out in a week or two. Back to work by the end of the spring.'

'Good, good. I'm glad to hear that.'

Culver Zahl shifted in his chair, easing round so he could view Schonfeld more directly. His beefy face looked florid under the bright office lights, and sitting so close, Schonfeld could see tiny blue veins criss-crossing Zahl's nose and cheeks.

'Jerry,' Zahl said in a quiet voice, 'I want you to tell the Secretary here about Harry Morrill.'

Schonfeld felt his throat suddenly contract. For one panic-stricken moment he felt he couldn't breathe. Harry Morrill. Jesus! The name conjured up terrors he could scarcely bear to contemplate. It was like having a curtain ripped from his mind, like being forced to stare helplessly into the abyss. It had been Harry who had started the whole degenerative process in the first place. Yes, if he was really honest with himself, if he faced things squarely and truthfully, it had all begun with Harry. Other things had contributed over the years, but it had been Harry who set him on the road to self-destruction.

'I know how painful this is for you, Jerry,' Zahl said, 'but it's important, extremely important, believe me, that we hear the truth in your own words.'

Schonfeld stared at the Secretary of State across the desktop. He could see the veins on the Secretary's neck. The Secretary was watching him intently, his broad face flat and expression-less.

'Harry Morrill was my best friend,' Schonfeld whispered. 'We worked together in the seventies.'

The Secretary of State nodded. 'So I understand,' he said encouragingly. He looked like a camp counsellor or some-body's uncle from out of town.

Schonfeld looked down and noticed his hands had begun to tremble. He dug his fingers into the tops of his thighs. 'Harry was one of the Company's university recruits,' he went on slowly. 'He came in on the student junior executive deal. He'd been out to the Himalayas on a mountaineering trip and knew a bit of the local area and the language so they sent the two of us into Tibet on a provocation exercise.'

The Secretary frowned. 'What's that?'

'It's a programme designed to stir up as much mischief as possible without directly involving the US. The idea was to arm the local dissidents and encourage them to set up an organised resistance movement.'

The Secretary turned to look at Zahl with an exclamation of surprise. 'You mean we really did have American agents operating inside the Tibetan frontier?'

Zahl sighed. 'Mr Secretary, what we're discussing here happened back in the seventies. It was a different world in those days. The Chinese were our enemies, not our allies. The agency devised this programme to embarrass the central committee in Peking. To tell the truth, it never came to much. Most of the operatives returned after only a month or two. And then, as our relations with the Chinese began to improve, the exercise gradually became obsolete.'

The Secretary considered the thought for a moment, then nodded and settled back in his chair, folding his hands across his stomach. 'Please go on, Mr Schonfeld,' he said. 'I'll try not to interrupt you again.'

Schonfeld chewed at his lower lip. For God's sake, he wished he could go on. He wished he could face the whole Godawful business the way the doctors had told him to. But every time he thought about it, he felt panic rising in his chest. 'I'm sorry, sir,' he whispered, 'this is . . . very painful for me.'

'Jerry,' Culver Zahl said in an earnest voice, 'What happened is over now, you must understand that. You've got to stop feeling guilty about the past. It's absolutely imperative that you tell us, in your own words, precisely what happened in December 1978.'

Schonfeld felt the world closing in. Again, he found it difficult to breathe. Maybe the air-conditioner wasn't working properly. Absently, he reached up and undid his shirt collar. He was still wearing his hospital uniform, a light blue tracksuit with a sunrise motif on the left-hand pocket.

What was he scared about? he thought. The past couldn't hurt any more. As Zahl had said, the past was over. There was no need for panic, no need for fear. It was only a question of getting it right. Remembering. He could do that surely. Of course he could.

Haltingly, and in a voice utterly drained of emotion, Schonfeld began to speak.

Tibet, December 1978
Schonfeld heard the shots as he crawled from the tent. They sounded muffled and far away, then he realised the impression was illusory, the noise having been absorbed by the heavy falls of snow. The land lay locked in a hush of wintry moonlight. Westward, Schonfeld could see the great curl of the Namgyal glacier gleaming like a jewel in the chill mountain night. Craggy peaks leaned into the dourly swirling sky.

Beside him, Chamdo had frozen in his tracks at the first staccato outburst, but now, reaching back, he picked up his submachine gun, his dark face tense and alert, his almond eyes glittering in the shadow clusters.

Schonfeld waited, holding his breath. The shots came again, less muffled this time, drawing closer. He heard a metallic click as Chamdo switched his safety catch to 'fire'. Schonfeld shook himself, rising to his feet. The night was silent now, the snow-capped peaks and gullies wrapped in the icebound stillness. Schonfeld knew the shots could mean only one thing. The raid had gone wrong.

Swiftly, he glanced around. The spot on which they had pitched the tent was protected on three sides by a jagged ice-glazed wall. Even in the darkness, Schonfeld could see the dull gleam of verglas on the pitted slabs. North, the land slopped steeply downwards, making it impossible for anyone approaching from that direction to spot them until the last possible moment. Nevertheless, if the Chinese came swarming down from the glacier, the tent would be unmistakable in the moonlight.

Quickly, Schonfeld made his decision. He and Chamdo had been left behind to guard the explosives. But if Morrill was in trouble, it was clearly Schonfeld's job to help him.

He ordered Chamdo to dismantle the tent and conceal it among the boulders, then he shouldered his carbine and strapped on his wooden snow *raquettes*, clipping his feet firmly into place.

'Where are you going?' Chamdo hissed, fumbling with the guyropes.

'To find out what the hell is going on,' Schonfeld told him.

'Remain in the gully. If the others return, join them. If not, we'll make fresh plans in the morning.'

He set off across the snow, plagued by a feeling of deep foreboding. The shots had been close. Too close. Whoever had fired them was almost within reaching distance.

It took Schonfeld forty minutes to traverse the tip of the glacier, and when he reached the spot where the snow ended and the first craggy outcrops began, he removed the *raquettes*, strapped them carefully across his shoulders, and began to scramble steadily upwards. The track dipped and bobbed to the spine of a narrow ridge. On its summit he paused, breathing heavily, and peered across the valley below. In the eerie moonlight, he spotted miniscule figures climbing up the precipitous hillslope.

Schonfeld fumbled in the leather case around his neck and took out his field glasses. Raising them to his eyes, he swivelled the lens into focus. Closer, the tiny figures looked more menacing. They were heavily-armed, and in the moonlight, their padded jackets and fur-lined caps gave them a bulkiness which seemed almost sub-human. Chinese.

Grunting with alarm, Schonfeld swung the glasses up the hillslope, following the line of screefalls and rocky outcrops. He spotted a crumpled figure sprawled among the boulders on the ridge tip, and felt his stomach tighten. Morrill. It had to be Morrill. And he was alone.

Quickly, Schonfeld slipped the glasses back into their leather case and began to scramble along the twisting roof, his breath rasping in his throat. Inside his nostrils, the tiny hairs froze into rigid needlepoints in the chill frosty air.

He heard Morrill groaning softly as he approached.

'Harry,' Schonfeld breathed, dropping to his side, 'what happened?'

Morrill didn't answer. His cheeks looked ghastly in the moonlight. His mouth was open, and spittle traced a glistening web over the beard stubble on his chin and throat. There was an ugly patch of scarlet on the front of his heavy Duvet.

'How bad are you hit?' Schonfeld whispered.

Morrill's lips moved almost imperceptibly. 'I think my ribs are busted.'

Schonfeld swore softly under his breath. 'What happened to the others?'

'They moved northward, to try and draw off the patrol.'

Schonfeld unzipped the front of Morrill's Duvet, peeling it back to examine the wound beneath. It looked ugly and dangerous, bone splinters peeking through the blue-rimmed flesh.

'Bad?' Morrill whispered weakly.

'Bad enough. There's damn all I can do here. Think you can walk?'

'Not a chance, coach. I've had it.'

Schonfeld sank back on his haunches, feeling a terrible weakness settle in his diaphragm. 'I can't leave you, Harry. The Chinese are coming up the ridge, for Christ's sake.'

Slowly, Morrill's eyes focused and he peered up at Schonfeld without speaking. Schonfeld knew what was going through his mind. Their orders had been explicit. Under no circumstances were any Americans to fall into Chinese hands.

Schonfeld felt panic rising in his chest. 'Come on, Harry,' he snapped, sliding his arm under Morrill's shoulders, 'let's get you on your feet.'

Morrill winced with pain as the movement wrenched his side. He pulled back, studying Schonfeld calmly in the moonlight. 'It's no use, Jerry.'

'For Christ's sake, at least let's give it a try.'

'I can't move, I tell you. My whole chest feels like it's coming apart. I'm sorry, coach.'

Schonfeld felt something catch at his lungs, as if the air had been inexplicably drained of oxygen. His body suddenly started to tremble.

Morrill peered at him closely, his eyes gentle in the moonlight. 'You can do it,' he whispered.

Schonfeld shook his head. 'I can't,' he choked.

'Sure you can.'

'No. No, no, no.'

'Come on, Jerry. Get it done and get the hell out of here.'

Suddenly, Schonfeld realised he was crying. Tears issued from his eyes and tumbled down his cheeks. 'I can't,' he wailed.

'Come on, Jerry. You know you've got to.'

Whimpering, Schonfeld lowered his head. Nausea swept through his stomach, and his vision blurred. The rocks seemed to ripple in and out like strips of india-rubber.

'I . . . daren't use the carbine,' he whispered. 'The Chinese are too close.'

21

Morrill nodded. His eyes looked strangely withdrawn, as if some essential part of him had slipped out of alignment. Without a word, he lifted his hand and Schonfeld saw, clutched between his fingers, the nylon cord Morrill kept strapped around his waist. The cord was standard equipment for operatives working in the field. It could be used for a diversity of purposes, restraining prisoners, binding fractures, fastening equipment together. It could also be used for strangulation. The classic method, the garrotte.

The sobs racking his chest, Schonfeld took the cord from Morrill's hand and began to twist it tightly around his fists. A strange numbness spread through his trunk, and he felt delirious as if his brain had ceased to function, leaving him not really a man any more but a piece of organic matter, unfeeling, unknowing.

When he left several minutes later, Morrill's face was turned to the sky. His cheeks were pale, his features still, and his eyes, staring sightlessly at the stars, displayed the blue-marbled milkiness of violent death.

As Schonfeld finished his story, his voice suddenly faltered and he bent forward, burying his face in his hands. Across the desk, the Secretary of State studied him in silence. He had spent his life making decisions which, put into practice, could affect the destinies of millions of people. But listening to Schonfeld, he realised with a chill that there were men making decisions far more desperate than his, and dealing with life and death in the most direct and violent manner. Schonfeld's action had been taken in the field, a war situation. Here in the sanctity of the crowded office, it sounded shocking and brutal.

'That's all?' the Secretary breathed as Schonfeld lapsed into silence.

Schonfeld nodded.

'And you're sure he was dead?'

'I'm sure.'

'How?'

Schonfeld looked at him. 'Mr Secretary, I know a dead man when I see one.'

'Are you a doctor, Mr Schonfeld? Have you had any direct medical experience in determining clinical death? The human body goes through various stages before one can definitely state

22

life has left it completely. From what I gather, it isn't easy strangling a man.'

Schonfeld looked desperately pale. He rubbed his checks with his fingertips and the massaging brought a semblance of colour to his pallid skin. 'I'm a pro, sir,' he said weakly. 'I know Harry Morrill is dead because I strangled him like a pro.'

'But you were upset. You said yourself you were crying. Isn't it just possible that in the excitement of the moment you went off without finishing the job?'

Schonfeld frowned. 'What are you getting at, Mr Secretary?'

The Secretary of State leaned forward. 'Jerry,' he said in a gentle voice, 'the Chinese claim not only that Harry Morrill is still alive, but that he's leading resistance attacks along the Tibetan frontier. Because of that, they've broken off vital science and technology talks with the United States.'

Schonfeld stared at him uncomprehendingly. 'I can't believe it,' he whispered.

'I realise how incredible it must sound, particularly to the man who's been under the impression for years that he killed him.'

'I'd swear Harry Morrill was dead,' Schonfeld muttered, shaking his head.

'Well, let's assume for the sake of argument that Harry Morrill, by whatever miracle, is *not* dead. Let's also assume that the raids are genuine, and that Morrill is, as the Chinese claim, leading them. Does that seem to you a reasonable proposition?'

Schonfeld's lips moved wordlessly, his eyes glistening with tears. His voice, when it came, sounded thin and strained. 'I . . . I just don't know, sir.'

The Secretary leaned back in his chair, locking his hands in front of him, interlacing the fingers. He looked like a preacher about to deliver a sermon.

'Gentlemen,' he declared, 'this man must be stopped. We can't afford to lose that Far East toehold. We sent him in there, it's up to us to get him out.'

He peered questioningly at Culver Zahl who shifted uncomfortably on his seat. 'Mr Secretary, we have no system of recall in such a primitive area. When the programme started back in the seventies, the idea was that all our operatives would withdraw under their own steam.'

'Can't you get a message through?'

'Have you any idea what that country's like? It's the wildest region in the whole of Tibet. No roads, no communications. It takes a week to travel a few dozen miles, that's if the blizzards don't wipe you out, or the bandits, or the militia.'

'Supposing we put in a man to find him?'

Zahl sighed. 'We could send in a whole goddamed army and they could wander around those peaks for years without getting any closer to Harry Morrill than you and I are right this minute.'

'Speaking personally,' Jack Hirsch grunted, 'I've always found the Chinese to be a reasonable people. Why don't we tell them the truth? Admit we had this programme back in the seventies, tell them what's happened, and ask for their help.'

The Secretary shook his head. 'Out of the question. Once we openly admit to this, they could use the information to blast US policy around the world. Whatever we decide upon must be handled delicately, and without Chinese knowledge or approval.'

A silence fell in the little office. Schonfeld heard the droning of a television set on the floor above. A clock chimed in the corridor, and someone passed by carrying a tray of glasses.

Schonfeld felt a heavy lassitude pervading his limbs. 'There is a way,' he announced suddenly.

They turned to look at him and he ran his fingers nervously down the front of his tracksuit. 'Morrill had a wife, a British girl whom I happen to know now works as a television producer in the north of England. Like Harry, she's a keen mountaineer. If we could persuade her to go to Tibet, and if by some miracle Harry really is alive, he'd be bound to hear of her arrival.'

'How's that?' the Secretary asked.

'The Himalayan telegraph. One yak-herder tells another. News spreads through those mountains with the speed of a prairie fire. Now I reckon that any man is bound to feel curious when he hears his wife is wandering around the peaks of Tibet. My guess is, if we can get Tracey Morrill out there, Harry will do his damnedest to make contact.'

The Secretary thought for a moment. His eyes were gleaming. 'By God, I think you've got it,' he whispered. 'She could go in through Nepal. She'd need visas and entry permits, of course. How long would that take?'

'Ordinarily, two to four weeks,' Zahl said, 'but I'm sure we can cut a few corners with the Nepalese embassy.'

'No,' the Secretary declared sharply, 'I don't want the CIA taking any part in this. The situation's volatile enough. It's a State Department matter and our people will handle it.'

'But Mr Secretary,' Jack Hirsch protested, 'we know nothing about this woman. What makes you think she'll even agree to go?'

'That's Friedman's job, Jack. Get him to fly to England first thing in the morning. It's up to Waldo to talk her into it.'

England, Friday 28 January
Tracey sat in the crowded control room and watched the panel of TV screens in front of her. The master screen was illuminated by a small red bulb. As Tracey studied the flickering images carefully, the camera on screen number three locked into position, picking up a vivid close-up of Jack Nicholson's face. The actor, momentarily shaken, was staring blankly into space. He had just been asked by the interviewer how he handled the problems of middle age and the question had confused him.

'Camera three,' Tracey hissed softly, 'get that blood. Get it.'

She pressed a button on the desk in front of her, and instantly the image on the master screen switched to a tight shot of Nicholson's features.

'Fifteen seconds to end credits,' the P A announced.

'Wind up Bertrand slowly,' Tracey commanded, speaking through her intercom to the studio floor manager.

Nicholson, having considered the question carefully, answered with a joke, his lips twisting into a puckish, mischievous smile. His confusion had vanished. He looked relaxed and sure of himself, a man enjoying his situation and the challenge of the moment.

Tracey listened to the interviewer expertly winding up as the PA chanted:

'Eight, seven, six, five, four . . .'

'Roll end-credits,' Tracey snapped. 'Fade mikes one and two. Pull back to camera four.'

The voices faded and music blared from the loudspeaker as the master screen displayed a long shot of the two participants chatting amiably while the names of the studio staff slid by in front of them.

'Thirty seconds to end-of-programme,' the PA announced.

Tracey watched the pointer on the panel wall flicking rhythmically. As the music rose in a crescendo, the picture on the master screen faded and a voice declared: 'That's it, folks. We're off the air.'

Leaning forward, Tracey switched on her loudspeaker. 'Thank you one and all,' she said. 'Anyone who's interested, there'll be drinks in the hospitality room afterwards.'

The light switched on and an air of subtle relief passed through the control room. The vision mixer leaned back in her chair, stretching languidly.

'Worked like a charm,' she muttered. 'Maybe we can sell it on the network.'

Tracey gathered her papers together and fastened them into her clipboard. She was trying to look composed. It was part of the image she liked to create. Some directors threw tantrums, others affected an air of almost casual disinterest whilst the programme was in progress. Tracey did none of these things. She was cool, efficient and professional. But once the end-credits had rolled, she had to work hard to hide the strain.

'I think I'd better go downstairs and make my presence felt,' she said. 'We don't want Mr Nicholson to think he's being neglected.'

She blinked as she stepped from the darkened control room into the brightness of the winter sunshine. It was something she never got used to, recording programmes in the early morning. In the old days, when everything had been live, she had geared herself to a slow build-up of tension culminating when the programme went on the air in the evening. But few transmissions were live any more. Even the simplest were taped as a matter of course. Tracey often regretted the passing of the old-time broadcasts.

She was a tall girl with high cheekbones, brown shoulder-length hair and a sensual, expressive mouth who had entered television after a brief period as a reporter on a local newspaper and had taken to the work with a facility which had surprised her. She had ascended rapidly from the position of researcher on the evening news magazine to the role of studio director, a job she handled with flair and imagination. She was, she knew, good at what she did, and this knowledge sustained her greatly. But Tracey Morrill seldom asked herself if she was happy. Since the death of her husband, she had thrown herself body and soul into her work. It was not that Harry's death had shattered her, not really. Quite the opposite, if the truth were known. They had lived together for such a little time, and she had certainly never understood him. But in a curious way, their marriage had been an anchor of sorts. Now that he had gone, there was only the work. Nothing else held any meaning.

Her achievements in such a fiercely competitive world had imbued her with a confidence she often wished would extend to the more personal areas of her life, for since her husband's death, even Tracey herself had to admit she had not been lucky with the opposite sex. There had been men, of course. Several. She was not the kind to shut herself in a nunnery. She had always loved the sensual things, the physical things. Not just sex. Climbing mountains, watching sunsets, feeling the wind in her hair. She sometimes felt they were bound together in some inextricable way. But the trouble was, she seldom responded to men unless the suitor was totally ruthless and utterly self-motivated, in which case Tracey, with the instinctive blindness of a lemming bound on its own destruction, would fall hook, line and sinker. She seemed to have a death wish where men were concerned. Whenever she met a decent one, kind, thoughtful, honest and straightforward, her interest appeared inexplicably to dwindle. She often wished her success could have been the other way around – happiness and stability with someone she loved, instead of accomplishment in a business so notoriously mercurial and insecure, but she accepted her position with the grace that lack of choice engenders, seeing in the acclaim of her colleagues the binding force which held her life together.

When she arrived at the hospitality room, Jack Nicholson was chatting amiably to the programme interviewer, Bertrand. Around them, sipping drinks, clustered the Nicholson entourage, agents, secretaries, managers, minders. Everyone was babbling brightly, congratulating each other on the brilliance of the programme. Nicholson himself was polite but withdrawn. He was an attractive man, she thought, even though some of those youthful good looks had begun to sag a little. Age, the great equaliser. And yet, somehow with men the ageing process became almost a virtue. What could be more attractive than a masculine lived-in face? It simply wasn't fair.

Tracey introduced herself and made polite conversation for a minute or two, then Nicholson glanced at his watch and decided it was time to leave. 'We have to be in Manchester by twelve,' he explained apologetically. 'This entire tour has been hung on a whistle-stop schedule.'

As Tracey escorted the group to the door, she thought: how easily I've slipped into the mould. There was a time, God knows, I would have run a mile with fright rather than face a man like Nicholson. Now I take it all in my stride, just like I've been born to it.

She ought to feel grateful for that, she supposed, but in some curious way the thought depressed her, as if the ease and facility with which she handled other people denoted the kind of superficial gloss she had always hated in the television industry. Am I becoming hard? she wondered.

At the studio entrance, she shook hands all round, allowed Nicholson to kiss her briefly on the cheek, then watched as the party clambered into their chartered limousine and pulled out into the stream of traffic.

Turning, she re-entered the lobby, humming softly under her breath. Her feeling of dissatisfaction had already faded. Everyone was a victim of the world they lived in, she thought. You couldn't avoid that. Outside influences, the demands of necessity. But in its brittle way, television imposed a different kind of pressure. The need to be sharp and ruthless. Fast on one's feet. Evasive and two-faced. God knew, she had never professed to be an angel. She liked the work, she did it well. But sometimes she wished . . . oh, how she wished she could hold on to her own identity.

The girl at the reception desk caught Tracey's eye. 'Someone's waiting to see you in the Visitors' Room,' she said.

'Man or woman?' Tracey asked.

'A Mr Waldo Friedman. Claims to be from the American State Department.'

Tracey frowned. 'Are you serious?'

'That's what his card said. I told him you were in the recording studio, but he insisted he'd wait all day if necessary.'

Tracey lifted her eyebrows. 'Well, we'd better find out what he's after, hadn't we?' she muttered.

The Visitors' Room was deserted except for a small man in a blue suit who was reading the magazines by the coffee table. He was solidly-built with a square face, pleasant features and grey hair balding over the forehead. He stood up as she entered.

'Mr Friedman?' she said, 'I'm Tracey Morrill.'

Smiling, the man took off the half-moon reading spectacles he was wearing and pushed them into his jacket pocket. He came forward, holding out his hand.

'Mrs Morrill, I'm glad you could see me.'

'The receptionist said you were from the American State Department?'

'That's correct.'

He fumbled in his wallet and handed her his ID card. She examined it briefly before passing it back. 'Are you sure this isn't some kind of mistake?'

'No mistake, Mrs Morrill. Not if you're the wife of Harold Wayne Morrill of Cincinatti, Ohio.'

He glanced around. 'Is there some place we can talk in private? Your office maybe?'

She laughed. 'My office is about as private as Piccadilly Circus. At the moment, it's bustling with producers trying to sort out the running order for tomorrow's LE show.'

'Then do you think we might take a stroll outside?'

She hesitated, eyeing him warily. 'Why should we?'

'Because what I have to tell you involves a matter of some delicacy, Mrs Morrill, and I can't afford to have our conversation overheard.'

She studied him in silence for a moment. He had a pleasant face, plain and reassuring. It was the kind of face a person instinctively trusted. 'Let me get my coat,' she said.

They left the studio and walked down the bank to the waterfront. Lines of seagulls cluttered the roofs of dark warehouses, creating splashes of white against the corrugated metal. A cargo ship chugged majestically through the oily river water, its banners waving. Skeletal dockcranes creaked and clattered, unloading cargo from a Norwegian freighter.

'I didn't realise the city was a port,' Friedman muttered.

'One of the biggest in the country. It's also a major ship-building centre. The yards lie near the mouth of the river.'

Friedman was silent for a moment as he strolled at her side. The smell of tar and leaking diesel fumes drifted into their nostrils.

'I see you've held on to your married name, Mrs Morrill,' he said at last.

'No reason not to. I'd already started working in journalism when Harry . . . when Harry died. It seemed pointless changing for change's sake.'

She glanced at him. 'What has my husband to do with all this?'

The wind caught a few strands of Friedman's grey hair, fluttering them over his eyes. Absently, he brushed them back. 'I'm afraid I have something of a shock for you. What would you say if I told you we are in possession of certain facts which suggest Harry Morrill may still be alive?'

She stopped walking and stared at him intently. 'What are you talking about?'

'You always imagined he'd been killed in a climbing accident, correct?'

She nodded.

'Were you aware, Mrs Morrill, that your husband worked for the CIA?'

'That's nonsense.'

'He didn't tell you?'

'Harry wasn't the type. He was . . .'

She tried to think of a word to describe Harry. Unworldly. That was the best she could do. It was his curious haunted air which had attracted her in the first place. And yet 'unworldly' wasn't accurate either. Harry had been nobody's fool. If he'd had any fault at all, it was simply that he had been an idealist in a world which had no further use for idealists.

'He just wasn't the type, that's all,' she finished lamely.

Friedman began to walk again, thrusting his hands into his jacket pockets.

'I realise how difficult it must be to accept the idea,' he told her. 'We always imagine we know our marriage partners better than anyone else. That's why it's such a shock when we experience moments of betrayal.'

'You don't understand. I scarcely knew Harry at all. We were children when we married. He was twenty-three, I was twenty-one. The whole thing lasted barely five months.'

'And then he died?'

'That's right. I felt bad about it at the time. But not the way you would expect to feel at the death of someone you really love. We spent too little time together. He was still a stranger.'

Friedman was quiet for a moment, and Tracey let her thoughts drift impulsively back to the man she had married. He had never been handsome; well, not really handsome, not in the filmstar sense. But he had carried about him a curious kind of dignity that had appealed to her from the very beginning. And yet, had she ever really known Harry Morrill? Was it possible for any human being to know a man so complex, so introvert? She had tried all right, she had tried hard in the early days. But Harry had wanted more than she could offer, a kind of purity to which she could never aspire.

Friedman paused as they reached the water's edge. He stood on the dock, peering down, his nostrils wrinkling as the odour of refuse and sewage drifted toward them. Gulls wheeled and dipped over the effluent, squawking shrilly.

'Mrs Morrill, I'm going to tell you something which I want you to treat with the strictest confidence. It involves certain aspects of international diplomacy which are sometimes necessary to our survival, but not always to our liking. At the time of your husband's death, he was not, as you'd imagined, a fledgling architect. He did not go to the Himalayas on a climbing trip, and he did not die by disappearing into a crevasse. He had been recruited into the CIA during his final term at university, and selected to take part in a special programme designed to create disorder along the Tibetan border.'

Tracey frowned at him. 'Are you telling me my husband was a spy?'

'Not exactly. But he *was* under government orders.'

'And now?'

'We'd assumed, like you, that he was dead. In 1978, Morrill was wounded during a raid on a Chinese military post. The orders from Washington were that no Americans were to fall into Chinese hands. Morrill's colleague strangled him with a piece of nylon cord.'

'My God,' Tracey breathed, staring at him with disbelief.

'I know, I know. My reaction was the same, Mrs Morrill. But these people live in a different world to you and me. To them, expediency is the important thing. Human beings scarcely matter. However, the Chinese are now claiming that Harry Morrill is still alive. It's possible, of course . . . just remotely possible . . . that our man didn't do a very good job. He was understandably upset at the time. He could have miscalculated. A new wave of violence has flared up along the

Tibetan border. The dissidents are hitting Chinese installations, then escaping back over the line into Nepal. The Chinese believe your husband is leading them.'

'It's incredible,' she whispered.

'I agree. If you want to know the truth, Mrs Morrill, until a day or so ago, I had no idea such things went on. But the problem we're facing here is this. The American State Department is currently negotiating with the Chinese on a series of science and technology agreements which would pave the way toward greater co-operation between our two countries. What's happening in Tibet is destroying the whole process. If your husband really is alive, we've got to pull him out of there.'

'Why come to me?'

'You are, I understand, a mountaineer yourself?'

'I've done a bit, but it's only a hobby.'

'Nevertheless, you are familiar with the problems of moving through high mountains.'

'You want me to go to Tibet?'

'That's what we're asking, Mrs Morrill. See if you can locate your husband, talk to him, explain that the past is over, the Chinese aren't our enemies any more. Explain how his actions are jeopardising relations between our two countries. And bring him back, Mrs Morrill, back where he belongs. I'm afraid, however, it will have to be done independently. Above all, we cannot ourselves be seen to be involved. We'll give you all the help we can before you set off, but once you're out there, you'll be on your own. Everything – arrangements, organisation, planning – will have to be handled by you.'

She stared at him. 'Give me one reason why.'

'He's your husband, Mrs Morrill.'

'He's a stranger. I can scarcely remember what he looked like. I told you, we were practically children.'

'Well, we'll cover your expenses, of course. And I've also been empowered to pay a substantial sum of money into your bank account once the expedition is successfully completed.'

'I don't need money, Mr Friedman. I make enough to keep me happy. There are more important things in life than the pursuit of wealth and riches.'

'Then what about adventure, Mrs Morrill? What climber can resist a chance to visit the highest mountains in the world?

Think of it. The home of Everest, Annapurna. You'll see peaks few westerners ever set eyes on.'

'I climb for pleasure,' she told him flatly. 'I can see all the peaks I want in the picture books.'

Friedman kicked a pebble into the water, watching it disappear with a soft sploosh. 'I'm told you're a talented director, Mrs Morrill. It must be frustrating to spend so much time tucked away in a tiny regional station in the middle of nowhere.'

Tracey said nothing. He turned to look at her, his lips twisting into a wry smile. 'I have certain connections with NBC,' he said.

'What kind of connections?'

'Friends.'

'And?'

'Locate your husband, bring him out of Tibet, and I'll do my damnedest to get you a post in New York.'

Tracey stared at him in silence. Damn the man. Was she really so easy to read?

Friedman's face assumed an expression of infinite patience. 'No need to decide right away,' he said. 'It's only four a.m. in Washington DC. There'll be no one at the office until after eight-thirty. You can let me have your answer then.'

Tracey's brain was reeling as she opened the apartment door. The meeting with Friedman had been a bombshell, taking her utterly by surprise. It had brought back aspects of her life she had thought long over. Her husband Harry. Her marriage. Their honeymoon in New Orleans. The memories seemed strange and disjointed, as if they had happened to somebody else. It had been a transitory affair, swept along by the impetus of the moment. They had touched only in bed, and then only for that frenzy of fulfilment. Elsewhere he'd seemed distant and aloof, a man she'd scarcely recognised, much less understood.

Tracey's feelings were in a turmoil. She had already told Friedman she accepted his offer. The possibility of the NBC post had been too tempting to refuse. Friedman, of course, had been delighted. She must leave at once, he'd said. Everything had been arranged. Visas, travel documents. She must contact the television studio and ask for an immediate leave of absence.

His briskness had angered her. How sure they had been of her decision. They had played her deftly, she thought, like a fish on a line.

And what would happen now if she found Harry still alive? Legally, their marriage was still binding. Would he expect to take up exactly where he'd left off? No chance. She had made up her mind on that point. There could be no question of a new beginning. She was a different person. Her hopes, dreams, aspirations had completely altered.

Brian was lying on the sofa as she entered the sitting room. He was sipping a can of beer and watching a boxing match on the television set. Brian was thickset and stocky, with curly hair and a heavy black beard. He worked as a programme artist in the television design department, and for fourteen months now they had been living together as man and wife.

Tracey had begun to despair about Brian. In the beginning, he had carried an air of nonconformity and rebellion she'd both recognised and approved of. He had seemed, during those early days, exciting and unusual, and she had laughed in admiration at the way he consistently defied authority and somehow managed to survive. But as the months progressed, their relationship had deteriorated. Brian, she discovered, had a possessive streak that was almost pathological. His attempts to restrict her, to bend her into the rigid structure of his own existence were destroying her life. They quarrelled bitterly and continuously, and she scarcely knew what held them together any more, unless it was Brian's reluctance to relinquish his power over her.

He looked up as she entered the room. 'I thought you said you were working late tonight,' he grunted.

'I had to come home and pack,' she told him, averting her eyes.

His brows lifted. 'Pack?' he echoed.

'I'm going to London. I have to leave immediately.'

He studied her in silence for a moment. Then he put down his beercan and eased himself higher on the sofa. 'Just hold on there a minute. We haven't even discussed this.'

'Brian,' she sighed, 'you're not my keeper. It's part of my job. You have no right to interfere with my job.'

'I've looked at the schedules,' he snapped. 'You're pencilled in on the studio list for the next two months.'

'It has nothing to do with the studio. I've asked for a leave of absence. I've been hired by a private agency to make a film in the Himalayas.'

'The Himalayas?' Brian almost choked. 'For Christ's sake, you could be gone for weeks!'

'I expect so.'

His eyes smouldered under the heavy brows. Rising to his feet, he walked forward and switched off the television set. 'You must take me for a bloody fool,' he muttered.

'Brian, don't be silly.'

'The Himalayas. You expect me to believe that shit?'

'Brian, please.'

'You're planning to leave me.'

Tracey felt her spirits sink as she recognised the mood he was in. Volatile and dangerous. She had been through it all before. 'No Brian,' she said wearily, 'I think I *should* leave you. I think we both realised a long time ago that this affair is already over. But one thing you can count on, I won't sneak away like a thief in the night.'

The assurance seemed to pacify him, but only for a moment. She saw the aggression creep back into his face and he growled: 'You think you're pretty hot stuff, don't you?'

'Brian, you're talking nonsense.'

'You think you're the hottest thing in British television.'

'You know that's not true.'

'You think I should fall down on my knees in gratitude just because you deign to recognise my existence.'

'Oh, for God's sake, Brian,' she snapped, and hurried into the bedroom.

She was holding on to her temper with an effort. If they quarrelled again, what in God's name would it accomplish? Yet she knew he wanted to, and her legs felt weak as the tension gathered inside her.

Why hadn't she left him months ago, when his savage outbursts had first started?

Standing on a chair, she lifted her suitcase from the top of the wardrobe and opening it, began to pack her things. After a moment, Brian appeared in the doorway. 'What are you doing?'

'What does it look like?'

'Put those clothes back in the drawer.'

'Go stuff yourself, Brian,' she answered mildly. 'You have no authority over me.'

'Damn you, I said put them back.'

Lunging forward, he grabbed at the suitcase. Tracey pulled it out of his reach and instantly, moving with a reflex action which startled her, he slapped her hard across the cheek.

'You . . . bastard,' she choked, her eyes moistening with fury.

For a fractional second they stood facing each other, Tracey's chest heaving, Brian's skin mottled with rage. Then without hesitation, she swung her fist and hit him squarely between the eyes. Blood spurted from his nostrils and she watched his lips draw back in a savage grin. Seizing her by the wrists, he threw her on the bed. 'You bitch,' he growled huskily.

She felt his hands sliding under her sweater, groping for her breasts, and tore wildly at his hair. She knew what was going to happen. Violence excited him, always had. He liked to feel her struggle, liked to taste his power over her. It was the unacceptable element in his nature. She shuddered with revulsion as she felt him touching her flesh. 'Stop that,' she hissed. 'Stop it, I tell you.'

But he was already tearing at her jeans, pulling them down over her tighs and knees. His eyes bulged insanely, and there were purple blotches on his cheeks. I won't let him rape me, she thought wildly. I'm not an animal. I won't let him treat me like an animal.

Desperately, she lashed out with her feet, but the heavy pressure of his muscular body held her helplessly in place.

He reached down to unzip himself and she felt the pressure of his erection against her thigh. Oh God, she thought, jabbing her elbow into his throat. His eyes tilted and his lips drew back in a grimace of pain. He groped up and pushed her arm away, twisting it viciously behind her neck. She smelled the odour of beer on his breath, felt the brush of his hair against her cheek, and with a quick dart of her head sank her teeth into his ear. He jerked back, yelling out loud, and she glimpsed the swift blur of his hand as he struck her forcefully across the mouth. Her brain jolted, her vision blurred. The salty sting of blood dribbled between her lips. She lay gasping, momentarily stunned, and taking advantage of her hesitation, he positioned himself between her legs and drove sharply inside her. She cried out as he entered, but he held her in place with his hands around her throat as his hips pumped rhythmically away. There was no finesse to his assault. She knew he cared little for her pleasure or his own. His motive was simple. Humiliation. He was establishing his 'rights', savouring his power, putting her in her place. She felt her body shudder with loathing.

The coupling ended almost as quickly as it had begun. His muscles tightened and she heard a guttural moaning sound issue from his throat as he went into a frenzied spasm and suddenly relaxed. For a long moment, he lay breathing deeply, then withdrawing his penis, he rolled over and zipped himself up.

Choking with anger, she watched him rise and stumble from the bedroom. A moment passed, then the outside door slammed as he left the apartment and clattered down the staircase to the street below. He was going to the pub. He would return later, drunker than ever. Suddenly, she realised she was trembling all over. Damn him, she was not the bastard's plaything. How could she ever have allowed such a destructive relationship to continue?

Rising from the bed, she took off the rest of her clothes and went into the shower. There was little point in waiting for morning, she thought. When Brian returned, there would be more quarrelling, more cursing, more fighting. She'd had enough. Enough to last her a lifetime. It was over at last. Whatever happened, she was never coming back.

Returning to the bedroom, she dressed quietly, packed her things and left the apartment for ever.

CHAPTER THREE

Dharmsala, India, Friday 28 January

The sound of gongs echoed through the palace corridors. The air was heavy with the odour of incense and melting butter. As Losang Gyatso entered the darkened prayer hall, he heard the chanting of the monks ringing in his ears like the gentle lapping of distant water. They were sitting in rows, crosslegged on the ground, each man reading from silk-bound scriptures in front of him. They were dressed, not in their traditional robes of orange and gold, but in modern Duvet jackets, padded over-trousers and heavy fur-lined boots designed for hard travelling at high-altitude.

As Losang listened, their voices rose into a single hypnotic chant – '*Om mani padme hum*' – 'Hail to the Jewel in the Lotus'. A bearer moved along the rows of kneeling figures, filling each man's bowl with sickly-sweet buttered tea. At the side of each bowl lay a single *torma*, a sacrificial cake decorated with cones of coloured butter and representing an offering to the gods for the lama's safety on the dangerous journey about to be undertaken. Around the walls, gold and vermilion pictures flickered eerily in the lamplight.

Losang stood in silence, watching the monks drain the rancid liquid from their bowls, then scrape out the sediment with their fingertips and rub it carefully into the skin on their faces. When they had finished, the bearer refilled the bowls and placed them back in position; this time they were left untouched – they would remain on the floor together with the *tormas* until the lamas' mission had been successfully completed.

Losang looked at his watch. It was nearly five o'clock. Dawn soon. Time to go. Gravely, he clapped his hands twice, and without a word the monks stopped their chanting and rose to their feet. They filed quietly from the darkened prayer hall, their soles scraping on the bare wood floor. Nobody spoke. In the hushed stillness of the pre-dawn morning, there was only the rustle of the lamas' clothing, the clatter of their boots and the muffled ringing of a distant gong. Somewhere in the darkness, a dog began to bark, its cry desolate and eerie drifting through the night.

Outside, the air was chill and bracing. A pale streak of grey glowed toward the east, but above the craggy mountain tips the sky was still studded with stars. On the forecourt, a line of Land Rovers stood in silent formation. Losang could see the turbanned heads of the drivers outlined through the dusty windshields. The Land Rovers had been packed with equipment and provisions, and strapped to the rear of the nearmost vehicle was an elaborately-carved sedan chair with a solitary flag fluttering from its tip. The flag carried the sacred symbol of the Dalai Lama.

Losang watched the monks spread themselves evenly around the line of vehicles, their shaved heads gleaming in the starlight. They were shivering with the cold and shrinking visibly beneath the folds of their heavy Duvets. Each man knew his place and stood in front of his allotted vehicle, awaiting Losang's command to board.

Losang himself scarcely noticed the chill. He was tingling with excitement, conscious that the months of planning and waiting were finally over. When he was satisfied everyone was ready, he clapped his hands again, the sound sharp and discordant on the early morning air.

A moment passed, then the palace door opened and a young boy emerged into the starlight. He was fourteen years old but might at first glance have been even younger, for his skin was soft and unblemished and his features held a curious innocence as if he had never in his life experienced a selfish emotion or harboured an uncharitable thought. Like the others, he was dressed in a Duvet jacket and padded overtrousers, but upon his head he wore an elaborate cap with the ear flaps turned back to resemble wings. The cap was studded with seed pearls and trimmed with strips of fine gold. As he emerged into the starlight, the monks bowed their heads and chanted softly: '*Om mani padme hum.*'

Losang watched the boy lift his arms in a gesture of spiritual blessing. Slowly, and with immense dignity, he began to cross the forecourt. Losang waited until he had almost reached the parapet, then he too bowed and said in a soft voice: 'The convoy is ready, Holiness.'

The boy looked at Losang, his almond eyes gleaming. He seemed sad, Losang thought, feeling surprised. He had expected excitement, anticipation. But sadness, never.

The boy turned and looked over the parapet at the village of Lower Dharmsala nestling on the slope below. The village lights had been extinguished, and only the blurred outlines of the buildings were visible against the bare rocky hillside. 'I have spent my entire life here,' he said at last. 'It is strange to turn one's back on the place of one's childhood.'

'You are returning to your homeland,' Losang told him gravely.

The boy smiled thinly. 'A homeland I have never seen? This is my home. Dharmsala. What lies beyond the mountains is a mystery to me.'

'You are the chosen one,' Losang reminded him.

The boy sighed and nodded. 'I must seek the path,' he agreed. 'But my heart is heavy to be leaving.'

Losang felt troubled. He studied the youthful features in the starlight.

'Your earlier identity is of little consequence now,' he whispered. 'You have been reborn.'

The boy stared at him calmly. 'You are right. The past no longer matters. Nothing matters but the way of universality, of perfect enlightenment. Yet it is not easy for a man to discover he is a god.'

He glanced down at the rooftops of the village, his eyes glistening. Then without a word, he turned from the parapet and walked to the Land Rover bearing the sedan chair. When he had settled himself in the passenger seat, the other lamas clambered into the remaining vehicles, Losang among them. The engines burst into life as the drivers switched on their ignitions. They engaged gears and swung in line out of the cindered forecourt on the the rutted road beyond.

The first part of their journey would take them through the mountains of Nepal, but after that, the Land Rovers would return to Dharmsala, and Losang and the lamas would continue their way on foot. Then their route would be hard and dangerous, their position desperate, their fate uncertain. Yet Losang never doubted for a moment they would succeed. After all, it was written in the scriptures.

Tibet's destiny was about to be fulfilled.

Nepal, Friday 4 February
The monastery stood on a rocky saddle surrounded by jagged,

snowcapped peaks. It was walled like a fortress, its golden roofs glinting in the sunlight. The arched gateway had been intricately carved out of seasoned rosewood, but time and the passing elements had worn away the paintwork until little remained of its original grandeur. Fractured cliffs protected the monastery's rear, whilst in front the ground dipped in a series of steep-sloping pastures which tumbled into the valley below.

Morrill stopped the guerrillas with a wave of his hand and stood staring at the buildings in silence, his dark eyes slitted in the sunlight. With no expression on his face, he slid the submachine gun from his shoulder and handed it to Chamdo. Chamdo took it without a word, cradling the weapon under his armpit. Morrill motioned the others to remain in the open, then climbed the sloping pasture toward the monastery gateway. He passed a *mani* or 'prayer wall' and, observing the proprieties, walked by on the lefthand side. The heavy, metal-studded door opened easily at his touch. Inside, the courtyard was empty. He could see the great golden dome of the prayer hall etched against the sky. A solitary *chorten* stood in the courtyard's centre, rising in a series of steps representing the seven stages Buddha had taken on his journey to Nirvana. Not a soul was in sight.

Pausing outside the prayer hall, Morrill took off his boots and padded barefooted up to the topmost step, then kneeling, he kissed the threshold. He entered the building, blinking rapidly at the sudden transition from daylight to darkness.

The prayer hall smelled mustily of stale incense. The walls were covered with paintings and elaborate carvings; some displaying men and women in the throes of sexual union, the nearest state to paradise a Buddhist could devise.

Dangling from the central pillars were flamboyant feathered head-dresses used by the monks for religious ceremonies, and in cubbyholes lining the walls Morrill could see the ancient scrolls, some many centuries old, which contained the secret scriptures of the Buddhist faith.

In the centre of the floor, completely alone and apparently in some kind of trance, knelt the high lama. He was dressed in an orange robe lined with gold. His head was shaved, his eyes were closed, his body immobile. He made no movement as Morrill padded softly toward him and knelt gently at his side. The lama's features looked calm and peaceful.

Clearing his throat, Morrill said. '*Om mani padme hum.*'

The high lama remained quite still, his eyes firmly shut. There was an air of simple serenity in his hollow cheeks, his thin lips, his sculptured skull. After a moment, he said: 'You should not have come here.'

'I had to come,' Morrill told him. 'I am confused, uncertain. I seek guidance and advice. You taught me once that killing is a crime against nature, but is it not possible that, used correctly, evil may sometimes destroy evil?'

'Evil destroys nothing except those who purvey it,' the high lama said.

Morrill was silent for a moment. He breathed deeply, filling his lungs with air.

'I want to be a true believer,' he muttered. 'I want to free my mortal life from the rigour of the spirit, but there are things inside me which refuse to be denied.'

'Deny those things,' the high lama answered without opening his eyes. 'Remember the seed syllable "Lam", symbol of the earth. It is the centre from which all living things evolve.'

Morrill stared at the sunlight streaming through the open doorway. Beyond the courtyard, he could see the sloping roofs of the monks' quarters where tall prayer flags fluttered in the wind.

'You have forgotten your teaching,' the lama said. 'A believer must attain quietude and serenity not only with himself, but also toward all living beings. To become an Enlightened One, he must participate in the experiences of others without abandoning his universality. Knowledge without love, without compassion, leads to spiritual death. The taking of life, animal, human or insect, destroys the way to inner completeness.'

'I have tried your way,' Morrill told him wearily.

'You have not tried enough.'

Morrill looked down at his folded knees, the smell of incense hanging in his nostrils. 'I owe you everything,' he said. 'You gave me life.'

'I gave you nothing. The *prana* is not a gift. Life and death are meaningless in themselves. There are only the concentric cycles of existence. Man must learn to be part of that, part of the universal consciousness which extends between space and motion, substance and emptiness. Only in this way can true serenity be achieved.'

'Your people are subjugated,' Morrill told him dully. 'Your

Holy Orders are repressed, and still you talk to me of pacifism and prayer. Is it so wrong for a man to take a stand for the things he believes in, to fight against oppression and injustice?'

'For the true believer, there is no such thing as oppression,' the lama said. 'His spirit is light and elusive as the air. He cannot be touched by the predatory nature of man.'

Morrill bent his head, his lank hair tumbled in a tangle across his pallid face. Beneath the heavy beard, his lips tightened into a grimace of silent pain. For a long moment, he remained totally still, his muscles tense and rigid, outlined against his skin.

At last, the high lama declared: 'You must go now. This is a place of peace, and while there is blood on your hands, you are a trespasser in the realms of holiness.'

Morrill looked at him. The high lama's eyes, still closed, had assumed the stoniness of a plaster cast. His limbs seemed to freeze inside their orange robes as if some elusive breath of life within him had suddenly departed.

Slowly, Morrill rose to his feet. He turned to peer at the scrolls behind him, then moving with a slow languid grace, crossed the threshold and stepped into the morning sunlight.

Harold Morrill's compulsive pursuit of purity could be traced to two sources, his father and his mother. He had been born on the west side of Lomstoun near Cincinatti, son of a doting creole woman who worshipped him with the impassioned fervour of one who had experienced the joys of giving birth at a dangerously late age, and a Polish building contractor who was out of work more often than he cared to relate and thrashed out his frustrations on the only creature he was able to get his hands on – his son. Morrill's father was not a brutal man by nature but he *was* a coarse insensitive figure who saw little harm in venting his anger in the most direct and physical way possible and who seldom stopped to question either the justice or the probity of his actions, particularly in relation to his own offspring.

This curious contrariety between a domineering father on the one hand and an over-indulgent, over-protective mother on the other produced in Morrill a conflict of emotions from which he was never to recover. He despised, almost from the moment he was old enough to appreciate such emotions, the

43

street of shoddy houses in which he was forced to spend his boyhood, and throughout his schooldays and the long years of his early youth dreamed constantly of escape to a world so pristine, so indefectible that only an idiot would have believed in its existence.

This belief however had been nurtured by his mother who never understood why she had married such a boorish clod of a husband in the first place and who, in her own esoteric way, held fiercely to the same kind of dream – a dream of a world not purer, as in Morrill's case, but more stable, peaceful and secure.

Strangely, Morrill's fixation in no way impeded his relationship with the other boys on the street. Though to them he appeared in every respect a creature of similar leanings, desires and interests, it was in his quieter, more solitary moments that his desperate yearning for a nobler form of existence began to assert itself.

When he was old enough to leave home, he did so gratefully, to the consternation of his mother and the bafflement of his father who had firmly expected him to enter the family business. Travelling south to Florida, he worked for a time as a labourer in a builder's yard, then moved to Louisiana where he secured a job in the New Orleans French Quarter selling trinkets to the tourists. These early experiences of making a living impressed upon young Morrill two unpalatable truths. The first was a conviction that peace and inner tranquillity did not lie in the dignity of labour as he had hitherto believed, the second was the realisation that life outside the suffocating confines of his Ohio home was infinitely more squalid, seedy and sordid than anything he had ever imagined.

He took an apartment on Dauphine Street, a ramshackle place where the furniture was falling to bits and where at night bugs came out and lay over everything like a shifting black carpet, and it was here, whilst ekeing out an existence at a few dollars a week that he first became aware of the fact that though the purity of the world was a misbegotten dream, the purity of the soul might well be a goal worth striving after. This idea was placed in his head by the couple who lived down the hall, a big rawboned merchant mariner named Slim and a Cherokee Indian lady who shared his apartment called Mary Two Hats; each was gifted with immense soulful purity in the sense that they were soused out of their minds pretty well most of the time.

Big Slim and Mary Two Hats took Morrill down to the local bar which was frequented by jazz musicians, drug peddlers, waiters, artists, connoisseurs, hangers-on and free-thinkers of every description. For the first time in his life, Morrill found himself in contact with people whose thoughts and ideas were no less outlandish than his own, and without pausing for a moment to consider the validity of these purveyors of wisdom, embraced everything they had to offer with an eagerness that bordered at best on the naive, at worst on the insane.

The bohemian life suited Morrill's temperament perfectly, but the fevered arguments and discussions in the tiny late-night bar brought him face to face with an alarming reality – he was woefully lacking in knowledge and education. It was this awareness, this feeling of inadequacy which led him to return to Ohio where, at his mother's persuasion, his father, who had at last managed to scrape together a tolerable balance of savings after working on a series of multi-storey housing developments, reluctantly agreed to put him through university.

But Morrill did not settle well into university life. He had become a solitary boy by nature, and though he had little trouble making friends, he chose to avoid them whenever necessary, turning his back on university leagues and societies and devoting himself instead to the thing which had attracted him in the first place, the pursuit of learning.

Academically speaking, Morrill was an exemplary student. Though his thinking processes were initially pedantic, he showed an amazing flair for knuckling down to intensive periods of hard work, and within weeks was soaring far head of his classmates. This progressive success did not of course endear him to his colleagues, but Morrill cared little either for their approval or their censure, and continued to apply himself with a fervour that delighted his tutors, puzzled his father, gratified his mother and totally drained Morrill himself.

So devoid did he become of humour, levity and physical indulgence that he ran the grave risk of ceasing to be human altogether – until, that is, he met the woman who was to become his wife.

Tracey Sugden was an English girl taking a two-year post-graduate history course in the United States as part of a student exchange deal. She was beautiful in the classic sense with perfectly sculptured features, an exquisite body, and a smile which made men forget their limitations and dream constantly of lofty ideals, higher emotions.

The first time Morrill saw her, he was struck by the purity of that smile. It seemed to him the simple essence of everything he had been striving for, and he knew in that moment, knew with a profound and burning intuition, that this was the girl he was meant to marry.

Their courtship was brief and fiery. The girl Tracey did not share Morrill's dreams of purity, did not in fact see herself as pure at all, and might have rejected him altogether had not Morrill overridden her uncertainties with the impetuosity of ten-ton truck, for Morrill in love was like a bull on the rampage and against such earnestness, such gallantry, such infinite and passionate devotion, no reasonable self-respecting girl conditioned to the precepts of home, family and a secure future really stood a chance.

They were married at the end of Morrill's penultimate semester and settled down to life as a pair of penniless newlyweds. Morrill reasoned he would graduate soon, and though he had no definite plans in the material sense, he felt sure that with his academic achievements and his nobility of purpose, life would surely provide.

In his final term at university, he was approached by two highly-sophisticated executives with a view to taking a post in the government service. It was part of a programme devised by the Central Intelligence Agency to seek out possible recruits among the nation's student population. Morrill was questioned several times in the seclusion of the university offices, and found his interviewers to be sensible impressive men who were sympathetic to Morrill's concepts of human dignity and universal benevolence. Before he had taken his final exams, Morrill had accepted a post with the agency based in Washington DC. It was a major step for Morrill who had always taken major steps impulsively, and having agreed and been accepted, he devoted himself to his new career with the same intensity he applied to everything else. It was, after all, purity of a sort, for what could be purer than the love of one's country, the willingness to work and if necessary die for the lofty traditions of patriotism and the common good? But Morrill, lost as he was in his aspirations of grandeur, had no idea that life, with a curious will of its own, displayed a disquieting capacity for interfering in the affairs of men, and that even the most perfect of virtues could, upon occasion, become hopelessly and inescapably tarnished.

CHAPTER FOUR

Tracey heard the engines change rhythm as the plane came in to land. Eagerly, she peered through the cabin window. She could see the airstrip below, and the rolling expanse of fields and brickworks which formed the Katmandu Valley. Around it, rippling mountains rose into the sky.

She felt tired yet excited; the flight had been interminable, but after a four-hour wait fretting and fuming amid the heat and flies in Delhi transit lounge, her first glimpse of the snow-capped ramparts of the Himalayas had revived her spirits, and she was humming softly as she waited to disembark.

It was the first time in her life she had travelled so far east, and certainly the first time she had taken part in such a dangerous enterprise. She was not doing it out of patriotism, she knew that. Nor out of love for her husband either, a man she had scarcely known and could barely remember. No, if anything, it had been her need to escape, to break away from the fetters of her life in England, to sever once and for all a relationship that had gone sour too quickly and dragged on too long. Nevertheless, she hoped she was not exchanging one lot of trouble for another.

The Tribhuvan arrival lounge was a scene of pandemonium and confusion. Robed women with ringed noses comforted squawling children. Elegant Sikhs in stately turbans waited in line to be checked at the Customs desk. Sprucely-uniformed Gurkhas wandered among the crowd, eyeing the newcomers with haughty disdain.

Tracey felt awed by the bombardment of unfamiliar sights,

sounds and smells, and stood uncertainly in the shadows, wondering what to do next. A tall man in a crumpled white suit approached her from the Passport desk. 'Mrs Morrill?' he asked, taking off his hat.

She nodded.

'My name is Jenkins, British Embassy. I've been asked to welcome you to Katmandu.'

She felt a wave of relief sweep through her.

'This your entire baggage?' Jenkins asked.

'Yes, it is.'

'Then let me help you. No need to bother with Customs. Those chaps take an age anyway.'

He picked up her rucksack and suitcase, smiling thinly. 'One of the great advantages of having a diplomatic passport, it helps to cut through the red tape at airports. Come on, I've got the car outside.'

She followed him throught the exit door and out to the bustling forecourt. Though it was barely February, the heat of the sun struck her like a hammer. Decrepit old buses lined the dusty sidewalk, turbanned tribesmen clinging to the roofracks. Rickshaw drivers, waiting for customers, clanged their bells incessantly. People were yelling and screaming at each other in a constant barrage of indecipherable sound, and Tracey blinked as she followed Jenkins through the milling throng.

'Ever been in Katmandu before?' Jenkins asked, raising his voice above the clamour.

'Never,' Tracey told him.

'It can be quite an experience, especially for someone seeing it for the first time.'

'I know. That's why I was so keen to accept this filming project.'

Jenkins peered at her with a faint smile on his lips. 'It's all right, Mrs Morrill, I understand your desire for secrecy, but as it happens, I've already been told why you're here.'

She frowned. 'I had no idea the British Embassy was involved in this.'

'Well, only in an indirect sense. We've been asked by the American State Department to smooth out the wrinkles, that sort of thing. Glad to help whenever we can. It's one of our little arrangements. The Americans scratch our backs, we scratch theirs. Here we are.'

Jenkins stopped before a shiny limousine with CC number-plates and a tiny flag fluttering from its bonnet. The driver was a Nepalese with a very dark face. He looked incongruous in his grey uniform and peaked chauffeur's cap.

Jenkins tossed her baggage into the rear. 'We've put you up at the Fire Dragon,' he said. 'It's not one of the more salubrious hotels in town, but the State Department asked us to be discreet and most of the other places are full of tourists at this time of year.'

Tracey clambered in, her senses fluttering. Everything seemed so incredibly different to the world she had left behind, and as they drove toward town, passing rickshaws, mopeds and ancient overladen buses, she peered eagerly through the window at lines of robed women crouching in the fertile-looking fields, scratching at the earth with primitive farming tools. It was like staring at a different age.

Tracey leaned back in her seat cushions. She had so much to do, planning, organising. She wondered if Jenkins would help. He seemed friendly enough.

'I have a problem,' she confided softly, watching the back of the driver's head. 'I have to go north into the mountains. To the province of Ghyankhala, over the border in Tibet.'

Jenkins nodded. He seemed unsurprised. 'We've been informed of the nature of your visit,' he said. 'The Americans have asked us to assist in any way we can. May I say, Mrs Morrill, I really don't envy you. The Ghyankhala is a highly dangerous area. Indeed, it's illegal for travellers to venture there. For one thing, the region is infested by Khampa bandits. They've made their living for centuries by murdering and stealing from pilgrims on their way to the holy city of Lhasa. It's impossibly wild, largely uninhabited, and even its deepest valleys lie at a height of twelve or thirteen thousand feet. Have you ever operated at altitude, Mrs Morrill?'

'Only in the Alps. Twelve thousand's the highest I've reached.'

'Well, the Himalayas begin where other mountains leave off. Make no mistake about it, altitude is a killer. Your brain and limbs lose contact with each other. You get shortness of breath, tiredness, nausea, severe headaches. Soon, you start floundering around like someone in the throes of an epileptic fit. Unless you drop to a lower level, your brain gradually swells until it crushes against the inside of your skull. Death follows swiftly.'

Tracey was silent as she stared through the window. She knew about altitude sickness. She had read about the symptoms and they frightened her. But it was too late now for second thoughts.

They drove into the city past tree-lined parks and extravagant temples. Beggars, dancers, fortune-tellers thronged the sidewalks in a seething hive of humanity. Noise blasted them from all directions, dogs barking, horns hooting, bells clanging, people shouting. As Tracey watched, a cow wandered into the middle of the road and lay casually down, making itself comfortable. The traffic detoured around it.

Tracey forced her mind on to the task in hand. 'I'll need Sherpas,' she said, 'and supplies. And extra equipment.'

'You'll need a damn sight more than that. It's illegal to enter the Himalays without a special permit issued by the government office in Katmandu. However, leave that to us. We'll arrange the necessary documentation. There are lots of trekking agencies which specialise in ferrying tourists into the higher peaks, but I suspect none will attempt a journey to the Ghyankhala.'

'What can I do then? I'll need a guide.'

'Let me scout around a bit. I'm sure we'll pick up a few freelances who aren't overly sensitive about their destination, providing the money's good enough.'

'How long is this journey going to take?'

'If you trek overland, a little more than a month.'

'My God,' Tracey breathed.

'Mrs Morrill,' Jenkins said patiently, 'I know you are an experienced mountaineer, but you have no conception of what that country is like. Every mile you cover will be across high-altitude passes which have no comparisons in Europe. There'll be few villages, so you'll have to carry your food by hand. And once you get above fifteen thousand feet, there'll be no trees either, so you'll have to carry your fuel too. The days will be searingly hot, the nights chillingly cold. Most of the time, you'll be operating at such a height that every step you take will feel as if you're wading through a sea of treacle.'

Tracey was quiet for a moment. The prospect of the long hike in daunted her. 'Can't I get there any quicker?' she asked.

'Overland? Out of the question.'

'Is there some other way?'

50

'I suppose you could always go by air.' He added hastily: 'Don't misunderstand me, there are no airstrips in the Ghyankhala. Putting down would be quite a problem.'

'But not impossible?'

'No, Mrs Morrill, with the right pilot, not impossible.'

She studied him carefully. 'Could you find me the right pilot?'

Jenkins' lips compressed and she watched the flesh whiten beneath his nose tip. 'There is one possibility,' he admitted. 'He's not ideal, by any means. We have a British flyer living here in Katmandu. Until recently, he was employed by the Royal Nepalese Airline people, taking tourists on flights over Everest. He is, I'm afraid, a bit on the wild side. His passengers kept coming back terrified out of their wits until, in the end, the authorities took away his licence. However, he's an excellent pilot, and he knows the Ghyankhala well. He used to run a lucrative sideline smuggling luxury goods to the Chinese communists over the border.'

'What's his name?' Tracey asked.

'Silas Ramdon. Here, I'll scribble down his address. He lives very close to your hotel.'

'Think he'll be interested?'

'I have a feeling he'll be delighted to grab any work he can get his hands on. The flight will be illegal, of course, but I hardly imagine you'll lose any sleep on that score.'

The hotel turned out to be a modern building constructed in the traditional Nepalese style. Its roofs sloped upwards in the manner of a massive pagoda. Jenkins joined Tracey at the reception desk as the houseboy carried her baggage upstairs. 'Be careful where you eat,' Jenkins warned. 'Hygiene is practically unknown in Katmandu. You can call me at the Embassy if you need anything. Meanwhile, I'll check around and see what I can come up with in regard to guides and porters. I'll be in touch if I have any news.'

'Thank you, Mr Jenkins, you've been very kind,' she said.

Upstairs in her room, Tracey stripped off her clothes and tried the ancient clattering shower. The water was freezing and came at her in a deluge, but after the interminable flight from London, she was grateful for any chance to feel clean again. She dried, put on fresh things, and sat in front of the window, staring into the street outside. How different it all seemed from the television world she had left behind. She sat perfectly still as the sun slowly dropped, the sky darkened, and the endless stream of rickshaws went clattering incessantly by. She was thinking about her husband, about a wild and desolate region called the Ghyankhala where Khampa brigands waited for unwary travellers and the altitude caused the brain to swell like a pumpkin. She sat like that for a very long time. Then she folded the shutters, lay on the bed, and closed her eyes in the gathering darkness.

The rickshaw driver dropped Tracey on the streetcorner. There were no lamps, and she stood in the shadows glancing nervously around. The little bungalow nestled among trim green lawns and heavy rhododendrons. A strange sound rose from the building's interior, drifting on the wind like a mournful dirge.

Hesitantly, Tracey opened the gate and walked slowly up the garden path. As she approached, the noise grew steadily in intensity. It was unlike anything she had ever heard before, a tuneless, discordant, droning noise which carried no discernible rhythm or melody.

Tracey tapped lightly on the door and waited. No one answered. The wailing went on, thin and formless on the cool mountain air. She knocked again. Still no response. Finally, she tried the handle, swung the door gently open and cautiously entered.

The interior widened into a large sitting room, the walls hung with animal rugs and numerous photographs. In the centre of the floor stood a man in light trousers and a pale tropical shirt. He was tall, his face deeply tanned and slightly hawkish in appearance, his hair tousled and greying at the temples. For the first time, Tracey realised the meaning of the eerie lament she had heard. The man was playing the violin. He was playing it very badly, but with great enthusiasm. As Tracey watched, his elbow bobbed, dipped and arched flamboyantly, and he tapped his foot to some frenetic rhythm only he appeared aware of. His eyes, peering out beneath a line of bushy brows, glittered like a man in the throes of some demented passion.

He seemed oblivious to Tracey's presence, and though she stood directly in his line of vision, displayed neither curiosity nor surprise. In an agony of indecision, she waited for the meaningless dirge to end. When at last he had finished, the man lowered his violin and peered at her expectantly. Tracey swallowed as she realised she was meant to applaud. Self-consciously, she clapped her hands together. The feebleness of her response was unmistakable, but it seemed to excite the man who said eagerly: 'Anything you'd care to hear?'

Tracey was taken aback. 'I . . . I really don't know,' she muttered.

'Anything at all. You hum it, and I'll play it. I have a natural ear for music.'

'What about "Rhapsody in Blue"?' she suggested.

'How does it go?

Tentatively, she whistled the opening bars and without a pause the man launched into a fevered rendering of Gershwin's immortal classic. The tune sounded exactly the same as the one before. In and out went the bow, up and down went his foot. Somewhere in the darkness outside, Tracey heard dogs howling in unison. I am in the presence of a madman, she thought.

Embarrassed, she waited for the performance to end. When at last the ear-jarring clamour drew to a close, the man stood smiling at her until again she gave a half-hearted clap, then he stepped to a violin case lying on the nearby table, and with a deep sigh, laid the instrument tenderly inside.

'When I was a boy,' he said without looking around, 'I used to dream of being a concert pianist. In those days, we couldn't afford a piano. Our family was terribly poor. So I drew a keyboard on the kitchen table and practised on that. One day they let me play at the church social. It was a shattering experience. I emptied the place completely. I suppose I'd probably have given up music altogether if I hadn't won this old fiddle here in a cardgame.'

He grinned at her, his eyes flashing. 'The minute I picked him up, I knew I'd found my métier at last. Whenever I feel low, whenever the world starts getting me down, I just scrape away at this old violin and he washes me clean like water.'

'That's . . . very fortunate,' Tracey muttered.

'Fond of music?' the man asked, turning.

'Very much.'

'I can play some more, if you like. I really don't mind.'

53

'No, no,' she said hastily, 'I wouldn't dream of imposing.'

'Fancy a drink?'

'That's very kind.'

'Whisky do?'

'Lovely.'

He half-filled a glass and added a tiny splash of soda. Then raising the bottle to his lips, he began to drink copiously, his adam's apple bobbing up and down. Tracey watched in amazement as he continued swallowing until the bottle was nearly half-empty.

'Who are you?' he asked, wiping his lips with his sleeve and handing her the glass. 'I don't usually receive visits from unattached ladies this late in the evening.'

Tracey took a deep breath. 'My name's Tracey Morrill. Are you Mr Ramdon?'

'Silas, everybody calls me. We don't stand on ceremony here. Best goddamned pilot in Nepal, till they took away my licence, the bastards. See this?' He moved to a framed photograph hanging on the wall. 'Know where that was taken? Everest. Twenty-one thousand feet. One of the highest fixed-wing landings in history. Could those bastards do it? Could they bloody hell. I've taken that kite into places you couldn't even dream of, and brought it out again.'

'So I understand,' Tracey said nervously, 'in fact, that's more or less what I want to discuss with you, Mr Ramdon.'

'Silas,' he corrected.

'Silas.'

He grinned. 'You want to hire my services?'

'If we can work out some kind of arrangement.'

'What's wrong? Aren't the Nepalese Airline people good enough for you?'

Tracey hesitated. 'Where I want to go is somewhat inaccessible and, I understand, rather difficult.'

'Difficult?' His eyes twinkled with amusement. 'You mean dangerous.'

She took a deep breath, 'Yes,' she admitted, 'I mean dangerous.'

He chuckled softly, coming forward to study her under the light. Close, he looked younger than she had first imagined, and there was a kind of innate shrewdness in his features which tended to offset his wild and reckless manner.

'Who are you?' he murmured, smiling.

'I told you. Tracey Morrill.'

'I mean who *are* you? Nobody hires me these days, unless they're desperate, or crazy, or both. Who gave you my name?'

'Mr Jenkins at the British Embassy.'

'Ah.'

The man laughed and tried to refill her glass. 'If Jenkins is recommending me, it can only mean one thing. He can't find anyone else. Therefore, what you're up to must be illegal.'

Tracey didn't answer. Something in Ramdon's attitude disturbed her.

Nervously, she watched as he knelt down to push the whisky bottle into the liquor cabinet. 'Where is it you wish to go?' he asked.

'The Ghyankhala,' she muttered.

He looked at her, his eyebrows lifting in astonishment. 'The Ghyankhala? Are you mad?'

'I have to get there somehow. It's terribly important.'

Ramdon laughed. 'As important as living? Because the chances are you won't be doing much of that.'

She went on hurriedly: 'I want you to transport a team of Sherpas and supplies as near to the summit of Tangpoche La pass as it's possible to land.'

'Just like that.'

'I realise it won't be simple, Mr Ramdon.'

'Silas,' he stated.

She waited, watching his face. Pursing his lips, he strolled casually across the thick goatskin rug, pushing his hands into his trouser pockets. When he reached the wall, he turned to stare at her again, studying her mildly with the infuriating glint still in his eye. 'If you want to go into Tibet,' he said, 'why go to the Ghyankhala? There are easier ways of entering, with or without papers.'

'That's not good enough.'

'Have you travelled in the Himalayas before Mrs Morrill?'

'No,' she told him.

'The lowest level of Ghyankhala province lies at twelve thousand feet. Even if I did manage to fly you up there, we'd have to put down in the snow. That's always tricky, even in the best of conditions, but up near Tangpoche La the country is wild and uncharted. What might look level from the air could turn out to be a minefield of crevasses and jagged outcrops.'

'You've done it before,' Tracey answered evenly.

'Who told you that?'

'Mr Jenkins.'

Ramdon gave a thin smile. 'Jenkins talks too much for his own good. Yes, I've done it before, when it suited my purpose. Trading illicitly with the Chinese when the money was good enough. That's one of the reasons they stopped my licence.'

'What was the other reason?' Tracey asked.

The smile left his face. A look of sullen resentment entered his eyes.

'They said I was too reckless,' he growled. 'Those bloody tourists used to get on my nerves. All they could do was yakker away like a bunch of chimpanzees. So I'd fly upside down once in a while to give them something to yakker about. The Nepalese Airline people didn't like it.'

'The tourists neither, I imagine,' Tracey said.

Ramdon gave an impatient gesture. 'You haven't told me what's so important about the Ghyankhala.'

'I'm looking for my husband. He went missing on a mountaineering expedition up there.'

'Then for God's sake, woman, he's probably dead by now. If the Chinese didn't arrest him, he'd freeze to death in those high-altitude temperatures.'

'I have reason to believe that he's still alive,' she stated stiffly.

'What reason?'

Tracey hesitated. 'I can't tell you that. It's sort of . . . secret.'

He chuckled dryly, and pressing his fingertips against his temple, shook his head from to side. 'Don't tell me your husband's one of those bloody CIA lunatics,' he muttered.

Tracey felt shaken. So Ramdon knew about the CIA. The realisation unnerved her and she stood for a moment in silence, trying to collect her wits.

Ramdon stopped smiling, peering at her closely, the light fading in his eyes. He looked almost apologetic, as if he sensed he had gone too far.

Shrugging wryly, he ran his palms down the front of his shirt.

'Hey listen,' he said, 'ever been to Katmandu before?'

She shook her head.

'Want me to show you the town?'

'I . . . I don't think so.'

'Come on. Best time to see it, at night. That way, you don't notice the dirty bits.'

Tracey hesitated. Without a pilot, she faced a gruelling month-long trek through high forbidding mountains. The prospect was not an alluring one. Whether she liked it or not, she needed this man.

'What d'you say?' he repeated. 'Shall I show you around?'

Gently, Tracey nodded. 'I think I'd enjoy that,' she agreed. Ramdon smiled, taking the empty glass from her hand. 'Let me get my coat,' he said.

They walked throught the maze of alleyways, temples and crowded bazaars which formed the old quarter of Katmandu. The streets heaved with people. Everywhere, there was a sense of life, movement, energy. Carved balconies hung like canopies above the bustling thorough-fares, and beneath them, merchants squatted in shadowy cubbyholes offering dates, apricots, figs, copper cooking pots, trinkets for the tourists. Small boys begged for alms, rubbing their bellies mournfully. Rickshaws trundled by, bells clanging. Passers-by retched and spat on the dusty flags.

'Is it always so noisy?' Tracey asked.

'The people like to remind themselves they're still alive.' Ramdon said.

'I wish they wouldn't spit so much.'

He grinned. 'Spitting's a way of life in Nepal. Everyone does it, from the lowliest beggar to the most genteel lady of society. You'll soon get used to it.'

His tanned cheeks seemed to merge into the shadows as she peered up at him curiously. 'How long have you lived here?'

'All my life, feels like. I was actually born in Sheffield though.'

'Never felt like going back?'

'I did once. Big mistake. I didn't fit in somehow.'

'I'm surprised they allow you to stay. Aren't there regulations about foreigners living in Nepal, residency permits, that sort of thing?'

'Oh sure. They never bothered me as long as I had my pilot's licence, but now that I'm grounded, I'm no longer any use to them. I expect they'll kick me out as soon as they get round to it.'

'Then where will you go?'

'I'll figure out someplace.'

A car swung toward them through the crowd, hooter blaring, and as Ramdon pulled her aside, she stumbled involuntarily against him. The car zipped by, the driver picking his way through the swirling mass of people, his hand pressed firmly on the horn. Tracey straightened, momentarily shaken. The unexpected contact had disturbed her. The hard resilience of Ramdon's sinewy flesh had been like an electric shock passing through her body. It took her a moment to compose herself, but Ramdon appeared not to have noticed. He was strolling on, peering casually into the night, his fingers lightly clutching her arm.

'You're not married?' she whispered.

He shook his head. 'I was once. She walked out on me. Said I was driving her crazy. Some people find me difficult to live with.'

I wonder why? Tracey thought, smiling gently.

The street widened into a crammed square filled with massive pagodas. Sacred cows wandered unchecked among the crowd. Directly in front, a uniformed Gurkha stood on guard outside a whitewashed building with stone lions at its entrance. Intricate latticework decorated it exterior.

'What is this place?' Tracey asked.

'It's the Temple of the Living Goddess, a very holy spot. Want to look inside?'

'Will they allow us in?'

'Oh sure, come on.'

She followed Ramdon through the doorway and under a low-beamed ceiling into a central courtyard. It was like standing in the middle of a tiny amphitheatre surrounded on all sides by elaborately-carved balconies.

'See that woodwork,' Ramdon said. 'It's many centuries old.'

'What about the Living Goddess, who is she?'

'Just a girl, an ordinary peasant girl selected for her devotion to the Buddhist scriptures. The lamas put her through a series of tests to judge her suitability. If she passes them with flying colours, she spends eight years shut up in those rooms up there, giving audiences to pilgrims from the surrounding valley.'

'You mean she never gets out?

'Only twice a year, at religious ceremonies.'

'So she's a prisoner then?'

'I suppose that's what it amounts to.'

'How awful.'

Ramdon nodded thoughtfully as if the notion had never occurred to him before. 'Can't be much fun from the girl's point of view,' he admitted. 'Most of them regard it as a period of servitude. It's a great honour for their parents, of course. Like to see her?'

'Is that possible?'

Ramdon cupped his hands to his mouth and shouted something in Nepalese. Three storeys up, the wooden window shutters slowly opened. A head popped out, almost indistinguishable in the heavy shadows. Tracey saw a young girl, her pale features scarcely formed, her coiled hair crowned by an elaborate headdress decorated with pearls. For a moment, they stared at each other in silence, the girl's eyes dark and unfathomable. Then the head withdrew and the shutter slowly closed.

'Is she allowed to marry?' Tracey whispered.

'Only when her term is over. And even then, it's generally believed that her husband must have strong blood and a good horoscope, otherwise he'll probably die.'

'I don't know how she stands it.'

Ramdon chuckled dryly as he led her back to the busy marketplace. 'You have to understand the Asiatic mind,' he said. 'In their world, patience is one of the greatest of virtues. In the Himalayan monasteries, you'll find lamas who spend their entire lives locked up in tiny cells barely three feet high. They believe it brings them closer to completeness.'

'What a waste,' Tracey breathed.

'Oh, I don't know. What the hell are we doing with our lives that's so bloody special? We're all prisoners of one kind or another. At least the lama chooses his cell. The rest of us are caught on a rack that's beyond our understanding.'

They spend the next couple of hours wandering among the curio shops and market stalls, Ramdon stopping occasionally to chat to beggars or passers-by. Everyone seemed to know him, that was the extraordinary thing, and he spoke Nepalese with an ease and fluency which surprised her. In the bustling streets of the old city, Ramdon's wildness seemed strangely subdued, as if he belonged here.

Watching him, she recalled the resilience of his body and her involuntary response. He was, undeniably, an attractive man. Compelling even. His lean cheeks and wolfish grin added a curious rapscallion quality to his features. If only he wasn't as nutty as a fruitcake, she thought.

He smiled down at her. 'Hungry?'

'Ravenous,' she said.

'Let's go eat then.'

He took her to a tiny restaurant crowded with people where the air was filled with the scent of incense. 'Tibetan cuisine,' he explained. 'You'd better get used to it.'

The waiters recognised Ramdon and showed them to their table, smiling. Around the small dais which served as a music stand, parties of American tourists were dining noisily. Tracey could hear their raucous voices echoing into the street beyond. A trio of musicians played Nepalese folk-songs.

Ramdon ordered a bottle of lusty red wine which he said came from the valley of the Songstan Mangpai. Tracey tried a sip and put the glass down on the table. She leaned back in her chair, peering around her happily. She was beginning to enjoy herself. The restaurant was full of life and vitality. She was also beginning to like Ramdon. With his suntanned face and unruly hair, when the light fell in a certain way he was, despite his wildness, indisputably handsome.

He smiled at her, his eyes twinkling above the candle-flame.

'How long have you been married?' he asked.

She shrugged. 'In practical terms, barely five months. I've been under the impression for years that my husband was killed in a climbing accident.'

'Until the CIA changed your mind?'

'That's right.'

'What do you do in England?'

'I'm a television producer.'

'You're kidding me.'

'No, it's true.'

'You must be quite an important lady.'

'Not really. It's only a small regional station.'

'Nevertheless, television producers don't grow on trees. I'm very impressed.'

She felt strangely embarrassed. 'Don't be. It's nothing to make a fuss about. Sometimes I wonder why I do it.'

'How's that?'

'Oh . . . it's not easy to explain. Working in television can be stimulating, I suppose, but there's a curious kind of impermanence to it, a feeling that everything you do is transitory, which tends to be rather unsatisfying. Also . . .' she hesitated. 'It can get pretty ruthless from time to time. I worry in case it makes me hard.'

'I can't imagine that.'

'Please understand, I'd hate to leave the business altogether. I do my job well.' She looked at him and added hastily: 'I hope that doesn't sound smug. It just happens to be the truth. I mean, why should I pretend to be modest when I know that I'm speaking the truth? But a lot of television people have a kind of superficial veneer I really can't stand. I'd like to hold on to my own identity, if I can.'

'Well, for what it's worth,' he said, 'I have a hunch nothing in the world could interfere with that.'

They ate soup and fried rice with some kind of meat which looked and tasted like spiced sausages. Afterwards, Ramdon ordered succulent buffalo steaks accompanied by a delicious salad. Tracey felt the wine going to her head. She peered at Ramdon happily. He was hardly a charming man, she thought. Too wild and reckless for one thing. His manner was blunt, often aggressive, but if he lacked finesse, if he seemed oblivious to some of the finer points of etiquette, she had to admit he was never boring. And he displayed occasional bouts of sardonic humour which set her rocking with laughter. What on earth am I thinking of? she wondered. This man is no good for me. He's the opposite to everything I need. He's unpredictable, unstable, probably amoral, and crazy into the bargain. And yet, in a curious sort of way, I like him. I wish I didn't, but the fact is, I can't help myself.

'Do you really do business with the Chinese communists?' she asked.

'Sometimes.'

'You don't feel guilty about that?'

'What in the hell for?'

'The Chinese are invaders. They have no right to be in Tibet.'

'Peking doesn't think so. The way they look at it, Tibet has always been part of the Chinese Republic. In case you haven't studied your history books, Britain and the United States thought so too until the communists took over.'

'Are you saying you approve of what they did?'

'Not entirely. But before the Chinese arrived, the people were living in a world as primitive and inequitable as medieval England. What wealth existed belonged to a tiny minority. The rest had to resign themselves to a lifetime of serfdom and slavery for a few miserable bowls of rice each week. The Chinese took away the power of the monasteries. They built roads and schools and hospitals. Today's Tibet, may not be free by western standards, but it's a damn sight more comfortable to live in.'

'You like them then, the Chinese?'

'I've always found them to be agreeable people.'

'You're a strange man,' she said, shaking her head.

'How's that?'

'Sometimes I think you're slightly insane. You talk as if all the things we cherish and believe in are part of some grotesque nightmare which has neither purpose nor meaning.'

Ramdon grinned crookedly. 'The madness you speak of doesn't lie with me,' he said. 'It's part of the human race. We deceive ourselves because the alternatives are just too frightening to talk about.'

At ten o'clock, the trio of folk musicians was replaced by a small western-style band which played selections from popular Broadway shows. This started the Americans applauding lustily.

Ramdon leaned back in his chair, dabbing at his lips with his napkin.

'You know, I think I feel a tune coming on,' he declared. Tracey felt panic rising in her throat. Oh my God no, she thought. She watched in dismay as Ramdon rose from the table and spoke briefly to the band-leader. Smiling, the man offered Ramdon his violin. The Americans cheered.

Ramdon turned to face them, clutching the instrument in his fingers.

'Is there anything in particular you'd like to hear?' he asked.

'How about "As Time Goes By"?' one of the Americans called.

Slowly, Ramdon lifted the violin to his shoulder, touching the strings delicately with his bow. The chatter died. Even the clinking of plates in the kitchen seemed to subside. Breathlessly, the restaurant waited.

Then Ramdon started to play.

Tracey pressed her fingertips against her forehead. I can't

believe this is happening, she thought, I just can't believe it.

Across the tables, she could see the smiles freezing on the Americans' faces. Their features assumed expressions of utter disbelief. Tracey sat in a paroxysm of embarrassment as Ramdon, like a man in a trance, drew his bow tunelessly over the strings, his lips twisting into a smile of pure ecstasy. The Americans looked at each other and started to giggle. Soon they were laughing furtively, caught in a bout of helpless hysteria.

Ramdon alone seemed oblivious to the din he was creating. He finished his recital with an extravagant flourish and waited for the audience's reaction. Tracey was the only one who clapped.

Unabashed, Ramdon bowed deeply, returned the violin to its stunned owner, and made his way back to the table. 'I thought those boys needed a little livening up,' he said. 'Music has to come from the heart.'

She watched him tucking in to the remains of his buffalo steak. He had the air of a man who had just delivered a virtuoso performance to a rapturous audience in Carnegie Hall. 'Mr Ramdon?' she said.

'Silas,' he corrected.

'Silas, you haven't told me yet if you'll accept my charter.'

'I thought I'd talked you out of that.'

'You can't talk me out of it. With or without your help, I have to go.'

'Then you're crazy. The Ghyankhala is one of the loneliest corners of the world. I'm doing you a favour by saying no.'

She felt her heart sink. 'You mean you refuse?'

'That's right.'

'Is it too much to demand why?'

Leaning forward, Ramdon helped himself to another portion of salad. He poured on a little oil and vinegar, then picked up his fork and continued eating.

'I don't have a plane any more, that's why. The authorities impounded it at Katmandu airport. If you want to know the truth, I owe money all over the place.'

'Well, the people I'm working for will pay you a generous commission. It'll help clear up your debts.'

'It's not as simple as that,' he stated, chewing placidly. 'If we don't have a flight plan, the Nepalese will refuse to release the aircraft, and we can't have a flight plan because it's illegal to travel to the Ghyankhala.'

Tracey thought for a moment. The prospect of a month-long overland trek appalled her. Ramdon was her only hope.

'Is your plane serviced and ready for use?' she asked.

He nodded. 'They keep it fully fuelled in case there's an emergency in the Dudh Khosi.'

She smiled with satisfaction. Sitting back in her chair, she regarded Ramdon pleasantly. 'In that case,' she said, 'I think it's high time we did something about that elusive aircraft of yours, Mr Ramdon.'

CHAPTER FIVE

The cave lay at the head of a steep-sided valley at a point where the cliffs joined the precipitous banks of loose rolling scree; the guerrillas had blocked the lower part of the entrance with boulders to disguise it from passing patrols and inquisitive aircraft, and thus protected, they used the cave to sleep in, partly as a shelter against the Himalayan weather and partly because it offered a simple escape route in case of emergency, a narrow chimney winding tortuously upwards to a rocky slab high on the mountain's western flank.

There were few travellers in such a desolate region and the Chinese patrolled it only in spring and early summer, but Morrill had insisted from the beginning that the cave must be guarded night and day, and with this in mind; the guerrillas, fourteen in all, a raggle-taggle collection scavenged from the scattered villages of the Ghyankhala, took it in turns to maintain pickets and keep watch over the steep winding valley below.

Holding his carbine in front of him, Chamdo slid down the screebank, a slim young man, bonily-limbed, with glossy black hair and smooth boyish features. He came from the village of Dusitang close to the western frontier of Bhyanlingma province.

Chamdo had not been born when the Chinese had invaded his homeland in the Year of the Iron Tiger, 7 November 1950, and he knew little of the life which had existed in this desolate region before that fateful takeover, but when he was nine years old, his father and five of his brothers had taken up arms against the Chinese, and retribution had been swift and brutal. Two of his brothers had been killed in the fighting, the others had been summarily executed, their heads slung from village doorposts like garlands of grisly flowers. His father had been strung up by his thumbs and slowly disembowelled, then live coals had been heaped inside his stomach as he dangled helplessly, still alive. Chamdo's mother and two sisters had been systematically raped and bayoneted.

Chamdo himself had managed to escape this horror, but the sight of his family's butchered corpses had left him with a memory he could never forget. Throughout his life, Chamdo hated the Chinese with a honed and seasoned passion. There was no limit to Chamdo's hatred, and no limit either to the lengths to which he would go to strike back at the barbarous intruders in his homeland. His hatred was divine in its purity, as immaculate in concept as Morrill's search for enlightenment and truth. But whilst Morrill was forever seeking new levels of awareness, his soul tortured and disturbed, Chamdo was comfortable in his malice, seeing in the coldness of his hatred the essential strength which guided and sustained him.

When Chamdo reached the cave, he found Tuseng sprawled in the entrance drinking *chang*, an alcoholic beverage brewed from rice and barley, the Tibetan equivalent of beer. Chamdo looked at the glass with distaste. He did not drink himself, and despised secretly all those who did. Chamdo touched neither alcohol nor tobacco. His credo was faultless in its intensity. Hate for his enemies. Hate for the murderers of his family. Hate for the conquerors of his country.

'Where is Morrill?' he asked in a sharp voice.

'Meditating,' Tuseng said, nodding toward the razor-sharp ridge which led to the mountain's tip. Frowning, Chamdo swept the line of buttresses with his eyes. On top of a large boulder, he could see a solitary figure sitting crosslegged, facing east. The figure appeared to be part of the rock itself.

'How long has he been up there?'

'Since morning,' Tuseng said.

Chamdo nodded. He was already familiar with his leader's mystical leanings. Only one thing transcended Chamdo's capacity for hate, and that was his understanding and regard for the American, Harold Morrill. Morrill had taken Chamdo's hatred and moulded it into a cohesive force. He had given him purpose and direction, a reason for living, and Chamdo had never forgotten that. He loved the rawboned American more than he had loved any human being before or since.

Slinging the carbine over his shoulder, Chamdo began to scramble rapidly toward the ridge top. He could see Morrill crouched on the shoulder, his lean frame motionless in the starlight, and with a curious persistence, Chamdo felt his mind drifting back to the fateful night he had discovered Morrill's body on the summit of this self-same ridge many years before.

The body lay among the rocks like a spread flower, the eyes, sightless, staring at the stars. In the moonlight, the cheeks looked like panels of alabaster.

Chamdo paused, gasping at the air. He stared at the figure in silence, his stomach bunching into a cold tight knot. Schonfeld had ordered him to dismantle the tent, but Schonfeld was a stranger, an interloper, and Chamdo took no orders from strangers.

Morrill was different. From the beginning, Morrill's fervour, his slow, quiet intensity had impressed Chamdo more than all the rhetoric in the world. Morrill belonged here. He understood.

Chamdo fell to his knees at the American's side, running his fingers over the cold forehead and the livid weal which encircled Morrill's throat. There was no sign of Schonfeld. It was painfully apparent what had happened, Schonfeld had garrotted his companion and left him behind for dead. Chamdo's lips settled into a thin tight line.

He froze as the murmur of voices lifted on the midnight air. He heard the scraping of boots, the clanking of accoutrements. The Chinese.

Breathlessly, Chamdo peered around. The ridge was narrow at this point, each side sloping precipitously toward the valley far below. There was no cover Chamdo could see. Then he spotted a narrow fissure leading into the rim of the cliff itself. Chamdo rose, and hooking his fists under the body's armpits, dragged it across the lip of the ridge and into the narrow crack. He had no idea how far the fissure extended, or if there would be footholds enough to keep them from sliding into eternity, but to his immense relief, he discovered a small ledge just below the fissure's opening, and using this as a support for his hips, he wriggled into the crack, clutching Morrill in his arms.

He was almost too late. At that precise moment, the first Chinese soldier appeared up the opposite slope, his frame deceptively bulky in his fur-lined jacket and padded over-leggings. Chamdo could see the man clearly outlined against the stars; his head was muffled beneath a hooded fur cap with a single red star sewn to its front.

He watched the man pause, glance swiftly around, and mutter something over his shoulder. Four more figures rose against the starlight, dressed like the first in heavy jackets and padded overtrousers. They looked like creatures from a distant universe, their outlandish shapes too grotesque to be considered human. For a moment, they chattered vociferously, their voices tinkling in a curious sing-song fashion on the icebound air, then they set off along the ridge in the opposite direction, and Chamdo breathed more easily as he watched them slowly fade from sight.

He waited until he was satisfied they had moved out of earshot before easing from the crack and dragging Morrill's body, like a sack of heavy firewood, back to the tip of the jagged ridge. For a moment, Chamdo sat among the boulders gathering his strength. The high altitude and the thinness of the oxygen had left his body weak and trembling. He studied the figure in front of him, feeling his spirits rapidly sink. Morrill's features looked grey and stony, the welt on his throat livid and unreal against the paleness of his skin.

Rising, Chamdo tilted the American against him, easing the heavy weight across his shoulders. Then, reeling crazily, he began to stagger slowly downwards, following the twisting line of the ridge through the eerie star-studded night.

It was almost dawn when Chamdo reached the monastery and hammered hard on the heavy metal-studded door. For a long time nothing happened, but Chamdo went on hammering until at last the door swung slowly inward and monks in orange robes carried Morrill's body over the threshold into the hall of the great prayer room. With the butter lamps flickering, they laid him on the floor, his head facing toward the east. Riven with exhaustion, Chamdo stood in silence with the others and stared down at the figure in front of him. Someone had closed Morrill's eyes, and except for the paleness of his cheeks and the savage scar on his throat, he might have been asleep.

The monks chanted softly, a meaningless dirge which Chamdo scarcely heard or understood. Tiger skins covered the walls, and bowls of holy water stood on a nearby altar. Incense sticks smouldered in the darkness. Behind Morrill rose the statues of three divinities clad in ceremonial scarves. Beneath their fiercesome features, a monk attired in a vest of bones pounded a tambourine made from a human skull.

Chamdo heard the muffled ringing of gongs, then drums murmured through the shadowy stillness, and into the prayer hall, two dancers, grotesquely clad in death's-head masks and extravagant multi-coloured costumes, shuffled weirdly, chanting hymns, swinging censers of incense and sprinkling holy water around the spot where Morrill lay.

The odour of incense and melted butter stung Chamdo's nostrils and his eyes began to water as he watched the dancers, cascades of ribbons jiggling from their limbs, weaving and twisting around the body in front of them.

Then suddenly the voices stilled and the dancers drew back into the darkness. A hush fell across the assembled throng, and Chamdo felt his pulses quicken as the high lama slowly entered the prayer hall. The high lama was an impressive, diminutive figure with a shaved skull and delicately-sculptured features. He was said to be a hundred-and-sixty-two years old.

Chamdo watched him stop at Morrill's head and stand studying the corpse in silence for a moment. Deep hollows marked the lama's cheekbones. His face seemed elongated, as if by some supernatural process his features had been stretched like plasticine many years ago. The faint wisp of a moustache decorated his upper lip. For a long time he stood there, staring at the figure in front of him. Then kneeling down, he bent forward and pressed his mouth against Morrill's lips. Chamdo stood watching as the high lama began to blow rhythmically into Morrill's motionless body.

The seconds stretched into minutes. The butter lamps flickered and the monks waited in silence. Chamdo was filled with a desperate lassitude. He was lulled into a trance by the odour of incense and the breathless hush of the moment.

An hour passed. The high lama's patience seemed endless. A breeze drifted through the open doorway, stirring his robes as he went on breathing *prana*, the life force, into Morrill's open mouth.

Gradually, the grey fingers of dawn crept over the threshold and Chamdo watched the rays settle on the lama's shaved skull, picking out the folds of his orange robe. Chamdo's eyes blinked. He could scarcely contain his sleepiness. Each time his lids closed, his brain seemed to reel like a see-saw, pitching him increasingly closer to the dark realms of slumber. Chamdo forced his mind to remain awake. His forehead wrinkled as he struggled to keep his eyes open. Then suddenly, his heart began to pound, for he noticed an almost imperceptible lift to Morrill's chest. He held his breath, peering desperately through the shadows. Had he been mistaken? Were his senses, reeling from exhaustion, beginning at last to desert him? No. The chest was lifting visibly now.

An exclamation of astonishment emerged from Chamdo's lips as softly, the monks began to chant. The chanting intensified, Morrill's breathing growing deeper, steadier, healthier. Slowly, the high lama straightened.

For a moment, he stood staring into the morning sunlight, then he turned to face Chamdo. 'You are from the village of Dusitang,' he said.

Chamdo was startled. He had seen the high lama only once in his life, and then from a great distance. He nodded.

'You fight with the disaffected ones against the Chinese.'

'Yes,' Chamdo admitted.

'This is a holy place. You are not welcome here.'

'I came only because of my friend,' Chamdo said. 'I had heard of the high lama's powers.'

The high lama inclined his head gravely. 'It was because your mission was one of mercy that you were admitted to the temple. Nevertheless, you must leave at once. Your friend will remain until he is fit enough to travel. Return again in three months. We will deliver him to you then.'

Chamdo stared down at Morrill breathing steadily on the prayer room floor. The pallor had gone from his cheeks and his skin was flushed with the glow of returning life.

'He is also wounded in the side,' Chamdo said. 'The bullet has passed through the flesh, but he has lost a great deal of blood.'

'We will attend to his injuries,' the high lama promised. 'He will be nursed back to health. But you must do as I say. Your presence here disturbs the life force and interrupts the healing process.'

Chamdo stared at him in silence for a moment. Then slowly, he nodded. 'I will return in three months' time,' he said.

And with the monks still chanting, he crossed the threshold and left the monastery by the heavy barred door.

Morrill woke from a deep sleep, opening his eyes and blinking uncertainly. He was in a room, small and cell-like, the walls plastered with dried mud, the ceilings hung with low wood beams. Sunlight streamed through the open window.

Blankets covered his body, bringing warmth to his aching limbs. Gently, he eased himself up on the narrow bunk and groaned as a sharp stab of pain lanced through his side. He glanced down, pulling the blanket away. He was naked, he saw, and a dressing had been strapped to the skin above his hip-bone.

Moaning softly, Morrill swung his legs over the side of the bed. He felt dreadful, worse than he could ever remember. There was a dull throbbing sensation in his temples and his neck felt as if it had been sawed in half.

He trailed his fingertips down the front of his throat and jumped with pain as they touched a curious swollen ridge just below the adam's apple. Rising, he moved to a small mirror hanging on the wall and peered at his face, haggard and unkempt. His cheeks were covered with beard stubble, his eyes red-rimmed and yellowish. Around his neck was a vicious circle of scarlet. Wonderingly, Morrill touched it again, letting his fingers linger more cautiously this time, puzzled at the meaning of the strange glistening scar. He remembered nothing. His last recollection was of setting out on the raid. Schonfeld and Chamdo had remained in the gully to guard the explosives. What happened after that was a mystery.

He glanced around the boxlike room. It was sparsely-furnished and primitive. There was a tiny stool with an unlit butter lamp standing upon it. A curtain slung across an alcove served as a wardrobe.

He moved to the window, pulling back the shutter and staring out at the awesome ramparts of the adjacent mountains. He had the curious feeling of floating on air. There was a sense of immense height, of depth and distance, space and perspective.

Morrill looked around. His clothes dangled from a hook on the door. Moving slowly, he took them down and began to dress. When he was ready, he edged to the door and gently tried the latch. It swung open with a muffled creak and Morrill blinked as he stared into an empty courtyard. Sunlight fell across a solitary *chorten*, a stone tower built to contain the ashes of pious Buddhists, rising like a pyramid at the compound's centre. Prayer flags fluttered in the breeze.

He eased into the sunlight, breathing deeply in the thin warm air. Buildings with slitted windows and sloping pagoda-shaped roofs lined three sides of the courtyard. On the fourth stood a large square-shaped structure dominated by a golden dome.

Suddenly Morrill understood. The dome in front of him was a prayer hall. He was standing in a lamasery. Behind, towering above the rooftops, rose the snowcapped peaks of the surrounding mountains.

Morrill's legs felt like indiarubber, and he had the notion that if he attempted to cross the courtyard unaided, he would tumble helplessly into the dust. His cell-like room, he saw, belonged to a row of similar cell-like rooms designed probably to house the younger novices.

As he stood there, trembling in uncertainty, he saw a man emerge into the sunlight, thin, delicately-formed, with a carefully-trimmed beard and a woolly skullcap. From a belt at the man's waist dangled a small leather pouch. He came forward, smiling at Morrill affably, 'Good morning,' he said in English.

Morrill looked at him. The man's appearance, his calm urbane manner confused him. 'Who are you?' he demanded.

'My name is Gendun. I have been detailed to take care of your needs.'

'You speak English.'

Gendun inclined his head graciously. 'I was educated at the mission school in the village of Cholatse near Delhi,' he explained. 'I learned the tongue of my instructors even before I learned my own.'

'What is this place?'

'You are at the lamasery of Cho Mangpai, three miles inside the Nepalese frontier. Though we are all Tibetan by birth, the monks fled here when the Chinese invaded our homeland. In Nepal we seek the true faith of universality and isolation. Naturally, we are sad that we had to leave our beloved valley of Lamringyhana, but one day, who knows, perhaps we will be able to return there.'

'How did I get here?' Morrill demanded.

'Your friend brought you, a man named Chamdo. You were badly hurt, very close to death.' The man smiled thinly. 'In fact, some say you were already dead, but here at Cho Mangpai we make no distinction between the body and the spirit. If the spirit lives, the flesh can be revived. It is a simple truth our forefathers taught us and we have believed it implicitly ever since.'

'Where is Chamdo?'

'He is gone from here. He will return again in the early summer. By then, hopefully, you will be well enough to travel.'

Morrill grunted and took a few experimental steps toward the *chorten*. He was feeling stronger now, but the ache in his throat and the dull throbbing in his skull continued with maddening persistence.

'You must not tire yourself,' Gendun warned. 'Your body will heal with time, but it must be given the right incentive. By all means walk a little, stretch your muscles and sinews, but take care not to overtax your strength.'

'How long have I been lying in that room?'

Gendun thought for a moment, his face calm and curiously youthful. 'Three weeks,' he said.

'My God,' Morrill breathed.

'The wound in your side is knitting nicely, but you must be careful not to wrench it. The scar on your neck, I fear, will remain with you always. Still, it is a small price to pay for the gift of life.'

'Am I free to come and go as I wish?'

'Naturally. You are a guest at Cho Mangpai, not a prisoner.'

'What lies beyond the gateway?'

Gendun smiled and offered his arm. 'Let's go see, shall we?'

Leaning heavily on the monk's shoulder, Morrill hobbled across the courtyard. A new sensation rose inside him. Hope. He was filled with an elusive excitement, like that which in childhood comes at the dawn of each new day.

They paused in the gateway for Morrill to get his breath. He glanced across a line of steeply-sloping pastures to a cluster of primitive dwelling houses clinging precariously to the mountainside. Terraces had been cut out of the incline, and on these, people were scratching at the earth with crude farming implements. Morrill saw a young girl shepherding a flock of goats across the hilly meadow. Woolly yaks grazed placidly in the grass, the bells on their necks tinkling on the bright morning air.

'Who are these people?' Morrill asked.

Gendun shrugged. 'Some of them are members of our monastery community tending to our flocks and vegetables. Others are tribespeople from Tibet who have come to trade rice and other commodities in return for religious guidance and instruction.'

He peered at Morrill keenly. 'Matters of the soul no longer survive in the Tibet of today,' he said. 'They have destroyed our lamaseries, destroyed our culture. The people, those who live near the frontier, come to the high lama for spiritual replenishment and reassurance.'

Morrill grunted and stepped through the gateway to the meadow beyond. He stood in silence, watching the people working on the terraced vegetable fields. They smiled at him shyly, their dark faces filled with a curious guileless innocence.

'You have everything you need here?' he breathed.

'Oh yes,' Gendun told him. 'The monastery is quite self-sufficient, but we do trade with visiting tribesmen for occasional luxuries. Cho Mangpai is a world in itself. Independence is, after all, necessary. We are so isolated, so removed from the principal pilgrims' paths.'

A young woman in bright coloured robes moved down the slope toward them. She was carrying an empty jug and Morrill realised she was going for water. She walked with a fluid elegance that made Morrill catch his breath. He looked at her, frowning, a strange sensation rising in his throat. The girl's face was exquisitely-featured and lacked the characteristic flatness of her countryfolk. Her lips were full, her cheeks rounded, her skin smooth as buttermilk. As she passed, she smiled at Morrill over her shoulder, her eyes merry and mischievous, and he felt something lurch in his diaphragm.

Gendun watched him, his lips twisting with humour. Gently, he disengaged his arm. 'I think, my friend, you are quite capable of taking care of yourself,' he said. 'Wander where you will, but remember, don't overdo things. We eat here at noon. Our food is plain but nourishing. Please don't be late. The high lama wishes to speak with you after you have dined.'

Still chuckling, Gendun turned and made his way back to the monastery gate. Morrill glanced down the hillslope after the retreating woman. Cautiously, he began to pick his way toward her. He watched her vanish into a fold in the ground and struggled to quicken his pace, gasping for breath in the high-altitude atmosphere. He reached the mouth of the little defile and saw her kneeling by the side of a tiny spring, holding the jug beneath its flow. As he approached, moving slowly, she smiled at him over the corner of her robe.

'What is your name?' he asked.

She laughed, her voice ringing on his senses like the tinkling of the water. How beautiful she is, he thought. How marvellously indefectible.

Something in the girl's manner awakened Morrill's dreams of purity. Moving closer, he eased himself down beside her. 'I am Morrill,' he said, tapping his chest. 'How are you called?'

She laughed again, turning her face away in a sudden fit of shyness.

'Baima,' she said without looking at him, her voice strangely muffled against the folds of her shawl.

Morrill could feel his heart wildly beating. 'Where are you from?'

'The village of Lamringyhana in the Ghyankhala.'

'Tibet?'

She nodded.

'What are you doing here in Nepal?'

'My father wishes to see the high lama. Men of wisdom and learning are no longer welcome in our province. We come here as often as we can.'

'Look at me,' Morrill told her.

Slowly, she turned her head. Her eyes held his, the pupils soft as the skins of black grapes. He thought: all my life, I've dreamed of meeting a girl like this.

Morrill felt his stomach tighten. 'Are you married?'

She shook her head, smiling roguishly. He knew the answer

meant little. Among the mountain people, marriage was a casual affair. As soon as a girl was old enough, she was free to choose a lover as she wished. Most young couples experimented before deciding whether or not to settle down with each other.

'You have a man?' he asked, his throat unaccountably dry and tense.

Again, she shook her head, the enigmatic smile still wrinkling her lips. He felt relief flood through him. For God's sake, he thought, I've scarcely set eyes on the woman. What in hell's name is happening to me?

But he knew. It was part of his reawakening. No accident had placed the woman here. It was meant to be, Morrill felt it.

'What about you?' she asked, keeping her voice deliberately light and casual.

Frowning, Morrill thought suddenly of his wife, Tracey. He had almost forgotten what she looked like. From the beginning, they had been strangers. He had talked her into marriage against her will. Impulsively, foolishly. Not thinking of the future. He had done it because it had seemed expedient. He had wanted things settled. Marriage. Children. The cornerstones of American society. He knew now he had made a mistake.

'I have no woman,' he said quietly.

The jug filled with water and the girl lifted it from the spring.

'Here, let me help you with that,' he muttered, reaching forward to take it from her hand. But as he straightened, lifting the heavy vessel to his shoulder, he felt his legs suddenly giving way beneath him and almost fell to the ground. She rescued the jug from his grasp, laughing gaily. 'You are still too weak,' she said, 'even for woman's work.'

He rubbed his hands on the sides of his pants. 'They told you about me?'

She nodded gently. 'Everyone in the mountains knows. They say you were brought here a corpse. The high lama gave you life.'

'That's nonsense.'

She shrugged as they walked slowly up the steep mountain path. 'There were many witnesses. You were dead on arrival. The lama breathed *prana* into your body.'

Instinctively, Morrill's fingers crept to the livid weal around his neck and a shudder ran through his stomach. 'Dead men can't live,' he muttered. 'Not in this world.'

'They say the high lama is not of this world. They say he lives in the air, and materialises only when he wishes others to see him. They say he has power over all natural things. He can quell storms, bring rain, heal the sick, raise crops.' She stared at him pointedly. 'And make dead men live again,' she added in a quiet tone.

Morrill did not answer. He fixed his gaze on the walls of the monastery above. But deep inside him, a strange uneasiness began to stir.

Lunch consisted of *tsampa* (parched ground barley moulded into balls), rice and spiced vegetables. There was water to drink and bitter incense-flavoured tea. Gendun explained that the eating of meat and fish were forbidden, for the lamas did not approve of taking of life.

They ate in the choral hall, the monks sitting cross-legged on cushions, clutching their bowls in front of them. No one spoke. Food was a necessity, Gendun said. The stimulator of life. The taking of it was not considered a social occasion.

The meal over, Morrill was escorted to see the high lama. He was still dreaming of Baima, the girl he had met by the waterhole, recalling her soft eyes, the steep curve of her cheeks, stirred by almost forgotten emotions. He knew with the deepest certainty that his old life was over, that he had been born again, and somehow, in the freshness of this strange new world, the girl Baima had become a compendium of all the things he had ever dreamed of, as alluring and elusive as the essence of life itself.

His spirits lifted as, following Gendun, he crossed the compound toward the great prayer hall and found the high lama waiting for him in the doorway. Morrill saw at a glance that the high lama was very old. And yet, his shaved head and sculptured features carried none of the parchment-like texture Morrill associated with the skins of elderly people. Though there were wrinkles around the eyes, deep lines flanking the corners of the mouth, the high lama's face looked strangely youthful, as if some curious force had given it an air of timelessness.

'I will leave you together,' Gendun said, inclining his head. 'You have much to talk about.'

Morrill stared at the high lama noting, now that he was close, how small and frail the man looked. At first glance he had seemed tall and dignified, but Morrill realised the impression had been deceptive. The lama's limbs were thin and fragile, yet there was a strange vitality in his features, a subtle strength that came not from self-assertion but from the passive acceptance of order and wisdom.

'How are you feeling, my son?' the high lama asked softly, his eyes twinkling. There was an air of irrepressible merriment in his wrinkled face.

'Disjointed,' Morrill admitted. 'I'm getting better though. I felt a damn sight worse this morning.'

The high lama smiled. 'Shall we sit here on the threshold?' he suggested. 'It pleases me to look across the high mountains.'

They settled themselves on the floor in the doorway, staring at the jagged peaks which reared beyond the monastery rooftops. A few fleecy clouds scurried across the topmost summits, but otherwise the sky was a faultless blue. The sun warmed their chests and faces. 'I guess I've got a lot to thank you for,' Morrill began uncertainly.

The lama silenced him with a gesture. 'Such a word has no meaning in our language. It has no place in the doctrine of universality or the power of consciousness. Here, we examine the enigmas of the body, but we seek always its liberation, and above all, the path of enlightenment toward completeness.'

'But you gave me life when . . .' Morrill hesitated, '. . . when I was close to death.'

The high lama smiled. 'How can that be, my son? True life can only be achieved by transformation. Existence itself must be channelled toward a vision so immense, so tranquil and beautiful that the spiritualisation of mind and body creates a radiant harmony. Until this has been achieved, life does not truly exist.'

Morrill shifted uncomfortably on his haunches. The conversation confused him. The high lama was still smiling pleasantly, but Morrill had the feeling some kind of response was expected on his part. 'I am not a religious man by nature,' he confessed. 'I was raised a Christain, but I guess I lost most of my beliefs along the way.'

'Why was that?' the lama inquired politely.

'No particular reason. I started thinking for myself, that's all. The spiritual side of life kind of loses its importance when you hold it up to the light of logic.'

The high lama laughed delightedly. 'A typically western concept,' he explained. 'You believe that the brain is the exclusive seat of consciousness. We however understand that there are many centres of awareness in which psychic and physical functions blend into each other. We deliberately stimulate these centres, and in this way transform our bodies.'

'For what purpose?' Morrill asked.

'For the greatest achievement of all. The experience of infinity. Our aim is to become conscious of indivisible completeness.'

Morrill was silent for a moment. He stared across the mountain peaks, aware of something awakening inside him. As a small boy, Morrill had been profoundly religious. Time and necessity had led him to turn his back on the teachings of his youth, but he had never forgotten his pursuit of purity. The truth was, Morrill had an innate capacity for spiritual issues.

'You know who I am?' he inquired softly.

The high lama nodded. 'You are one of the disaffected ones, the men who make war on the Chinese.'

'But still you welcome me here.'

'You are not waging war at the moment. You are simply a human being who is hurt and needs help. You are also, I think, on the brink of spiritual unfoldment.'

Morrill frowned on him. 'What are you talking about?'

'Just as the lotus, hidden deep within the darkness of the earth, turns toward the sun, I believe you are already turning toward a higher awareness. The way of the warrior is repugnant to you. You have an infinite capacity for suffering, but the attainment of peace lies in overcoming the limitations of one's mind. Everything created by the brain is illusory. We must alter the patterns of our thinking until we become conscious of a higher, purer, exalted vision. Of reality.'

Morrill stared down at the floor. Gently, he traced a line in the dust with his finger. 'How long will I be allowed to stay here?' he asked.

'You will know yourself when it is time for you to leave.'

Morrill nodded. As he stared across the rippling mountains, he felt a lightness within him, a sense of transcendence, a feeling of purpose he had never before experienced. 'I have a feeling,' he said, 'I would like to remain for ever.'

CHAPTER SIX

As the days went by, Morrill found his strength steadily returning. The lamasery's ordered pattern of existence gave him a
feeling of serenity and contentment. The breathtaking splen-
dour of the surrounding mountains was like a salve to his senses
and he would sit for hours watching the sun cast slivers of
scarlet and gold over their snowcapped tips; never in his life had
he experienced such an effusion of peace and well-being.

The monks themselves tended to avoid his presence when
they could, for social exchanges, whilst not exactly frowned
upon, were regarded as an intrusion on days spent largely in
meditation and prayer. As evening fell, Morrill would listen to
their chantings in the altar room and watch the sun sink beyond
the rim of the distant hills.

Life was sacred in Cho Mangpai; no living thing, no matter
how small, was ever deliberately hurt. If a butterfly fluttered
into a bowl of tea, the lamas scurried to scoop it out before the
hapless insect drowned. Wild creatures injured in the mountains or starved by the long ravages of winter were taken in and
cared for.

The lamas took four fundamental vows: to reject violence, to
refrain from theft, to speak the truth and to practice celibacy.
Celibacy was considered the most important.

Junior monks were not permitted to enter the lamasery until
they had been given a *sung-du*, a strip of cloth with blessings
printed upon it which they wore about the neck. If a monk
broke his vows, his *sung-du* was taken from him and he had to
leave the premises while the other lamas assembled in the altar
room to pray for his forgiveness.

In addition to the *sung-du*, each lama was given a *dhanda*, a
written manuscript amounting to a personal character assessment. If a lama's *dhanda* placed him in the caste of tea-maker or
altar cleaner, then that would be his principal role in addition
to his religious studies. None of the monks worked on the land;
cultivating the soil involved killing of insects, so the vegetable
terraces were maintained by lay members of the community.

Some lamas undertook long periods of solitary meditation,
locked in lonely cells deep in the mountain's flank. Here they
lived on *tsampa* and tea, devoting their spiritual energies to

contemplation of the Holy Trinity, *Kunchok-Sum* (Buddha), *Dharma* (The Law), and *Sangha* (the Religious Society).

The lamas also performed the rights of *kusang* and *tsewang* designed to prolong life and bring spiritual happiness. Juniper leaves and sandalwood were burned to produce smoke, *tsampa* and *chang* were offered as sacrifices to the gods, cymbals were clashed and trumpets blown to ensure good luck; in this way, the lamas called upon the god of life, *Tsepakme*, and asked for his blessing.

From time to time, tribesmen were brought to the lamasery possessed by evil spirits. On such occasions, the lamas would exorcise the unfortunate sufferer by chanting tantric *mantras* and touching him with their *phurpas* or sceptres. These *mantras* were kept a strict secret, for it was commonly believed that they contained immense destructive potential and wrongly used could be both physically and psychically dangerous.

Throughout his early weeks at Cho Mangpai, Morrill's only companion, apart from the high lama himself, was Gendun, whose gregarious disposition was equally matched by an inordinate desire to practise his English. For hours, the two men wandered the surrounding meadows discussing the conceptions of mind and matter, body, soul and spiritual consciousness.

Only rarely did their talk linger upon worldly things, but one day, after Morrill had been explaining the motives behind his guerrilla activities, Gendun told him of his own experiences during the Chinese occupation.

'Initially,' he admitted, 'the invaders behaved with great restraint. There was no theft, no violence, no raping of Tibetan women. But they warned us that Marxism must replace the teachings of Buddha. Buddha himself was denounced as a reactionary. We began to fear the destruction of our religion and way of life. Armed resistance spread through the east. Chinese supply-columns were attacked, military outposts destroyed. The Chinese retaliated by burning the monasteries, submitting our holy lamas to public humiliation. In March 1959, the rumour spread through Lhasa that the Chinese were planning to kidnap the Dalai Lama. The people flocked in their thousands to the summer palace and formed a cordon around it. The Chinese brought up artillery and began to shell the building. Happily, the Dalai Lama had escaped the evening before, but many thousands of our people were slaughtered in the bombardment and their bodies strewn around the palace grounds and walls. By March 23rd, our attempts at insurrection had been bloodily crushed.'

It was a story Morrill had heard many times before. The Chinese suppression of the 1959 rebellion had been savage and ruthless, yet Gendun spoke without any trace of bitterness as if he had somehow managed to distance himself from the past in a manner which rendered him immune from destructive emotions. The occasion was an unusual one however. As a rule they spoke little of such earthly matters, concentrating instead on psychic and spiritual interpretation and wisdom. Gendun proved an agreeable companion whose arguments obliged Morrill to adopt an ever-expanding approach to the world, to life and to existence. He felt awed by the mystic nature of Cho Mangpai, as if at last he had found something timeless and imperishable to which he could attune himself.

His only other interest during those blissful days of early spring was the girl Baima whom he had met at the waterhole. Each morning, at precisely the same hour, they joined each other at the lamasery gate and strayed until lunchtime, following the mountain tracks over the meadows and surrounding hillsides. Baima, he quickly discovered, was utterly artless in the ways of the outside world; though she displayed the same instincts and emotions as members of her sex anywhere, she carried also a freshness and vitality Morrill found irresistible, and before long he realised he was falling in love with her.

Love was a curious emotion to a man like Morrill; he had never experienced it before, not in the real sense, the true sense, for his marriage had been merely the assuaging of a need within him, an attempt to reach that level of purity to which he desperately aspired, but now, with Baima, he felt trapped by an inexorable yearning which refused to let him go.

Both Gendun and the high lama regarded Morrill's infatuation with undisguised amusement. They encouraged his association with the girl, for it was plain to everyone concerned that Morrill's new-found happiness was contributing greatly to the healing of his wound.

At last however, Baima told Morrill that the time had come for her to leave Cho Mangpai. Her father had completed his business there. The following morning, they would return over the Tibetan border to their village at Lamringyhana.

Morrill felt dismay fill him. In the past few weeks, he had taken Baima's presence almost for granted, and it seemed strange now to think of life without her. It was almost as if Morrill's existence had been divided neatly into two parts. The first had been boyhood and young manhood, the second his moment of awaking at Cho Mangpai. He had entered another world – his mind and emotions had undergone a complete transformation. Baima was part of that. She belonged here as he belonged. He could not bear to think of her leaving.

That night he met her under the stars, and holding her in his arms, kissed her longingly on the mouth. 'Stay,' he pleaded. 'There is no earthly reason for you to return to Lamringyhana.'

But Baima shook her head. 'My father is old and weak. The journey is arduous and there is much to carry. We are poor people. We cannot afford to hire porters.'

'In that case,' swore Morrill, 'I will come to you at Lamringyhana as soon as I am strong enough to travel. I will leave here and cross the pass at Tangpoche La. Then we will be together always.'

The notion sustained him; in his emptiness, he was conscious of a sense of happiness deferred, as if everything, the culmination of his expanding hopes, his gnawing needs, would come to them both if he would only wait, for with waiting came patience, and with patience the greatest of virtues could be realised.

Next morning, he stood at the lamasery gate watching Baima and her father vanish into the drifting mist. They stopped only once, on the rim of a distant hill, and he thought he glimpsed her waving. But in a moment they had disappeared from sight and he was left alone with his pain.

He went to see the high lama and told him he wished to pursue the path of completeness and inner tranquillity. The lama was pleased and promised to give him instruction. Each morning, Morrill studied spiritual unfoldment and the Tibetan system of meditation. He learned the principles of space and movement, the various dimensions of consciousness, the laws of creative reality, the psychic functions of *prana* and the sacred ideals of the *Bodhisattva*.

Morrill's studies created within him a satisfying sense of balance, a stability which had never existed in his previous life. It was as if everything he had ever done had been moving inexorably toward this point of fulfilment. Slowly his personality changed. He grew calm and tranquil, tolerant of the requirements and well-being of others. It was as if a veil had been lifted from the world, taking him into a reality that was at once subliminal and in harmony with the universe.

As spring lengthened, the rhododendrons burst into blooms, and across the rolling pastures the hillsides looked like panels of fire. The scent of blossoms hung perpetually on the sun-warmed air. Morrill had never in his life felt so content. And then, in the second week of May, Chamdo returned. Gendun came to Morrill's room to warn him. 'He is waiting by the gate,' Gendun said. 'The high lama has forbidden him to step within the monastery walls.'

Morrill felt no immediate sense of alarm. In the bliss of his new awareness, he had forgotten Chamdo completely. Now the memory of his erstwhile comrade came like a fractured image from some distant childhood dream.

Slowly, Morrill crossed the courtyard. Chamdo was standing on the pasture outside, his face lean and emaciated, his eyes haunted, his clothing hanging in rags. In places, his breeches had been ripped clean away, displaying bare legs smeared with patches of dried mud. He peered up at Morrill speculatively, clutching his carbine in front of his thighs. 'How well you look,' he declared.

'I *am* well,' Morrill told him. 'I have been renewed.'

'And the wound?'

'It is healed.'

Chamdo nodded, his eyes wary. He had detected a change in Morrill, one he did not fully understand. For a moment, he studied his friend in silence, filled with a sense of foreboding, a conviction that things had altered in some elusive, indeterminate way. 'We have been fighting very hard,' he muttered. 'We have stolen many guns and a great deal of ammunition. The Chinese sent in numerous patrols to find us, but always we outwitted them.'

Morrill nodded without answering. Chamdo peered down at the ground and then at the sky. He felt the crisis coming, sensed it hanging between them, unspoken, but as tangible as an electric charge. Chamdo scarcely knew how to react. 'We need you,' he said softly. 'We have the weapons and the will, but we need you to guide us, to lead us.'

Morrill shook his head. 'I am not coming back,' he stated.

Chamdo frowned. In his dirty unkempt state, he looked like a hunted animal. 'You must,' he whispered.

'No. It is over for me now.'

'But it was you who came to us in the beginning. It was you who promised liberty, freedom.'

'I was wrong to promise those things. I know now they can never be achieved by violence.'

Chamdo straightened, anger rising inside him; his body felt light, drained of blood, and the muscles in his legs contracted impulsively as if he had been pushed beyond the boundaries of reason. 'What have they done to you here?' he demanded. 'What nonsense have they poured into your head?'

Morrill sighed. 'I cannot make you understand, my friend. All I can say is, the man you see before you is different in every imaginable way to the one you left behind. The war is wrong. True enlightenment, true freedom comes not from the struggles of men, but from the unfettering of the soul.'

There was no hope in Chamdo's mind; though he stood for more than two hours arguing, cajoling, threatening, pleading, he knew with the instinctive discernment one human being sometimes glimpses in another that Morrill's decision was irrevocable. At last, bitter and defeated, Chamdo turned and made his way wearily down to the valley floor.

Afterwards, news reached the lamasery occasionally of fighting beyond the frontier. They heard of bridges being blown, patrols attacked, roads destroyed, military outposts set on fire. For Morrill, lost in his great pursuit of completeness, the stories were like fantasies from a different age. He did not think of Chamdo again for a very long time.

When the summer was at its height, a small party of lamas crossed the border into Tibet. It was the traditional journey of *rupa-kaya* when the monks carried their holy message to the scattered villages of Ghyankhala province. The expedition was always conducted in secret, for the high lama knew that many thousands of monks had been imprisoned by the Chinese in their attempts to destroy the rigid structure of the old religious order, yet despite the hazards of the journey, the young lamas considered it a pilgrimage of profound spiritual significance and there was seldom any shortage of volunteers.

When Morrill heard preparations were taking place, he asked the high lama if he might accompany the deputation as far as the village of Lamringyhana. Despite his absorption with the search for enlightenment, he had not forgotten the young girl Baima. At times, when he recalled the perfect symmetry of her features, he was consumed by a terrible longing that begged to be assuaged, and though, dutifully, he turned his mind, like a true *Bodhistattva* to the liberation of his soul, his body carried him remorselessly back to the tyranny of the flesh. He was sure he loved her. Nothing in the world could compare with the purity of that love.

The high lama was amused at Morrill's ardour. Convinced that the American's wound was now sufficiently healed, he gave his consent gladly, and even went so far as to provide Morrill with gifts for the young lady's parents, a bamboo-framed hat for the mother, covered with red cloth and skeins of coral, turquoise and seed-pearls, and for the father a hair shirt with four-foot long sleeves to protect the hands from the mountain cold.

The trip was to be led and supervised by Gendun himself, for in the lamasery calendar it occupied a position of immense importance, the only point in the year when the monks carried their holy influence into the realms of their beloved homeland.

The entire monastery turned out to see them leave. Vast hordes of orange-robed monks stood in front of the lamasery wall beating cymbals and blowing enormous ten-foot long horns which emitted weird wailing noises into the thin mountain air. Their baggage was carried by a team of woolly-flanked yaks, the bells on their necks tinkling delightfully as they stumbled down the steep rolling pastures and into the valley below.

Morrill was glad to be on the move again. Though the monastery had brought him immense happiness, it felt good to be venturing forth on what he felt sure was a completely new episode in his life.

The trail rose steeply across a pass of barely melted snow, and though Morrill's body was now attuned to thin oxygen and high altitude, his ears began to ring at eighteen thousand feet and he was glad when the pass levelled out and the trail began to dip again.

They passed through several yak-herders' villages, pausing to spend a night at each. The people welcomed them with gifts of food and hot buttered tea. In the market-places, the monks gave their instruction and handed out red ceremonial scarves which the villagers retained as sacred talismans.

Despite the beauty of the landscape and the warmth of the Tibetan hospitality, Morrill was impatient to reach Lamringyhana. The memory of Baima was constantly on his mind. He had only to close his eyes to see the dark density of her hair, hear the delightful resonance of her laughter.

Gendun was amused at Morrill's impetuosity. 'Have you learned nothing from our teaching?' he asked wickedly. 'Earthly joy and earthly consciousness are transitory only. A man must transcend the timebound passions of the real world. Only then can he experience true love.'

But Morrill was beyond convincing. Day after day, he fretted and fumed as the village of Lamringyhana drew slowly, tantalisingly nearer. At last, they traversed the final pass and glimpsed Lamringyhana lying in the valley below them, the houses scattered, their sloping roofs shining in the sunlight. Prayer flags fluttered in the breeze, and Morrill could see twin *chortens* guarding the village's entrance. His body was trembling with excitement and the long, slow descent down the steep, winding trail seemed endless. When at last they reached the village outskirts, the inhabitants turned out to meet them, and Morrill eagerly scanned the flock of laughing faces for a glimpse of Baima, but she was nowhere to be seen.

For a while, the monks went through their customary procedure of blowing their horns, ringing their bells and beating their skull tambourines, then Gendun, still smiling with amusement, took Morrill through the narrow streets to Baima's home.

The house was a lavish one by Tibetan standards, though primitively furnished and oppressively hot. A yak-dung stove stood in the corner belching out smoke. As was customary, the smoke filled the entire building, drifting gradually through the slitted rooftiles.

He and Gendun were received courteously by Baima's family, but Baima herself was nowhere in sight. Baima's mother served them buttered tea and *tsampa*. In the choking darkness, Morrill recognised Baima's father, but the two other men present were strangers to him. He asked Gendun who they were.

'They are Baima's mother's alternative husbands,' Gendun told him casually.

Morrill stared, frowning. 'You can't be serious?'

'But of course I am serious, my friend. It is part of the custom here that when a woman marries, she is allowed to take two of the bridegroom's younger brothers as deputy spouses.'

'That's obscene,' Morril declared.

Gendun gently stroked his beard, his eyes twinkling merrily. 'Why is it that westerners seems perfectly capable of accepting the concept of polygamy – the practice of having more than one wife – but Tibetan polyandry, more than one husband, produces expressions of astonishment and disbelief? It is considered a virtuous system here and makes a great deal of sense. In a country of few natural resources, it limits the population. In this way, though the people are poor, true poverty, true starvation is very rare.'

'What about Baima? Does she have more than one man too?'

Gendun chuckled. 'Do not worry about Baima, my friend. Until she marries, the question will never arise.'

Morrill shifted impatiently on his haunches, blinking in the oppressive smoke-filled atmosphere. 'Where is she?' he demanded. 'Why isn't she here? Can't you at least ask her whereabouts?'

'I already have,' Gendun smiled gently. 'Where would you expect a dutiful daughter to be at this time of day? Naturally, she is tending the yaks on the high pasture.'

'Where?' Morrill snapped, seizing his wrist.

Gendun's eyes danced. Deliberately, he hesitated as he sipped at his bowl of butter tea. 'Not too far,' he admitted, 'for a man with strength in his legs and passion in his heart. You follow the valley track until it rises beyond the river. The grazing lands lie on the high plateau.'

Morrill did not bother to say goodbye. He heard Gendun's lilting laughter following him as he hurried down the narrow track between the lines of dry stone walling. Lamringyhana was not a true village in the western sense; it consisted of little more than a few scattered huts linked together by a myriad network of walled enclosures. The enclosures were, for the most part, uncultivated. They existed principally for grazing and for the protection of livestock during the winter months.

It took Morrill only minutes to leave the last of the buildings behind. At this point, the valley was shaped like a steep-sided star, with rippling glaciers, hanging icefields and snow-streaked buttresses rising precipitously on the left. To the right, the incline was no less gentle, but the climb levelled into the pancake flatness of a broad mesa.

Morrill followed the track steadily upwards and when he reached the summit he paused, gasping, his heart hammering wildly in his chest. Yaks grazed among the stunted hillgrass, their bells tinkling on the high-altitude air.

He spotted a figure standing alone in the sunlight. Choking with excitement, Morrill began to run toward it. As he approached, the figure took on form and substance. Baima. He saw her look at him, surprise flooding her features. Then the surprise gave way to an expression of undisguised delight.

Tears of happiness were streaming down her cheeks by the time he reached her. Without hesitation, Morrill swept her into his arms and kissed her wildly on the mouth.

'You've come,' she cried. 'You promised you would, and now you have.'

She was talking and weeping in turns. Morrill felt his own excitement almost bubbling over. 'I couldn't find you in the village,' he gasped. 'I thought you'd gone. I thought they'd married you off to some bastard from another valley.'

'I told you I would wait,' she laughed, wiping the tears from her face. 'How little faith, to suspect I would leave so quickly.'

Morrill wanted to shout out loud with joy. The long weeks at the monastery, the interminable trek through the mountain villages had filled him with a profound frustration that had built up slowly with each passing day; now the sense of release, of fear dispelled, anxiety halted, was dazzling in its intensity.

They had much to talk about, he quickly discovered. His weeks of study had filled him with a burning desire to impart his new-found knowledge, and he chatted endlessly about the high lama's teaching while Baima listened with amusement; she understood little of what he said, but his earnestness, the enthusiasm which radiated within him, touched her deeply.

She told him about her own experiences which, by comparison, seemed commonplace and mundane, her long journey back to the village, her father attempts to trade a few yaks, the devil dancers who had visited the village for the 'unveiling of spring' ceremony; there was an almost childlike innocence in her manner which Morrill found charming.

Toward evening, when they had talked themselves hoarse, they fell into a curious silence. A new feeling had entered Morrill's senses, one he scarcely knew how to control. He was filled with a fierce physical awareness. He had waited too long, deferred too much. His emotions were greedy and impatient.

She was watching him shyly, her dark eyes suddenly deep and sombre, and he knew she experienced it too. Gently, he kissed her on the mouth. For the moment, she scarcely responded, and then, with a suddenness that took him by surprise, she began to return his caresses passionately.

Morrill felt the craving mounting within him. The blood pounded in his throat as he tore at her thin cotton dress, exposing the small plump breasts. Gasping, he ran his lips down the steep curve of her throat, his fingers kneading her yielding flesh. Her head was thrown back, her lips open, emitting soft mewing sounds.

There was no finesse to Morrill's approach. He was beyond reason, beyond coherence. He could feel her palms on the small of his back, her breasts pressed hard against his chest, her mouth warm and moist upon his ear, whispering indecipherable messages of love.

On that windswept Tibetan plateau, as his body went through the timeworn ceremony of the ages, Harold Morrill felt that his path to completeness had at last been achieved.

The marriage was discussed that very same evening. It was to be a much more casual affair than Morrill had expected. As Gendun explained, the policy was to let the lovers continue their relationship without commitments on either side for at least six months. If the girl became pregnant, the marriage ritual could then take place.

'Supposing she doesn't?' Morrill asked.

Gendun gave an elaborate gesture. 'In that case, why saddle yourselves with unnecessary responsibilities? Remain together as long as you wish. Without children, men and women are free to please themselves.'

Morrill nodded, satisfied with the proposal. They would wait until the middle of winter. If, by then, Baima was expecting a child then he, Morrill, would marry her. It did not occur to Morrill that he was already married. The earlier experiences of his life, his relationship with his wife Tracey, seemed confused and hazy. At times he felt they had happened to a different person.

Gendun and the lamas left the following morning to continue their pilgrimage. Morrill escorted them to the edge of the village. Gendun stroked his beard, his eyes twinkling merrily. 'You know it is our belief that the nearest a man can come to paradise is through physical union with another being,' he said.

Morrill nodded gravely. 'In that case, I shall endeavour to get close to paradise at every available opportunity', he promised.

He watched them set off along the steep mountain track, their orange robes startlingly vivid in the early-morning sunshine. Their yaks, laden with the lamas' belongings, stumbled along in front of them. They crossed the ridge, mounted a small col flanked by two jagged columns of rock, then they were gone.

Morrill settled easily into the simple pattern of village life. The monastery had sustained him with its fascinating dissemination of knowledge and wisdom. In the village, he found a new strength, a new identity marked by a pattern of existence so fundamental in its concept that for the second time in a mere matter of months Morrill felt he had been reborn.

The seasons passed tranquilly, summer lengthening into early autumn. Morrill learned to look after the yaks, driving them on to the high pastures each morning. He learned to smear dung over the dry-stone walls, baking it in the sunlight into fuel for the cooking fires. He learned to drink *chang* and *rakshi* with the village elders and discuss the merits of high and low grazing, the weather omens for the coming winter and the virtues of trading with the Chinese.

And always there was Baima. Morrill found her a never-ending source of discovery and delight. He waited impatiently for each day to end so he could be with her again. In the past, he had always been a solitary man, driven by forces he scarcely understood, his nature restless and unsettled. He had searched constantly for serenity of mind, conformity of purpose. With Baima, he knew that search was over.

They lived with the family in the rough-walled dwelling house. Morrill found the arrangement something of an embarrassment in the beginning, for there were no bedrooms, and at night the cattle occupied the lower floor whilst the family slept together on a long bench stretching the entire length of the upstairs room. At first, Morrill confined his lovemaking to the open air, contriving to meet Baima in the empty pastures or on the hillslopes overlooking the deserted plateau; he refrained from touching her at night, and rejected her amorous advances with a determination that sent her into fits of nocturnal giggling. Baima's mother, on the other hand, displayed no such timorousness, and would happily enter into bouts of enthusiastic coupling with any of her three husbands whilst the others lay blissfully asleep. At length, Morrill forgot his shyness and began to enter into the spirit of things, embracing Baima with a fervour that brought nods of approval from her father and uncles.

At the end of eight weeks, Baima, to Morrill's delight, informed him she was pregnant, and arrangements were rapidly made for the wedding ceremony to take place. First however, there was the customary celebration of conception, which by tradition the bride's mother and father held for the neighbouring yak-herders. Tibetans rarely missed any chance for a party, Morrill had already discovered.

The festivities took place in the middle of the week so as not to interfere with the fortnightly yak-trading. The guests arrived from all corners of the surrounding area, and even from as far away as the Zhaojiabang valley. In the cloistered darkness of the upstairs room, with the wood floor vibrating ominously, they ate and drank and talked till dawn. Toward midnight, the customary singing began. It was started by the women who beat tambourines and plucked primitively-fashioned lutes. As Baima's mother moved from group to group distributing *chang*, some of the men began to dance, their sinewy figures weaving elegantly in the lamplight, their movements imbued with a grace and fluidity that contrasted strangely with their rough clothing.

Morrill felt himself rapidly becoming drunk. He sat cradling his glass of milky *chang*, listening to the wailing dirge of the women, smelling the overpowering odour of cooked rice, melting butter and unwashed clothing. At length, when his head began to spin, he eased himself up and made his way down the creaking ladder into the chill freshness of the high-altitude night. The sky was studded with stars, and all around him, the jagged mountain peaks glistened eerily. A thin scattering of snow had fallen, and yaks huddled together in the darkness, their bells making muffled ringing sounds as gently they swayed to and fro. Standing alone in front of the house, Morrill was entranced by the beauty of the moment. He felt as if everything in his life had been moving with an inexorable persistence toward this point. He had left the world of material possessions and returned to the essential beginning of things. He had cast off the trappings of civilisation and embraced the simplicity of nature. He had a woman who loved him, a family who revered him, a religion which sustained him, and soon, God willing, he would have a child to cheer him. It was like the fulfilment of some long-forgotten prophecy, and it seemed to Morrill at that moment that he was closer to paradise than he had been in his entire life.

In the first weeks of autumn, Gendun and the lamas returned from their pilgrimage. They were anxious to reach the monastery before the high passes became blocked by the winter snows. Morrill greeted Gendun warmly. He had grown increasingly fond of the Tibetan monk whose enthusiasm for the English language was matched only by his appetite for pulling Morrill's leg.

Gendun expressed satisfaction and delight when he heard of Morrill's forthcoming marriage, but declined an invitation to stay for the ceremony, explaining their need to reach the lamasery before the weather worsened.

'Also, there is another danger,' he told Morrill gravely.

'Your old friend Chamdo has become quite a menace in the province. It is said he resents the influence we have had upon you. He blames us for taking away your mind. He has threatened violence against the lamas, and for this reason I am anxious to reach Nepal as quickly as possible.'

Morrill laughed lightly. 'Chamdo would never harm a holy man. It would be contrary to everything he believes in.'

'Nevertheless, he is desperate, that Chamdo. He has been fashioned and nurtured by hatred.'

Morrill was thoughtful for a moment. 'If you really are concerned for your safety,' he said, 'maybe I should venture with you as far as the frontier. You'll be okay once you cross the borderline. Chamdo would never attempt any kind of mischief

92

in Nepalese territory. It's his only escape route when the Chinese get too close for comfort.'

Gendun was hesitant. 'I can't ask you to leave your woman at such a time,' he protested.

'Nonsense,' Morrill said. 'If we keep a steady pace, I can be there and back within five days.'

So it was arranged that the following morning Morrill would escort the party of lamas to the Nepalese frontier. He said goodbye to Baima who provided him with a bag of food and warm clothing for the return journey, and in the first flush of dawn set off up the steep exit ridge which led out of the precipitous little valley. Three days later, he bid Gendun goodbye on the Nepalese border and returned swiftly the way he had come. Already, the weather was worsening, and the days were growing colder. Sharp snow flurries swept in from the east, and several times Morrill was caught in blizzards so dense he found difficulty in keeping to the defined track. Despite the vagaries of the elements however, he managed to reach Lamringyhana, as he had prophesied, on the evening of the fifth day. There was a mist over the valley that night, obscuring the village from the ridge above, and the first intimation he had of disaster was a glimpse of Lamringyhana's outbuildings burnt to charcoal in the first shades of approaching dark.

Morrill felt his stomach tense and a sudden spasm of fear shoot into his skull. Where the dwellings had stood, there was nothing but shapeless heaps of rubble and charred rafters caked with soot. There was no sign of a living thing, not even a dog. Panic seared Morrill's chest. Baima, he thought. Sweet suffering Jesus, Baima.

He stumbled forward, quickening his pace. Between the lines of dry-stone walls he saw their house, or what was left of it, a pathetic heap of stones, smoke-blackened and shapeless, support-struts tilted obscenely into the sky.

Almost demented, Morrill dropped his pack and scrambled over the pile of refuse, looking for the building's occupants. He was weeping openly, tears streaming down his haggard cheeks. His brain seemed strangely unhinged, as if everything was happening in slow motion. The vision of Baima floated in his senses, her features hazy and undefined.

Desperately, his fingers clawed and scratched at the shifting rubble, tearing aside bricks, window-frames, bits of shattered furniture, until at last he found the bodies tucked against the outside wall. In accordance with Tibetan custom, they had been dismembered, the flesh peeled from their bones to feed the vultures and jackals. Morrill counted the remains of five corpses, and an inarticulate cry of protest emerged from his lips.

In a daze, he stumbled around the village looking for survivors. He found a young woman and her infant son who had managed to escape to the high pastures. Chinese soldiers had come with the dawn, she said, looking for Morrill. They had assembled the villagers in the market-place and interrogated them each in turn. When they realised Morrill had escaped, they had set about executing everyone in sight. The assassinations had been random and casual. Baima, her mother, father and two uncles had been the first to be shot. Some of the villagers had managed to escape, but those who didn't, women, children, old people, even the animals, had been dispatched with the bland unconcern of beasts at a slaughter-house.

Later, after the Chinese had gone, the survivors had returned to salvage what they could and to carry out the Tibetan custom of dismembering their dead. Now the village was tainted with evil spirits and death. Most of the remaining habitants had moved into the neighbouring valleys. Her husband was up in the high pastures gathering the yaks. In the morning, they too would depart for the village of Dusitang.

Morrill listened to this story with a mixture of horror and disbelief. Five days ago, his life had seemed a blessed fusion of all the things he had ever dreamed of. Suddenly, in one grief-stricken moment, it had been shattered beyond repair. The pain in his chest seemed to be tearing him apart. He thought of Baima, her gentle eyes, her tinkling laughter, and his body shuddered as a series of anguished spasms drove through him.

He waited until the woman had gone, then sitting on the blackened rubble of their home, he threw back his head and howled like a wolf in the darkness . . .

Chamdo stopped when he reached Morrill's side. Morrill was sitting motionless on the rock, staring into the night. If he was aware of Chamdo's presence, he gave no sign. Etched against the starlight, the two men made an eerie tableau.

Years had passed since Morrill had returned to Chamdo, but

the American had never been the same again. Gone was the earnest exuberance, the nervous intelligence Chamdo had so respected and admired. The new Morrill was a man tormented. He had found the purity he so fervently sought. The purity of hate. Now Morrill hated as Chamdo hated, but while Chamdo's hatred was a searing flame, sustaining him through the weary months of attack, counter-attack and flight, Morrill's filled him with a complexity of emotions he neither knew how to handle nor bothered to control.

Sadly, Chamdo studied his friend in the moonlight. Morrill still yearned for the purity of the soul, but in his veins ran the destructive purity of hate, and Chamdo knew the polarity of the two was irreconcilable. The American could embrace one or the other, but until he did, his brain would remain in limbo, tortured by the continual conflict within him.

Gently, Chamdo touched Morrill's shoulder and Morrill woke from his reverie with a start. He peered upward, his eyes gleaming above the haggard cheekbones.

'It's time to go,' Chamdo said in a soft voice.

For a moment, Morrill was silent, then he nodded. Rising to his feet, he picked up his submachine gun, slung it across his shoulder, and together the two men walked down the twisting footpath, their boots echoing weirdly in the stillness of the mountain air.

CHAPTER SEVEN

It was dark when Ramdon stopped the truck. The howling of wild dogs echoed in his ears and behind them, the lights of the city glowed in the night sky. Through the windscreen, Tracey would see the airport ahead. There were no lights in the windows of the terminal building and only a single Gurkha patrolled the traffic forecourt, his floppy wide-brimmed hat curiously shapeless and distorted in the starlight.

'This is as far as we go,' Ramdon said.

In the darkness of the driving cab, his face looked wolfish. Again, Tracey was filled with the uncomfortable notion that Ramdon might be mad. It seemed ironic in a way. Of all the pilots she could have chosen, she'd ended up with Ramdon. Why did he have to look so crazy all the time?

A clammy feeling of dread settled over Tracey's body. She knew it was a wild thing to do. Even Ramdon himself had been doubtful when she'd suggested it. '*Steal* the plane?' he echoed. 'Are you out of your mind?'

Well, maybe she was at that. Maybe her stay in Katmandu had somehow unhinged her. Of course, once they'd settled on a suitable remuneration, Ramdon had more or less entered into the spirit of the thing. She supposed the criminality of the act rather appealed to him. He was that sort of man.

Lucky for him, she thought dryly. But if anything went wrong, she might as well face the fact she would end up in a Nepalese jail, and there would be no help then from the US State Department. She would be on her own, isolated and defenceless.

Her legs were trembling as she clambered from the driving cab into the cool of the mountain night. Squatting on packs of camping equipment in the back of the truck sat the five guides and Sherpas Jenkins had hired the day before, small wiry men from Namche Bazar and the Dudh Khosi. They wore tattered, heavily-stained clothing and tiny cloth skullcaps. Their feet were bare, their faces dirty, and each carried, thrust into the belt at his waist, a wicked-looking *khukri* or Gurkha knife. They stared down at her in silence, their eyes sombre in the darkness, and instinctively Tracey shivered. With Ramdon here, they obeyed her orders without question, but once he dropped them on Tangpoche La pass, would she still command their attention and respect? Tracey was no stranger to authority; in the television studio where she worked, she controlled people many years her senior, but here in the mountains she was in different world, and the realisation frightened her.

Ramdon tumbled from the driving cab and hissed something at the men in the rear. Instantly, they scrambled over the side of the truck and began to unload the equipment. Ramdon took a blanket from the back of his seat and crossed the small strip of empty ground to where the airport's perimeter fence stood etched against the starlight. Tracey joined him, her senses tensing. 'Will there be no one on patrol?' she whispered.

His teeth flashed in the darkness. 'Oh, they'll be patrolling all night, but they've got an awesome expanse of field to cover. With a bit of luck, we'll be in the air before they know it.'

Tracey eyed the wire fence dubiously. It was at least fifteen feet high and along the top she discerned three separate strands of ugly barbed wire.

Ramdon looped the blanket around his neck, and without hesitation began to mount the fence, hooking his fingers through the tight wire loops. She could hear the metal creaking and his breath rasping in his throat as he grunted with the strain. When he reached the fence rim, he hung back on one hand, carefully drew the blanket from around his neck, and with infinite patience, draped it over the prickly strands of barbed wire, masking their wicked points. She glimpsed his face peering down at her. 'Come on,' he hissed.

Swallowing hard, Tracey took hold of the wire and slowly began to climb. She felt the harsh strands biting into her fingers and her toes dug at the tiny metal rings. When she reached Ramdon's side, he hooked his hands under her armpits and forced her over the blanketed rim. On the other side, she paused for a moment, gasping hard, then closing her eyes, let herself fall. Her feet hit the ground and she bent her knees, taking the strain. The impact jarred her body, rolling her over in the dust. She looked up and and saw the Sherpas following swiftly, passing the trekking packs from one to the other.

Ramdon dropped to her side with a muffled grunt. 'Right,' he hissed, 'let's find out what they've done with that kite.'

She followed him across the open runway. There were no lights, the airport had been closed till morning. Tracey saw the menacing shape of the hangar looming out of the darkness, and Ramdon peered back at her, grinning wildly, sweat tracing rivulets of moisture down his sunbaked skin.

'Okay?' he hissed.

She nodded, scarcely daring to speak. She was shaking all over. Behind her, she heard the sound of the Sherpas scrambling in their wake, their wiry bodies bent almost double beneath the heavy trekking packs. It seemed incredible such small men could carry so much, she thought. The cooking utensils clanged dully in the stillness, but Ramdon scarcely seemed to notice. He found the door of the hangar secured by an old-fashioned padlock and jimmied it easily, sliding the heavy panel aside. In the shadows, Tracey could see the shapes of the aircraft huddled in rows beneath the girdered roof. Ramdon moved among them, his boots echoing against the concrete floor. Tracey waited in the doorway with the Sherpas, holding her breath as her heart pounded against her ribcage.

When Ramdon returned, he was frowning with puzzlement. 'Bloody thing's not here,' he whispered. 'They've got everything but the kitchen sink, but no sign of old gravel-guts.'

'It must be here,' she insisted fiercely, panic rising in her chest.

'Don't get your knickers in a twist. They probably moved her someplace else. Let's take a look at the apron.'

Tracey followed Ramdon across the grassy verge. From time to time, she glanced toward the empty terminal windows, filled with the worrying thought that at any moment a security guard might casually enter and glance in their direction.

Ramdon himself seemed oblivious to the danger. He was sauntering along as if he had every right to be here. In the crisp night air, she smelled whisky fumes on his breath. Damn the man, he'd been drinking again. Had he no sense of responsibility?

There was no denying Ramdon worried her. She liked the man, more than 'liked', if the truth were known. But physical attraction wasn't enough to gamble one's life on. Silas Ramdon might be captivating in the sexual sense, but he was also unstable and unpredictable and she was beginning to regret the fact that Jenkins had recommended him in the first place.

The Sherpas scurried along behind them, their heads obscured by the heavy trekking packs, their bare feet making no sound as they padded through the darkness. Ahead, Tracey saw the shadows merge and solidify. As she drew closer, her eyes discerned the outline of a small aircraft.

'There she is,' Ramdon exclaimed with satisfaction. 'They must have been using her. They do that sometimes, when there's an overload of trekking parties on the Lukla run.'

Tracey stared at the plane in dismay. It looked battered and decrepit, its wings and fuselage on the point of falling to bits. 'Supposing they've used all the fuel?' she whispered.

'Oh, they'll keep her topped up.' Ramdon promised, 'just in case there's an emergency.'

Reaching underneath, he undid the cargo hatches. 'Get

those trekking packs on board. We'll strap them into place afterwards.'

Tracey felt her spirits flounder as she slipped beneath the port wing and followed Ramdon into the cockpit. The interior of the aircraft looked even more ramshackle than the outside. She stared in alarm at wires dangling from the ceiling and empty beer cans crumpled and discarded on the mudstained deck.

'How's my old beauty,' Ramdon chuckled, patting the instrument panel with his hand. 'Miss old Silas, did you? Thought he'd run off and abandoned you forever?'

In the rear of the plane, the Sherpas dragged the trekking packs on board and carefully locked the cargo hatch.

'Sit down,' Ramdon told her, leaning forward to scan the fuel gauge.

She settled herself in the co-pilot's seat. 'Where's the seat-belt?' she asked.

'What the hell do you want a seatbelt for? Don't you trust me?'

'Every aircraft should have a seatbelt. It's the law.'

'For Christ's sake, if we worried about the law, we wouldn't even be here. Hang on to your pants. They'll give you a damn sight more security than any bloody seatbelt.'

Ramdon started the engine and checked the gauges. Tracey felt the hull vibrating beneath her feet. Her mouth seemed dry. Anxiously, she peered through the windshield at the buildings on her left. There was no sign of life. It was a miracle they hadn't been heard. In such stillness, even the faintest of sounds carried.

Ramdon started to rev the engines. The noise made an ear-splitting roar. Desperately, Tracey held her breath. Ramdon revved harder. He was grinning wolfishly, his face wild and demented.

For God's sake, she thought, they must have heard us by now. Why aren't they doing something, reacting, responding?

Then suddenly Tracey blinked, shading her eyes as a search-beam of light shot across the tarmac from the control tower, picking them up in its blinding glare. At the same instant, a siren began to howl, its discordant wailing echoing across the empty runway.

Ramdon released the brakes and the plane started to move.

Even above the siren's scream, Tracey could hear men shouting. She saw dusky figures running toward them, Ghurkas with rifles caught in the glare of the searchlight beam.

Ramdon taxied to the leeward end of the runway and began his take-off, singing wildly: 'As I lay in distress, I watched a maid undress, She had the map of Scotland tattooed on her chest . . .'

Through the side window, Tracey saw jeeps hurtling across the open apron. Fear rose through her. Her body started to tremble. She could see the end of the strip coming up fast. The plane was still on the ground. Ramdon hauled back the stick. 'Come on, you old bastard,' he grunted, 'get your arse in the air.'

Still they did not rise. The siren was incessant now, ringing in her ears. She heard the ragged stutter of gunfire. My God, they're shooting, she thought wildly. It was like watching a film taking place in slow motion. Nothing seemed real any more – the screech of the siren, the glare of the lights, the spurts of flame from the rifle muzzles, Ramdon cursing and singing in turns – it was like a nightmare etched in her consciousness. We'll never make it, she thought, oh God, we'll never make it.

Then slowly the plane lifted. Ramdon's voice, still singing lustily, echoed in her ears: '. . . and further down, I did spy, That shady little nest where Nelson lost his eye . . .'

Looking back, Tracey could see sharp little flashes as the machine guns spluttered. Something hit the aircrafft along the side of the fuselage, shaking it violently. Ramdon paused in his singing to swear.

'Bastards are shooting better'n I thought. Damn near got us there.'

Tracey glared at him. In the light from the control panel, she could see him grinning. The tension inside her began to dissolve and waves of relief flooded through her body in a breathless rush. As Ramdon banked the aircraft toward the east, the searchbeam behind them faded steadily into the darkness.

Tracey realised something was wrong when the engine started to stutter. She had been dozing fitfully, her brain crammed with weird dreamlike images which popped in and out of her head like tiddly-winks.

Startled, she opened her eyes. Dawn had broken, and a pale sheen of daylight glowed through the windshield. She peered downwards, swallowing swiftly. They were flying low over jagged snowcapped peaks. There was nothing to see but craggy mountains and tumbling valleys. The land looked desolate, awe-inspiring, and she shivered as she glimpsed darkly-swirling stormclouds gathering menacingly over the topmost tips.

Beside her, Ramdon was swearing at the controls. She could hear the Sherpas chattering excitedly, then the engines hic-cupped, died, caught again.

'What's wrong?' she asked, sitting upright.

'Christ knows. Looks like we got hit more badly than I thought. Those bullets have done something to the fuel intake.'

'How far have we still to go?'

'That's Tangpoche La pass dead ahead. You can see it curl-ing beneath the angel-shaped glacier.'

Tracey peered through the windshield. She spotted a narrow track vanishing into empty snow. It looked so desolate, so unimaginably exposed that, watching, she felt her blood freeze.

'Can't you put her down?'

'We've got no choice,' he told her frankly. 'Either we land now, or fall out of the air like a stone. I'm going to try and bellyflop her into the snow. Get back with the others and find something to hold on to. It might get a little bumpy.'

'Supposing there are rocks down there?'

'Stop looking on the black side, lady. I tend to panic very easily.'

Tracey felt sick with fright as she eased out of the cockpit and jammed herself tightly on the aircraft deck. She hooked her arm around the hull struts and gritted her teeth, her body trem-bling. She could see the Sherpas' faces, pale with fright. They had stopped chattering now, each man retreating deep within himself as slowly the plane began to lose altitude.

Tracey watched snow flurries whipping past the porthole windows. She could see Ramdon battling with the controls. In front of his head, the windshield was rapidly coating with ice. Jagged peaks swayed into her vision and instinctively Tracey closed her eyes. She waited, holding her breath, for the impact to come.

There was no warning, no preliminary shudder. Just a spine-jarring, brain-stunning crash and a breathless whooshing sen-sation as they careered dizzily forward. Tracey could see snow

cascading across the windows. Above the rattle of accoutrements and the screech of tortured metal, she heard a strange,
unidentifiable sound and realised she was screaming. They
went on rocketing forward in a dizzy rush, bits of the fuselage
breaking up and scattering wildly across the milky surface.
Ramdon was bellowing like a madman, wrestling with the controls. Tracey felt as if her brain had shaken loose inside her
skull. Her vision seemed to shudder violently and she chewed
hard at her lip till her mouth filled with salty sting of blood.
Suddenly, the entire flank of the aircraft opened up and icy air
scoured her cheeks and throat. Snow billowed in through the
jagged gap, covering the occupants from head to foot. Tracey
struggled to keep her head aloft, feeling the icy particles biting
into her skin. The snow was everywhere, tumbling over and
around them in a suffocating shroud.

Then slowly, almost imperceptibly, she felt their momentum
slacken. They spun sideways in a screech of tearing metal and
slithered abruptly to a halt. A heavy silence filled the tiny cabin.
Tracey sat stunned, watching the Sherpas brushing snow from
their faces and limbs. Ramdon was leaning back in the pilot's
seat, his forehead bleeding where the windshield had caught it.
'What a bloody landing,' he exclaimed jubilantly. 'Did you see
that? A piece of bloody genius.'

Wincing, Tracey moved. She eased herself upwards through
the snow, running her hands down the length of her body.
Everything intact, thank God. No bones broken. But the plane
itself was a mess. Jagged corners of metal reared against the
steel-grey sky. Fractured struts swayed eerily in the brain-
numbing wind.

Tracey dragged herself forward, carving a path through the
snow. 'Are you all right?' she asked Ramdon.

He was still sitting in the pilot's seat, his face flushed and
exhilarated.

'Sure, I'm all right. Why shouldn't I be all right? That was
the most fantastic bit of flying I've seen in my whole life.'

'Well, before you start congratulating yourself,' she said
dryly, 'you'd better take a look at this old crate of yours.'

The light died in Ramdon's eyes. She watched him turn and
survey the damage, his features clouding bleakly.

'Not much left, is there?' Tracey muttered.

Inwardly, she wanted to shout out loud with joy and relief.

The plane was a write-off. Ramdon couldn't leave them even if wanted to. She wouldn't have to face the mountains alone after all.

'This is going to take some explaining when I get back to Katmandu,' he mumbled.

'Well, there's no way on earth of you flying back. I'm afraid whether you like it or not, you'll have to come along with us.'

'Just a minute,' he grunted, 'this is above and beyond the call of duty.'

'You're the one who pranged the kite, old boy,' she said in an exaggerated pilot's accent.

'I just hope those employers of yours will settle on a satisfactory bonus.'

'First, we've got to survive. Then we'll talk about a bonus.'

Frowning, he clambered out of the pilot's seat. The sherpas were moving experimentally around the deck. 'Anyone hurt?' Ramdon asked.

'I think they're all okay,' Tracey said.

'What about Merlin?'

She frowned. 'Merlin?'

Carefully, Ramdon rooted among the trekbags until he found the one he was looking for. Unlacing the top, he took out a battered violin case and opening it up, examined the instrument inside.

Tracey stared at him in disbelief. 'My God,' she breathed, 'you mean you've brought that ridiculous fiddle along?'

Ramdon looked affronted. 'You don't know what you're saying. This is the only thing that keeps me sane.'

'That's what worries me about you,' she told him dryly.

In the harsh chill of the early dawn, they began to unload the equipment. Ramdon had climbing boots and padded arctic clothing stowed in a cubby-hole at the cabin's rear. Insurance against emergencies, he explained, pulling them on. He seemed surprisingly resigned to his unexpected maroonment. In fact, the narrowness of their escape had imbued them all with an intoxicated air of well-being and their spirits were high, almost jaunty, the Sherpas laughing and chatting happily, their voices helping to disperse the tension.

The snowfield on which they had landed lay on a narrow saddle between two mountain peaks. A ragged trail in the snow, littered with bits of wrecked fuselage, marked the length of

103

their skid. Above, winding tortuously beneath the rim of the massive glacier, a narrow track bobbed and dipped over Tangpoche La Pass.

Ramdon rummaged around inside the aircraft and came out with a long-barrelled Mannlichen rifle. An ammunition pouch dangled from his shoulder. 'Never know when we might need this,' he muttered cheerfully. 'Even if the Chinese don't shoot us, the bandits might. I don't believe in turning the other cheek.'

'How far is the frontier?' Tracey asked.

'That's it at the top of the pass.'

'Supposing there's a customs post?'

'Are you kidding? This is the end of the world.'

Tracey pursed her lips. The track looked dangerous and forbidding, and the altitude was beginning to make her head throb. Her high spirits at finding herself still alive faded rapidly. They still had an awesome distance to cover, and once on the other side of that pass, they would be moving through enemy territory. The prospect frightened her, but briskly she zipped up her Duvet jacket and eyed the porters standing in front of her. 'Well, what on earth are we waiting for?' she snapped. 'We've got to get up there sooner or later, so we might as well get started.'

Tall crags leaned into the sunlight, towering high above the shadowy chasm. Beyond the rim of the pass, the snowcapped mountains rose pyramid-like, etched against the sky. Spumes of snow drifted from their summits and fleecy clouds gathered at their tips.

Tracey's back felt as if it were breaking. She had been walking for hours, following Ramdon over the steep hump of Tangpoche La, the Sherpas following in silence, falling back under the awesome load of their heavy packs. Though the way was cluttered with snow, they walked barefooted, oblivious to the biting cold.

The shock of the plane crash had left Tracey feeling faintly dazed. Despite the exertion, she shivered as she felt the high-altitude air biting through her Duvet. She scarcely knew what she was doing here. Somewhere in that tundra wilderness ahead, she knew her husband was hiding, but she hadn't the vaguest idea how to contact him. Everything depended on chance, on the news of her approach preceding her. It seemed a clumsy way of doing things, but she could think of nothing else.

She stared at Ramdon striding along in front. He had the rifle slung from one shoulder, the violin from the other. She scarcely knew what to make of Ramdon. He was an enigma, an exasperating bear of a man.

As if he realised she was thinking about him, he turned toward her, grinning.

'Feeling okay?'

She nodded. 'Bit breathless.'

'That's the height. This pass rises to eighteen thousand feet. Lucky you took those pills. Working out at this altitude can finish you off if you're not used to it.'

For the past three days, Ramdon had been feeding her diuretic tablets.

'They'll make you pee a lot,' he'd warned, 'but at least they'll cut down the chances of altitude sickness.'

She peered about her curiously. Everywhere she looked, there were high peaks and precipitous valleys, a wilderness of ice, rock and snow. 'Are we in Tibet yet?' she asked.

'Sure. We crossed the line at the summit.'

'Do people actually live here?'

'A few. Down in the valleys. Mostly though, they're scattered to the north. This is the most isolated region in the country. See that triangular peak over there?'

'The one with hardly any snow on it?'

'That's right. Looks only a mile or two away, doesn't it? It would take you eight to nine days' hard travelling to reach it. The Tibetans call it Chomolungma.'

'What does that mean?' she asked.

'Goddess Mother of the Earth.'

'How lyrical.'

He smiled. 'We've got a different name. We call it Mount Everest.'

'Everest?' She looked at him. 'You mean that's really the top of the world?'

'That's right. Chomolungma.'

Tracey stared fascinated at the mountain's distant hump. A faint wisp of mist hung above its summit like regal lace. She found it difficult to realise she was peering at the highest point on earth.

The hours passed steadily, as the track levelled into a broad saucer of land flanked on all sides by glistening seracs, Tracey felt her strength growing. She was getting into her stride now. The altitude bothered her less acutely. Her head still ached, there was still a slight breathlessness in her chest, but the awful draining lassitude pervading her limbs had begun at last to dissolve. For the first time, she began to notice the beauty of the landscape. She had never seen anything like it, she thought. Even the Alps, with their towering pinnacles, were no match for these mighty giants.

They walked all day following the track across rugged hill-slopes, and when night fell, they made camp at the side of a bubbling stream, Tracey sprawling exhausted in the grass whilst the Sherpas, working with the tireless precision of men born to such hardships, prepared a supper of curry and rice. With the coming of dark, the temperature dropped acutely, and once the meal was over Tracey made no attempt to prolong conversation but crawled into her tent and huddled shivering inside her sleeping bag. She slept badly, though not because of the cold; Ramdon had warned her that the thin oxygen made slumber practically impossible, and throughout the long hours of darkness she tossed and turned, listening to the distant moaning of the wind. When morning came, she joined the Sherpas at the cooking fire and gobbled down a hasty breakfast of boiled porridge, then, with the first streak of dawn lighting the eastern sky, she helped them dismantle the tents, pack up the cooking gear and continue on their way.

All through the long hours of morning they walked tirelessly, following the track around ice-canyons and hummocks of silvery moraine. Clouds gathered on the mountaintops, and snow flurries whipped east and west like flocks of wild birds.

Toward noon, Ramdon drew alongside, his thin cheeks flushed with exertion.

'You're bearing up well. You must be used to this.'

'I used to go climbing with my husband,' she said. 'Mountains are no novelty to me.'

'Just the same, don't push yourself too hard. You've got to give your body a chance to acclimatise to the altitude.'

They walked along in silence for a moment, then Ramdon, in a voice so soft she scarcely heard him, said: 'What kind of a man was he, your husband?'

She glanced at him sideways. 'Why do you ask?'

'Just curious.'

Tracey shrugged. 'This may sound a little strange, but I scarcely knew him. We were together for only five months.'

'You can get to know a person pretty well in five months.'

'Not Harry. He was . . . a quiet man.'

'Introvert?'

'Very. He seldom talked much about himself. He was always gentle, always fun to be with, but I don't think I ever touched beneath the surface.'

'Did you love him?'

'I thought so at the time.'

'And now?'

'How can you love a stranger? Thinking back, I can hardly even remember what he looked like.'

Ramdon's eyes fixed on the trail ahead. A tangle of hair tumbled over his forehead and absently he brushed it back. Tracey slowed her pace, sweating freely as she climbed. The going was tougher here. Mist curled among the mountain flanks, smudging the topmost tips into a bleary haze that oozed into the sky with no dividing line.'

She studied Ramdon curiously. 'What about *your* wife, Mr Ramdon?' she muttered.

'I thought I told you to call me Silas.'

'Very well, Silas. Why are you always so secretive?'

'I'm not secretive. Don't want to bore you, that's all.'

'Was she Nepalese?'

'No, British. I met her in Vancouver, Canada. I was flying men out to the logging camps for the timber people.'

'Don't tell me your wife was a lumberjack.'

'No, she was a nurse. We had a bad accident one day. Young choker had his leg sliced off by a drag-chain. We fixed a tourniquet on the stump and I flew him down to hospital in Vancouver. That's when I met Sally.'

'What was she like?'

'Different. What the Americans would call . . . kooky.'

'You must have made quite a pair,' Tracey grunted.

'Well, it was kind of a bumpy marriage. If you want to know the truth, I wasn't around a hell of a lot. That was the year I was running in supplies to the rebels in Chad. Pretty profitable at the time until the French put a stop to it.'

'And Sally?'

'She got fed up in the end. Took off with a diver working on the oil-rigs in the Gulf of Mexico.'

'Did you miss her?'

He grinned. 'Not so's you'd notice,' he said.

She never knew when to take him seriously, she thought. That was Ramdon through and through. Exasperating to the end. It would take a saint to stay married to such a man. And yet – the truth was inescapable – Ramdon, whichever way you looked at it, was a damned attractive man. Not in the filmstar sense – his face was too bashed-about to be called handsome – but he was appealing in a vital masculine way. Even his craziness was appealing. She could see at a glance why Sally had fallen in love with him.

Still, she had no intention of doing that. No intention at all. She'd had enough rapscallions in her life without including Silas Ramdon.

In the late afternoon, as they made their way steeply downwards through boulder-studded pastures, they spotted a cluster of black nomad tents in the valley below.

'People,' she hissed.

They were the first human beings they had seen since crashlanding on the snowfield, and Tracey felt a tremor of excitement. Ramdon however looked grim and wary. He eased the Mannlichen from his shoulder and held it in the crook of his arm.

Tracey stared at him. 'What are you doing?' she asked. 'Those people aren't our enemies. They're Tibetans, not Chinese.'

'This is Khampa country,' Ramdon told her gruffly. 'Until we're sure who we're talking to, everyone around here is our enemy.'

Dogs started to bark as they moved slowly closer. A woman emerged from one of the tents and shaded her eyes from the sun, peering up at them as they wandered down the winding track. She called something in a high wailing voice and instantly six or seven men crawled out of the tents' interiors. They moved toward the travellers, chattering excitedly. Glancing back, Tracey noticed worried frowns on the faces of the Sherpas.

The nomads gathered around them, fingering their clothing, patting their packs, grinning happily and jabbering in a continual babble of sound. Tracey studied them curiously in turn. Like the Sherpas, they were small and wiry, their clothes smeared with grease and dirt. They wore purple scarves and fur hats with the ear-flaps turned up to look like wings, and they emitted a powerful odour of sweat, incense and smoke.

Ramdon talked to them briefly. They gabbled back at him, laughing and giggling.

'Who are they?' she asked.

'They say they're traders from the Dharadari on their way to Dusitang.'

'You believe them?'

'Who knows? They could be telling the truth.'

'They look friendly enough anyhow.'

'Don't let those smiles deceive you. They're checking us out, weighing our value. They've clocked my rifle all right. What they're wondering is, have you got a pistol tucked inside your pockets. If they try to pat you, dissuade them. Better if they think we're fully armed.'

'You're not seriously suggesting these happy people are bandits?'

'If they're not, what the hell are they doing here? They're a long way from Dusitang, which is where they claim to be going. My bet is, they're Khampas all right, and they can't believe their luck having us drop into their laps like a catch of prime fish.'

The sombreness of Ramdon's manner convinced Tracey that the friendliness of their welcome was not to be altogether trusted and she was wary and tense as the nomads produced a flagon of milky *chang* and passed it around, grinning happily.

Ramdon rested for only a short while, then they said goodbye to their hosts and set off once more, leaving the valley behind and climbing the flank of a narrow ridge which wound toward the higher summits. The nomads made no attempt to interfere, but stood on the valley floor waving cheerily as they slowly ascended. Nevertheless, Tracey felt relieved when the miniscule figures finally faded from sight.

The strain of the climb was beginning to tell on her at last. She felt her thigh muscles wobbling, and a searing pain seemed to settle in her chest.

'Can't we . . . go . . . a bit slower?' she gasped.

'Worn out already?' Ramdon grunted. 'How far do you think you'd have got if I hadn't come along?'

'We'd probably be a damn sight better off,' she retorted angrily. 'Your crazy flying damn near killed us all, and now when this is over, we've no way of getting home again.'

'Don't worry,' Ramdon told her cheerily, 'it's only a month's trek to Katmandu. We'll make it all right. Now stop talking and get a move on. I want to put as much distance between us and those Khampas as we possibly can.'

'You still think they're bandits?'

'I'd stake my life on it.'

'Well, they'd be foolish to try anything. They wouldn't stand a chance against that rifle of yours.'

Ramdon laughed shortly. 'Don't let those innocent looks fool you. They had rifles all right, hidden inside their tents. The CIA shipped dozens of weapons in here back in the seventies, hoping the Khampas would start some kind of holy war along the Tibetan frontier. The idiots hadn't considered the fact that the Khampas have been bandits for centuries. Oh, they started a war all right, but it wasn't against the Chinese. They used those rifles on any poor bastard who happened to stray into their territory.'

'You think they'll come after us?'

'Damn right they will.'

'Can we escape?'

'If we move fast enough, maybe they'll figure we're not worth the effort.'

The pushed desperately on and when nightfall came, Tracey felt completely exhausted. Never in her life had she known such weariness. Oblivious to her discomfort, Ramdon forged ahead like a man burning with some hidden fever.

'It's no use,' she croaked, 'I'll have to stop.'

He turned toward her, his face darkening. 'The track dips down beyond the summit of the pass,' he said. 'If we can reach the valley, it'll be warmer there and safer too.'

'I can't possibly go another step.'

His eyes flickered over her in the darkness, noting the state she was in.

'Here,' he said, slipping an arm around her waist, 'lean against me. We'll forget the valley. There's a hut at the top of the rise. It'll give us a shelter of sorts.'

110

She shuffled along at his side, feeling the warmth of his body pressed against hers. It had a comforting glow to it, that warmth. She snuggled beneath the crook of his arm, her fingers tracing the sharp corners of his hip, seeking solace, encouragement. Again, despite her depleted state, she was conscious of Ramdon's nearness arousing strange yearnings inside her. She tried not to think about that, but it was hard fighting the inexorable pull of his presence, especially when he was so close.

Ahead, the track levelled out and on the desolate summit, cairns cluttered the mountain's surface and tattered prayer flags fluttered in the wind. A stone hut stood at the side of the trail, its walls crumbling, its bricks glistening with ice. Tracey uttered a little cry of thankfulness as she realised the roof was relatively intact and would offer a primitive sanctuary from the biting cold.

Inside, there was nothing, no furniture, no cupboards, no upstairs floor. Just an open space with dark circles on the ground where earlier travellers had built their cooking fires.

'What is this place?' she asked.

'Caravanserai,' Ramdon told her. 'A shelter for pilgrims crossing the border trail.'

'Nobody lives here?'

'Somebody probably did once, but not any more. The Khampas have seen to that.'

The Sherpas came in and dumped their packs on the floor. They didn't bother to rest, but started immediately to build a fire in the corner. Tracey sprawled exhausted against the wall. Every part of her body seemed to throb with a dull infernal ache. In silence, she watched Ramdon open his violin case.

'What are you doing?' she demanded.

'I thought a little tune might brighten the boys up.'

'For God's sake, supposing the Khampas are out there?'

'Well, they do say music soothes the savage beast.'

Tracey couldn't believe it. Was the man completely out of his mind? In her exhausted state, she felt her anger flaring. 'Put that bloody thing away,' she snapped. 'I've heard enough of your playing to last me a lifetime.'

Ramdon stared at her in silence for a moment, then looking hurt and indignant, he pushed the instrument back to its holder.

They dined on rice and spiced vegetables, but Tracey barely

picked at hers. The strain of the climb and the rarified atmosphere had destroyed her appetite. All she wanted was to lie down and rest.

As the night lengthened, the cold intensified. Tracey had never known such cold. It was like being inside a refrigerator. Ice glistened clearly on the dry-stone walling, and their breath hung like a vapour on the frostbound air. Wryly, she thought of her life at the television studio. A different world there. Glamorous. Comfortable. No real hardships, not physical ones anyway. She must have been crazy, letting herself in for this.

She took out a sleeping bag and unrolled it in the darkness, then struggled inside, still wearing her Duvet jacket, and pulled the hood up around her face.

'Who's keeping watch?' she asked.

'I will, for an hour or two,' Ramdon said. 'After that, the Sherpas can take turns.'

'Me too. I don't want to be an encumbrance.'

'Maybe tomorrow. Tonight you're all done in. Better grab what rest you can. It might be the only chance you'll get.'

Tracey started to protest, but her voice trailed gently away. The long day's marathon had utterly defeated her, and though she struggled hard to remain awake, she felt herself sinking rapidly, inexorably, into a deep untroubled slumber.

CHAPTER EIGHT

The crack of a gunshot woke her less than an hour later. She heard the sharp report in the darkness, then something pinged into the wall above. Instantly, she was wide awake. The Sherpas were scrambling furiously among the shadows. Ramdon crouched at the window, the Mannlichen resting across the ledge. As she watched, his finger squeezed the trigger, and a spurt of flame lit the tiny room.

'Missed him, the bastard,' Ramdon exclaimed. Tracey fought with the zip of her sleeping bag. Frantically, she wriggled free and joined Ramdon at the window. 'What is it?' she hissed.

'Keep your head down,' he warned. 'They're out there, the sods.'

'Khampas?'

He nodded. 'I thought we'd lost them. I should have known better.'

'How well are they armed?'

'Can't tell for sure. That rifle sounded like a .303.'

'Is that good or bad?'

'Bad for us if the bastard knows how to use it. But at least it's not one of the modern jobs. Maybe the CIA didn't reach these people. If their weapons are old-fashioned, we've still got a chance.'

Tracey was about to speak again when a second shot rang out and the bullet chipped the stonework above her head.

'Close,' Ramdon breathed. 'Keep away from the window. If you get your brains blown out, I won't get paid.'

'What are we going to do?' Tracey asked.

'Well, we can't stay here. When daylight comes, they'll be able to pick us off at their leisure. I think we ought to run for it. We can leave the trail completely and head into the valley straight down the mountainside.'

'Isn't that dangerous?' she muttered dubiously. 'I mean, in the dark we could fall over a precipice or something.'

'That's what I'm counting on. With a bit of luck, it'll stop those buggers following us.'

He snapped something sharply at the Sherpas. They chattered back at him, protesting, Tracey guessed, the rashness of such a move. But Ramdon shouted them down and pointed at the trek-packs.

Hastily, they stuffed in what was left of the equipment and strapped them to their shoulders. More shots rang out, the bullets hissing harmlessly over the rooftop. Ramdon fired in reply, reloading the Mannlichen from the ammunition pouch at his hip.

'Everybody ready?' he demanded.

Tracey felt tense and nervous. Her tiredness was gone. Now she was conscious only of a feeling of dread. The thought of moving into the open, of sliding helplessly down the darkened hillslope terrified her, but she hid her fear for Ramdon's sake. She knew the Sherpas were scared enough already; the slightest provocation could scatter them, panic-stricken, into the night.

They eased out through the back doorway, inching cautiously down the steadily-steepening incline, their feet slithering on the icy surface. Boulders reared out of the gloom, their craggy shapes weirdly distorted in the silvery moonlight. Below, the earth dropped with a terrifying abruptness. Into what? Tracey wondered. Eternity?

She was finding it difficult to maintain her balance. Behind her, the Sherpas were floundering too. Loaded down with the heavy packs, they were sliding and slipping in helpless disarray.

Only Ramdon seemed sure of himself. He moved in front of them, picking his way with uncanny certainty. He found a screeslope and clattered across it, the violin case bobbing against his spine. They followed as best they could, the rattle of the boulders rolling like thunder on the hushed icebound air. If the Khampas were listening, they'd hear them clearly, Tracey realised, and instinctively quickened her pace. She could see the top of Ramdon's head bobbing just below. The route had steepened now, and they were scrambling furiously over a series of jagged sharktooth rocks. She dared not hesitate even for a moment. To pause meant to think, to think meant to panic, and to panic meant to fall.

Below, the void loomed menacingly, a heavy curtain of impenetrable blackness. Supposing they came to a cliff-top? Descent would be out of the question. The over-burdened porters were struggling enough as it was. She hoped to God Ramdon knew what he was doing. A simple slip could lead to total disaster. A loose rock. An ill-judged foothold. Anything.

From above, she heard a cry of terror and alarm and stopped, looking back. A Sherpa had fallen and was rolling helplessly, his body tumbling and slithering between the massive boulders. His trek-pack bounced viciously and plummeted earthwards in a graceful arc, vanishing into the gloom. The man was screaming in terror and clawing at the ground. Without thinking, Tracey jammed herself against the mountain slope, positioning her body directly in his path. She reached out, holding on to the rocks on either side, her heart thumping as she waited for the impact.

The man hit her across the shoulders, tumbled over her right breast, and with a gurgle of relief, clawed at her waist. Tracey felt him slither to a halt. Her skin felt numb where his weight had thumped her.

Ramdon turned back toward them, his eyes glittering in the starlight. He seized the Sherpa and helped him to his feet. The man babbled at Ramdon incoherently. Ramdon hugged him gently around the neck.

'Is he all right?' Tracey croaked.

'Scared, that's all. He got the shock of his life. But he's unhurt, thanks to you.'

He added, smiling thinly: 'That was pretty quick thinking. If you hadn't stopped the poor sod, he'd be halfway to hell by now.'

She didn't answer. She was shaken badly, and trying not to show it.

They pushed on in silence, the air rent by the harsh rasp of their laboured breathing. The incline grew steeper. The Sherpas were experiencing some difficulty now in remaining upright. Tracey shuddered to imagine the strain of the heavy packs upon their spindly legs. She was grateful that at least she had only herself to worry about.

Soon, Ramdon slithered to a standstill. She found him crouched on a tiny ledge, peering dismally into the gloom.

'What's up?' she gasped, easing alongside.

'Looks like we're stuck,' he told her.

He nodded at the slope ahead, and Tracey felt her stomach contract as she glimpsed a slab of contourless rock completely blocking their route. The slab slid into a perpendicular wall, disappearing into the darkness below.

'Damn,' she muttered.

'Not a foothold anywhere,' Ramdon said. 'We'll never get the packs across.'

'We could use ropes,' she suggested.

'Sure. But one of us would have to traverse the slab first.'

Tracey moved forward, inching along the narrow ledge. Calmly, she studied the slab in the starlight. It looked unclimbable, its smooth surface utterly devoid of cracks. She leaned back, peering at a small rocky projection above. This was her kind of problem, she thought. She'd spent enough moments of her life in situations just like this, working out routes on tricky rock-pitches.

'Maybe it's possible,' she whispered.

Ramdon glared at her. 'Without footholds? Only for flies.'

'Fetch the ropes,' she told him.

'What are you going to do?'

'Ever heard of Hans Dülfer? He perfected the rope-traverse technique on the West Wall of the Totenkirchl.'

Ramdon smiled thinly. 'I forgot you were a mountaineer,' he muttered.

Without another word, he turned back along the ledge and met the first of the Sherpas descending the incline above. Tracey's muscles had begun unaccountably to shudder. There was no point deceiving herself, she thought. She was scared, she might as well admit it. The slab looked treacherous in the extreme. But the thought of going back, of facing that interminable ascent only to find the Khampas waiting for them at the summit strengthened her resolve. They had to traverse the slab. It was their only chance.

Ramdon returned, carrying one of the nylon ropes. She tied the end around her waist, knotting it expertly. 'Now the pitons.'

Ramdon snapped something at the nearmost Sherpa who took off his trek-pack and began to rummage inside. He handed Ramdon a cluster of glistening metal spikes.

'Stick them into my Duvet pocket,' she ordered. 'I'll need slings as well.'

A supply of nylon cords joined together by metal karabiners were passed across to her and she looped them over her neck. Then, moving as cautiously as she could, she began to ascend the rock-face immediately above. There was a narrow crack in the chilly surface; it was only a matter of inches wide, barely enough to get her fingers in, but using this as a support, she inched up bit by bit until she had reached the rocky projection above the rim of the vertical slab. As Ramdon watched from below, Tracey felt carefully around. She found a spot where the rock curved inward, and hammered in a piton. When she was satisfied the peg would hold, she clipped on the rope and eased herself gently back to the ledge. Ramdon studied her in silence.

For a moment, she stood perfectly still, breathing deeply, the rope stretched above her to the rocky knob. Then, sucking in the air, she moved toward the precipice.

'Hey,' Ramdon said, 'you're not moving out on that thing?'

'I'll be safe enough,' she promised, 'I'm using the rope as a diagonal support.

He peered at the line taut above her, clearly unconvinced. 'I hope to God you know what you're doing,' he muttered.

'Trust me.'

With her heart thumping wildly, Tracey edged herself out onto the perpendicular wall. She felt the rope tugging at her waist and leaned against it, using the gravitational pull to steady her balance. She ordered herself not to look downwards. If she did that, if she glimpsed for one moment the awesome void below, she knew her courage would desert her.

Step by step, Tracey eased across the massive slab, straining hard against the rope. From time to time, she paused to hammer in a piton, clipping on one of the nylon slings to hold the second rope when her traverse was completed. If her friends at the TV studio could see her now, she thought. She was always so restrained there. A perfect lady, temperate and controlled. Not the type at all to be dangling from precipices. Panic kept rising in her chest, but with a determined effort of will she fought it back and continued resolutely on.

There was nothing to see below. Even if she looked, there was only an empty pall of blackness lightened here and there by a bulging outcrop which framed the deathly route to oblivion. She ignored the emptiness beneath her feet, concentrating instead on the few square yards on which she moved, easing her body inch by inch across the glistening, ice-glazed surface. Almost there, she thought. A few more feet and she'd have it. She could see a good solid stance at the far edge, wide enough to take their entire party if necessary, and beyond that the incline slackened into a more navigable grade.

Then, at the precise moment she was preparing for the final pitch, the wind suddenly hit her like a battering ram. There was no warning. It came like a rogue tornado, roaring out of the valley below. Desperately, she clung to the cliff-face, her body shaking violently.

'Tracey, come back,' Ramdon bellowed.

She shook her head as, gritting her teeth, she waited for the wind to slacken, then, taking advantage of the momentary lull, leaned across the rock and groped frantically for the crack at the slab's outer rim. She felt her fingers slide into the narrow fissure. 'I've got it,' she yelled.

Edging across the last few feet, she stumbled on to the rocky platform, gasping for breath. Relief flooded through her. She'd done it. Thank God.

'Are you okay?' Ramdon shouted from the opposite side.

'I think so.'

She pulled herself together. No time for rest. She had to bring the others across before the wind picked up again.

First, she took the packs over on a double rope. The manoeuvre was difficult and irritatingly slow. By the time the first of the Sherpas was ready to attempt the traverse, more than two hours had elapsed and the wind was gathering strength with every minute.

Tracey belayed herself to the rock with a nylon sling. She could see the Sherpa's face clearly in the starlight. It was pale with fright. She knew he was safe enough – she had him firmly on the rope and he could use the second line as a handrail for the difficult move across – but she sympathised with his feelings. Anyone would be terrified, she thought, on that awesome vertical expanse.

When she was ready, she called to him to begin. The Sherpa was small and skinny as a monkey. His youthful features looked tense with strain as he eased himself on to the ice-glazed wall. Tracey leaned back against the slab, the rope stretched taut across her shoulders. She drew it in as the Sherpa slowly approached. His movements were jerky and irregular, and she could see his fists gripping the line, the knuckles gleaming white through his skin.

He moved gingerly, ducking his head against the squally gusts lashing into his face from the valley below. For a moment, she thought he was going to make it safely then, without warning, one of the pitons suddenly broke loose. It burst from the rock with the sharpness of a bullet, tumbling the man from his perch as the handrope slackened in his grasp.

The man gave a squawk of alarm, dangling helplessly from the loosened line, his legs kicking and twisting in thin air.

'Hold on!' Tracey yelled. 'Don't look down, just hold on!'

She could see the man's eyes bulging crazily in their sockets. She could see his mouth hanging open in terror. She could see the thin line of spittle covering his lips. Then his grip loosened and he plummeted earthward like a stone.

With a gasp, Tracey rammed herself against the cliff and gritted her teeth, waiting for the strain. The rope swung beneath her, but nothing happened. There was no tightness across her shoulder, no lurching tug from the pendulum-like figure below. The line trailed loosely over the tip of the rocky platform.

Cautiously, Tracey allowed herself to relax. The Sherpa must have landed on something, she realised, a ledge, a rocky outcrop. She eased to the rim of the platform and peered downwards. There was nothing to see, only the line disappearing beneath a bulging fold of rock.

'Is he alive?' Ramdon shouted.

'Can't tell,' she called. 'There's an overhang there.'

Tracey thought for a moment, then carefully she untied herself from the rope and fixed it to the rock with pitons. Drawing the second rope across the slab, she pegged that too, and slipped it between her thighs, pulling it S-wise around the back of her legs.

'What are you doing?' Ramdon yelled.

'I'm going down on the double rope.'

'You little fool. You'll be killed.'

Tracey ignored him. Easing backwards, she let herself over the edge of the cliff. Leaning against the line, she began to dance down the wall in ten and fifteen-foot jumps, abseiling gracefully like a spider on a thread. She felt frighteningly exposed. The wind bit at her cheeks, scattering her hair wildly. The harsh line dug into the flesh on the back of her thigh as she tried not to think of the emptiness below, to concentrate instead on the simple function of edging downwards.

Then, as she drew beyond the lip of the overhang, she saw immediately what had happened. The Sherpa had landed in a bush sprouting out of the cliff-face, and was trapped precariously in its spindly branches, terrified out of his wits but apparently unhurt.

Tracey drew alongside and stopped. Her body spun on the rope and she reached out, using the cliff as a steadier. 'Speak English?' she asked.

The man stared at her blankly, then shook his head. Tracey sighed.

'First we've got to get you into a safer position.'

She glanced quickly around. Above the bush was a small defile, barely a foot across. It looked dangerously exposed, but it was better than waiting for the shrub's roots to tear themselves loose. She leaned sideways, sticking out her arm. 'Here, give me your hand,' she ordered.

The Sherpa took it gratefully, and Tracey leaned back on the rope, pulling him upwards out of his prickly perch. He scrambled into the narrow defile and huddled back against the rock, his cheeks pale with fear. Tracey ran her hands down the length of his limbs.

'No bones broken anyhow,' she grunted. 'That's a nasty cut on your forehead, but I think you'll live.'

She pushed beside him on the narrow ledge. 'Now we've got to get you above that overhang,' she said, 'and the only simple way is up the rope.'

She took two of the nylon slings from around her neck and carefully fashioned a pair of prusik knots, attaching them carefully to the loosely dangling line.

'Let me show you this,' she murmured. 'It's called a prusikloop. You put your foot in it, see? Now when you lift your leg upwards, the sling slides easily up the rope, but once you rest your weight on the loop, the knot locks tight around the nylon strand. Bit like climbing a ladder really, except that you pull the steps along with you as you go. Think you can do that?'

She knew the man hadn't understood a word she'd said, but her demonstration had been graphically clear, and he looked at her, nodding confidently.

'Let's see you try,' she said.

Easing up from the ledge, he pushed his toes into the nylon loops and began to clamber up the hanging rope. He moved uncertainly at first, finding the unfamiliar technique difficult to adjust to, but once he'd mastered his balance, he climbed with gathering confidence. Tracey crouched below, calling encouragement. 'Good, that's good. Take your time, there's no hurry. Look around a bit, that's it. Go on now, you've done it.'

She watched the Sherpa ease himself over the overhang's bulge and reach the corner of the rocky platform. Tracey sighed. Taking the two remaining slings from around her neck, she followed swiftly in the Sherpa's wake, prusiking up the the slender line. Her body twisted and turned, spinning on the rope like a button on a thread. The strand was so slender it was difficult to maintain any sense of balance, but she managed it gradually, forcing her hips to remain upright, letting her legs do the work until, gasping and heaving, she dragged herself over the rim and on to the rocky shelf.

The rest of the team traversed the slab without incident. Ramdon was the last to cross. When he reached the platform, he seized her in his arms and kissed her wildly on the mouth. 'My God, you've got the nerve of the devil. You had me scared out of my wits. I never for a minute believed you would make it.'

She smiled at him thinly. 'You should have more faith in me.'

'I will in future,' he promised.

Conscious suddenly that he was still holding her, she broke loose from his grasp and glanced around, struggling to recover her composure. 'Which way now?' she muttered uncertainly.

'Straight down. The gradient seems to slacken below the overhang. Looks like a gentle slope from here on.'

The rest of the descent was conducted at a more leisurely pace, and when dawn broke they had reached the valley floor. Tracey felt weary and disorientated. The strain of the long flight, the hazardous rescue beneath the cliff had shattered her nerves completely. But the thing she remembered most – and the realisation startled her – was not the shocked look on the young Sherpa's face, or the touch of the ice-glazed rock, or the harsh rasp of the nylon rope. It was the memory of Ramdon's kiss.

Through the window, the lights of Peking cast an iridescent glow across the night sky. The clamour of bicycle bells echoed from the street below, awakening Lin Hua's senses. In the next office, someone was playing a radio and the noise sent vibrations across the bare wood floor.

Lin Hua was tired. He had been working very hard. He always worked obsessively and with a total dedication which left him, when day was done, emotionally drained and utterly exhausted. He had been told by his doctor that such Herculean efforts were no longer necessary in the Popular People's Republic, that a more moderate approach might be advisable for his health's sake, but Lin Hua could not help himself; he worked hard because he had always done so, even as a child, and the habits of a lifetime were difficult to break.

Lin Hua was forty-one years old. He was not a tall man, but

he carried himself with such an air of dignity that people often took him for being larger than he actually was; his body was slender in build with narrow shoulders, an exceedingly thin waist and long, elegant hands which his wife, Li Hsiao-yu, often described as 'artistic' but which Lin Hua himself, from the moment he had been conscious of such things, had regarded as disturbingly effeminate. Not that there was anything unmasculine in Lin Hua's metabolism; he was a quiet man, not overly given to fits of aggressiveness, but in sexual matters his appetites were scrupulously orthodox – nevertheless, he carried an air of sensitivity and gentleness which had troubled him greatly in his early life, and which troubled him still if the truth were known, though now, with the passions of his youth slipping quietly behind him, he found the less positive traits of his nature – he always thought of them as traits – disturbing him less and less.

He despised violence, always had, even in his student days when, as a dutiful disciple of the Cultural Revolution, he had served a stint in the People's Liberation Army, learning to drill and shoot with deadly precision. Such practices had been repugnant to Lin Hua, but he had applied himself with his customary zeal, for he was a devout communist who believed implicitly in the order of the socialist state.

He had begun his civilian life as a lawyer in Shanghai, but with the Chinese occupation of Tibet had been absorbed into the Peking Administrative Office of the T.A.R., the Tibetan Autonomous Region, and assigned the task of rewriting the Tibetan vocabulary in the manner which her Chinese conquerors could easily understand. Lin Hua's qualifications for such a daunting endeavour lay in his early boyhood which had been spent in the city of Gyangtse on the high Tibetan plain where his father had worked as a merchant trader. However, the problem of translation proved to be a monumental one both in practice and theory, for there were no words in the Tibetan language to describe such phrases as 'state consciousness', 'capitalistic decadence', 'anti-imperialism' or 'monopolistic bourgeoisie'. Still, he had persevered until his efforts had induced the Central Committee to appoint him Officer with Special Responsibility for Tibetan Affairs, with the result that Lin Hua had never returned to Shanghai; he had settled down instead in the Chinese capital with his wife and two sons. His sons were sixteen and seventeen respectively, and soon they would attend the Central Academy of Fine Arts. In China, all artists were employed by the communist state. Depending upon his sons' ability, they would be classified as either 'amateurs' or 'professionals'. 'Amateur' artists were allowed to paint only part of the time, and had to regard their calling as secondary to their role as state employee. 'Professionals', on the other hand, were paid a monthly salary for their efforts and assigned to a government department. It was a system Lin Hua both accepted and approved of. He had no time for the freedom of the individual. In the western world, the capitalists beat their brains out in their efforts to swindle each other. Here, life was so simple; a man placed his fate in the hands of the Committee, lived according to the dictates of revolutionary brotherhood, and in return the state provided him with all the good things, the deeply comforting and comfortable things which life had to offer.

Lin Hua was about to close the book he was reading and place it in his drawer when he heard footsteps clattering in the passageway outside. He blinked. At such a late hour, the building should have been empty. The cleaning women did not arrive until early morning and the security guards seldom bothered him, for Lin Hua's dedication to his work was a departmental legend.

Frowning, Lin Hua was about to rise from his seat when, with a resounding crash, the office door burst suddenly open and three men stood framed in the passage light. Two wore civilian suits, the third wore the uniform of a military colonel. They stood looking down at Lin Hua who, taken by surprise, had frozen in the act of rising and was now poised awkwardly between his chair and desktop.

'Lin Hua?' one of the men barked.

He was pale-cheeked and heavy-shouldered, his face raddled by some indeterminate skin disease. His chin was broad and bulged unhealthily at the corners, the rolls of his neck swelling balloon-like above the starched confines of his shirt collar.

Lin Hua nodded uneasily.

'You are to come with us,' the man stated.

Lin Hua blinked at him. 'Now?'

'At once.'

'But . . .'

Lin Hua glanced at his watch. 'It is almost nine o'clock.'

'It makes no difference. We are here on the orders of the Public Security Bureau.'

Lin Hua felt a chill spreading through his stomach. The Public Security Bureau was responsible for maintaining order throughout China's provinces. In recent years, they had displayed an increasing tendency to parade felons through the streets before dispatching them, in places of public execution, with a single shot through the back of the neck. Not that he had committed any crime, but in the curious complexity of the class struggle a man could sometimes find himself guilty without being consciously aware of it.

In a daze, Lin Hua pushed back his chair and lifted his raincoat from the wall-peg. 'Will this take long?' he inquired. 'My wife is waiting. I promised to be home for dinner.'

'Your wife has been informed,' the man told him crisply. 'She is no longer expecting you.'

Lin Hua felt his spirits plummet. Stories of disappearances drifted through his brain. Citizens who had misread the party line were spirited away on re-educational programmes. Some never returned.

Realising his hands were trembling, Lin Hua pushed them into his raincoat pockets. 'Where are you taking me?' he asked.

'Ask no questions,' the man snapped. 'You will be told everything when necessary.'

They walked downstairs together, the colonel leading the way. In the lobby, the security guard watched curiously as they crossed the marbled floor and left by the revolving doors. Outside, a large car stood parked at the kerbside. On its bonnet fluttered the flag of the Revolutionary Council.

Lin Hua was ordered into the passenger seat. The colonel took the driving wheel, the two civilians clambered into the rear. Lin Hua's body was trembling visibly as they drove along the Avenue of Perpetual Peace. He was not afraid, he kept telling himself, not truly afraid. It was just the uncertainty. A man needed to know. Any man. Even a good communist who placed his faith in the benevolence of the state. Committees, like governments, were only human, and human beings made mistakes. Lin Hua's cheeks blanched at the thought. If a mix-up had taken place, he could be immured for ever through no fault of his own.

They skirted Tian An Men Square, passing the red walls of the Imperial City and the Gate of Heavenly Peace and drove out of town, leaving the main bulk of the traffic behind. The roads grew dark and narrow. Flooded rice-paddies flitted by, mud-villages, straw huts, farmhouses with windows shuttered against the night. Their head-lamps carved cones of light through the murky darkness.

Nobody spoke. When Lin Hua tried to start a conversation he was ordered brusquely to be quiet. The almost machine-like precision of the three men unnerved him and he felt nausea starting in his stomach, sweeping through his body in waves.

For almost an hour they drove in silence, then suddenly, without warning, the colonel swung off the main road and steered along a narrow track that weaved and dipped through the darkness. Lin Hua saw the pale glow of lights ahead and a roaring in his ears. Framed against the sky, he glimpsed a concrete control tower, its windows blazing. He blinked. An airfield.

There were three official airports in Peking, two domestic and one military, but this was the first time Lin Hua had been aware of a fourth.

The colonel drew to a halt at the edge of the apron and Lin Hua was ordered to get out. Uncertainly, he stood by the car door, shivering in the chill night air. He could see the pale outline of an aircraft framed against the sky.

'This way,' the colonel said, taking his arm.

They walked across the concrete, the roar of the aircraft's engines masking the clatter of their feet. At the doorway, Lin Hua stopped and looked back, his hair blowing wildly in the wind. 'Where am I going?' he shouted, his voice almost obliterated by the thunderous clamour surrounding him.

The colonel shook his head. 'Everything will be explained later,' he bellowed.

A young rating in a padded flying suit helped Lin Hua into the cabin and settled him in a chair, strapping his seatbelt into place. The hatch was closed and a moment later, the plane began to move. There was no prelude to take-off. It was as if the entire airfield had been waiting for his arrival. Lin Hua glimpsed the three men who had brought him here standing by their automobile as he taxied down the runway, then the flaps dipped, the aircraft lifted, and Lin Hua watched the starburst of lights which marked the location of Peking city tilting far to the west.

Resignedly, he settled back in his chair. There was little he could do, he reasoned, until the plane landed. His record was impeccable. He had nothing to be ashamed of. Why then should he feel afraid? If a mistake had been made – and in Lin Hua's mind there could be no other explanation – he would simply explain the truth and place himself like a good comrade at the mercy of the Bureau.

Toward midnight, the rating brought him a bowl of rice and some fish. Lin Hua ate hungrily. The nausea had settled in his stomach and after the food he felt better. After all, one did not feed a man one intended to dispose of.

The roar of the engines hung in Lin Hua's senses, making him drowsy. He eased the seatbelt into a more comfortable position, and closing his eyes, drifted into sleep. He woke once during the night when the pilot put down to refuel, but when he undid his seatbelt and prepared to disembark, the rating ordered him back to his chair.

Next time he awoke, it was early dawn. He peered through the porthole window at a desolate plateau streaked with ice and snow. There was no sign of cultivation, no sign of human presence at all. The landscape seemed endless, a vast feature-less sprawl that rambled depressingly on and on. Far ahead, Lin Hua could see the snowcapped peaks of distant mountains. They reared against the sky like the ramparts of some incred-ible fortress.

The green light above the pilot's cockpit switched to red and the rating clambered back to his seat, strapping himself firmly into place. They were coming in to land.

Lin Hua stared out balefully as the plane put down on a tiny concrete runway and the pilot taxied to a halt in front of a cluster of tin-roofed buildings glinting in the sun. The rating signalled Lin Hua to rise.

Mystified, Lin Hua followed him through the open hatch-way, catching his breath as the wind hit him like a piercing blade. He felt snow pellets fluttering against his cheeks and, still wrapped in the gaberdine raincoat, his body began to shake violently.

In front of the buildings stood a military truck. The driver, a small olive-skinned young man with a red star on the front of

126

his cap, climbed out and saluted casually. He opened the rear door for Lin Hua to clamber in.

Lin Hua settled back in the seat cushions, his breath leaving a misty cloud on the icebound air. He was relieved when the driver started up the engine and the truck's heater pumped waves of blessed warmth into the passenger cab.

They left the airstrip behind, driving along a primitive road which followed the route of a winding river. The landscape looked dour and desolate. There were few trees, and the stunted grass was coated with patches of frost. Lin Hua watched the distant mountains draw steadily closer.

Toward noon, he spotted a sprawl of buildings on the far horizon. They nestled in the lap of softly-undulating hills. As he approached, he saw a massive mud-brown structure, studded with windows and twisting staircases, towering over the rest of the city. Lin Hua had seen pictures of the building many times before at the Council offices in Peking. It was the Potala Palace. He was approaching Lhasa, capital of Tibet. Even in his boyhood, he had never ventured so deep into the Tibetan interior.

They drove in through a network of carefully-ordered streets flanked by houses with metal roofs, then leaving the outskirts behind, they moved into the old part of the town where Lin Hua peered fascinated at the terraced dwellings with their sloping walls and narrow coffin-like windows. The mighty span of the Potala Palace hovered above them like a living presence. Lin Hua could see the sunlight glinting on its golden roofs. He knew from his reading it had been started in the seventh century and was said to contain more than a thousand rooms, ten thousand altars and two hundred thousand statues. During the Cultural revolution, when the Chinese Red Guards had destroyed most of Tibet's major monasteries, the Potala had somehow managed to survive. Its very name meant 'High heavenly realm', for it rose seven hundred feet above the surrounding rooftops.

Lin Hua's driver drew to a halt beneath the massive steps. Waiting at the foot of the stairway was a man in the uniform of an army major. He was barrel-chested and heavy-jowled, and his face carried the bloated, indolent air of an inveterate sensualist. His lips were thick, his eyes small and narrow, and he wore a thin moustache which seemed to emphasise his brutish features.

As Lin Hua climbed out of the truck, he felt his spirits sink once more. The major looked the kind of individual Lin Hua instinctively distrusted. All through his life he had suffered indignities at the hands of such men. They were callous in their concepts, inflexible in their attitudes, contentious in their nature. As if to confirm this impression, Lin Hua detected an immediate glimmer of distaste in the major's small eyes.

'You know what this is?' the major asked in a guttural voice, waving at the building behind him.

Lin Hua nodded. 'The Potala Palace. I had not realised it was still occupied.'

'It is not occupied. It is maintained as a museum by the Cultural Relics Commission, but there are no hotels in Lhasa and you will be more comfortable here than at the military barracks.'

Turning, the major began to climb the stairs, and Lin Hua, realising he was meant to follow, scrambled hurriedly after him. The steps seemed endless, and Lin Hua, unused to Lhasa's altitude of twelve thousand feet, quickly found himself gasping for air. The major gave no sign that he noticed Lin Hua's distress. He went on climbing steadily, making no attempt to slow his pace.

'My orderly will take you to your quarters later,' he announced. 'First, I want to show you something.'

When they reached the rooftop door, Lin Hua's chest was heaving and he was filled with the disquietening conviction that he was going to faint. Holding on to his senses with an effort, he followed the major along a series of narrow echoing corridors flanked by elaborate ceremonial rooms.

'I am Major Tang A-hsi,' his host informed him. 'I command the military operations in the area. You have been sent here because it is thought that your knowledge of Tibet may help me in a matter of great importance.'

He glanced back at Lin Hua. 'You were in the army yourself, once, I understand.'

'Many years ago,' Lin Hua admitted breathlessly.

The major's gaze lingered on his narrow frame and Lin Hua saw his expression of contempt intensify. He knew the man was maintaining his politeness with an effort.

'We have tried to make you comfortable here,' Tang A-hsi said. 'It gets very cold at night and I'm afraid fuel is scarce in Lhasa. There are no forests in the surrounding area, and most of the residents burn dried yak-dung, but we have furnished your bed with heavy blankets, and have also installed an oxygen tank in case you have trouble with the altitude.'

'You are very kind,' Lin Hua said.

'It is not a kindness. It is a matter of expedience. You will be useless to me if you become ill.'

The corridor ended, and perched in the corner Lin Hua spotted a beautiful ornate chest, decorated with an intricate lacework of gold. On its lid stood a human skull, the crown studded with jewels, the eye sockets lined with beaten silver. Lin Hua gave an involuntary exclamation of surprise and touched the skull gently with his fingertips.

The major watched him, smiling thinly. 'The face of death,' he muttered.

'Not really,' Lin Hua said. 'To the Tibetans, the skull symbolises the impermanence of the body. They see the human frame as only one of many vessels the spirit must occupy in its journey of reincarnation.'

The major grunted. 'A primitive people, still racked by medieval superstition. They have no conception of hygiene. They remain dirty by nature, and refuse to be educated out of their decadent ways. They still cling obstinately for instance to the notion of serfdom, refusing to accept the fact that they have already been liberated.'

Lin Hua knew the major's view was a popular military one and precisely what Lin Hua expected from such a man. He had met soldiers like Tang A-hsi in all the provinces of the republic, and without exception, their outlooks were the same. Moulded and fashioned by the Cultural Revolution, they believed what they were told to believe.

He followed the major down a narrow staircase and into a second corridor wider than the first. Tang A-hsi paused in front of a massive mural depicting mythical figures embellished with scarlet and gold. He signalled Lin Hua to step past him through an open doorway. Blinking, Lin Hua entered a tiny room with yellow tapestries hanging from the walls. He stared in silence at a small bed with a metal headboard, a crude dresser with two statues of Buddha on its top, a calendar displaying the date *Monday 31st*, and a clock on which the pointers had stopped at ten minutes past one.

'This is the bedroom of the Dalai Lama,' Tang A-hsi said.

'We have kept it exactly as it was when he fled the country in 1959.'

Lin Hua studied the primitive furnishings in amazement. 'Extraordinary. It is such a simple room.'

'They are a simple people,' the major grunted, 'trapped in the meshes of theocracy.'

He moved in front of the dresser and ran his fingers casually over one of the tiny Buddhas. 'You understand the significance of the Dalai Lama?' he asked.

'I understand it very well. The name was given by a sixteenth-century Mongol ruler and means 'ocean of wisdom.' It is rare to find a country in which both religious and ministerial power is concentrated in one person. The Dalai Lama meant a great deal to the Tibetan people. He was more than their ruler, more than their king. He was also their god. His death must have devastated them.'

Tang A-hsi chuckled unpleasantly. 'He was a deity, was he not? How can a deity die? Surely in a society based on reincarnation, his soul must live on?'

Lin Hua felt puzzled. He had no idea why the major was pursuing this extraordinary dialogue.

Cautiously, he answered: 'That is true. When a Dalai Lama passes away, his followers believe his spirit enters the body of a young boy.'

'They search their realm to find that boy, correct?'

'I understand so.'

'And when they do?'

'He is put through a rigid examination. He is called upon to select personal articles belonging to the former Dalai Lama. If he recognises them without hesitation, and if he can answer the questions of the Tsedrung monks, then he is carried here to Lhasa and consecrated at the holiest of all Tibetan shrines, the Jokhang. He then enters an intensive period of religious training before assuming power at the age of eighteen.'

The major nodded, satisfied. Lin Hua felt he had just passed some undefined test.

'During the life of the previous Dalai Lama,' the major said, 'he was repeatedly invited by the Central Committee to return to his homeland, did you know that?'

Lin Hua nodded.

'Always, he refused,' Tang A-hsi continued, 'insisting on

Tibet's total independence from China. He ignored the fact that Tibet has been part of China for centuries.'

Lin Hua had heard the argument many times before. Indeed, it represented the central premise on which his entire department was based.

'In your opinion,' the major said, 'what would happen if a new Dalai Lama appeared here in Lhasa?'

Lin Hua frowned. 'Surely such a thing is impossible.'

'Not quite. He could be a reincarnation. The boy whose body the god-king has entered.'

Lin Hua sucked in his breath. 'Then the people would rise. We would have a revolution on our hands.'

'That is my feeling precisely. It is also the feeling of the Central Committee.'

Lin Hua felt his pulses racing. Suddenly he knew what the major was going to say. Tang A-hsi picked up the tiny Buddha and studied it closely in the filtered daylight. When he spoke, his voice had changed timbre. Its tone was harsh, crisp and businesslike.

'Our intelligence sources in India have informed us that a party of Tibetan monks is at the moment travelling toward Lhasa with the new Dalai Lama. They intend to consecrate him at the Jokhang. We have no idea which route they are following or at what point they intend to cross the Tibetan border, but our job is to locate them, arrest them, and deliver them quietly to Peking before the country erupts like a powder keg.'

The border post stood at the head of a wide valley, commanding an excellent view of the Pilgrims' trail and the river below. On one side, pine-studded mountains rose in a clumsy jumble to the deep scar of a forbidding glacier. On the other, the land tumbled downwards, levelling uneasily into the bedrock flatness of the valley floor.

Losang Gyatso stood behind a rock and studied the border post thoughtfully. A solitary flag fluttered from its roofmast, and on the verandah Losang could see the trim outline of a soldier, his polished boots and gleaming webbing belt reflecting the sun's rays in shimmers of refracted light.

Pursing his lips, Losang moved back down the trail to where the line of Duvet-clad lamas waited in patient silence. On a

131

carved sedan chair, supported at each end by motionless monks, the young boy sat watching Losang's approach. When Losang reached the sedan chair, he bowed deeply. 'The border post is just around the bend,' he declared. 'It will be necessary to leave the trail at this point and detour through the trees.'

The boy regarded him with an air of calm solemnity. 'Do they know we are here?'

'I doubt it, Holiness. The post does not appear to be heavily manned. Beyond lie the mountains of the Ghyankhala. Few pilgrims travel this road so there is little need for the Chinese to be vigilant.'

The boy nodded. He delivered an order in a gentle tone and without a word the four bearers settled the chair carefully on the ground. The boy eased himself up and stood at Losang's side. He pointed to the mountain tips ahead.

'Tibet?' he whispered.

Losang inclined his head, his face flushed with excitement. 'We are within a mile of our homeland,' he confirmed. 'From this point on, we must proceed with great caution.'

The boy gave an impatient snort. 'You said yourself we carry the protection of the gods. Since the Chinese have no gods to instruct them, how then can they be a match for us?'

'That is true, Holiness,' Losang agreed, 'but sometimes it is prudent to give the gods a little help. There is nothing to fear here in the Ghyankhala, but if the Chinese learn of our coming, they can intercept us easily when we reach the high plain.'

'Very well, I will listen to your advice,' the boy agreed. 'This intrigue is still new to me, and I am anxious to see the homeland you speak of so warmly.'

Losang delivered a sharp order and they moved off through the trees, following a zig-zag route steadily up the hillside. The four men carrying the sedan chair stumbled and slithered as they manoeuvred their heavy burden beneath the overhanging branches.

The boy moved easily at Losang's side. He was young and strong, and seemed oblivious to the altitude. At one point, the trees broke into a series of little clearings, and Losang glimpsed the sloping tiles of the border post far below. Something caught in his throat as he realised they were back in his beloved Tibet. Impulsively, he threw himself to the ground and bending forward, kissed the earth. The other monks did likewise. The boy stood looking at them, his face creased by a puzzled frown. He seemed bemused by such an effusive display, but without a word, he too dropped to his knees, following their example.

'We are home.' Losang breathed softly.

'Home?' the boy muttered. His eyes flittered across the pine-studded hillside. It looked no different to the mountains of Nepal. One land was much the same as another, he thought. One crossed frontiers and dividing lines, but the earth itself didn't alter.

'Can't you feel it?' Losang asked him.

'I feel nothing. I was born in India.'

'But you are the chosen one. This is the country of your ancestors.'

'I feel nothing,' the boy repeated stubbornly.

Frowning, Losang studied him in silence for a moment. He was about to speak again when suddenly a shout rang out, reverberating across the hillside. Startled, Losang turned, his heart thumping wildly. To his dismay, he saw men scrambling toward them through the trees. They wore khaki uniforms and little fur caps.

Losang wanted to cry out loud at the injustice of it. To have come so far, endured so much, only to be arrested on the borderline.

He watched the soldiers fan out along the line of motionless monks, brandishing their rifles menacingly. Losang counted eight in all. Beneath their caps, their faces looked flat and hostile.

'Chinese?' the boy whispered.

Losang shook his head. 'Worse,' he said. 'Tibetan militia. The trained monkeys who dance to the music of Peking.'

The militia commander was a young man with a narrow scar above his lips. He moved toward Losang who rose slowly to his feet. In his fist, the commander clutched an ugly revolver. 'Who are you?' he demanded in a rough voice. 'What are you doing here?'

Losang cleared his throat. 'Pilgrims,' he announced, 'on our way to the Holy city.'

The commander's eyes did not falter. 'Why have you left the trail?'

Losang shrugged helplessly. 'We did not mean to leave it. We strayed from the path in the early morning, while it was still dark. We've been trying to find our way back ever since.'

Losang glimpsed the disbelief in the commander's eyes and felt his spirit sink. It had been a lame excuse and he new it. The path was clear and well-defined. Even in the darkness, it would be difficult to miss.

'You have papers?' the commander demanded harshly.

Losang hesitated. 'We have come from the kingdom of Nepal. Under the trade agreement with the Chinese Republic, we have no need of papers.'

'You are lying,' the man told him flatly. 'You are not pilgrims and you are not lost. You have come this way to avoid being questioned at the border post.'

'You are mistaken,' Losang protested weakly, but the commander stepped back, waving his revolver.

'You are all under arrest. Place your hands on your heads and turn around.'

Losang hesitated. The man's expression was hostile and dangerous. He had been trained to follow orders without question. Losang knew if he notified the Chinese of their presence, everything would be lost. There was only one answer. It was risky, but they had no choice. The commander was still a Tibetan, no matter how the Chinese had conditioned him.

Softly, Losang said to the boy: 'Show the commander your rosary.'

The boy glanced at Losang's face then without a word, unzipped the front of his Duvet and slipped the rosary from his neck. Stepping forward, he held it in front of the commander's chin. For a moment, the man looked blank, his small eyes fixing in puzzlement on the decorative little necklace dangling from the boy's fingers. Losang watched the various emotions flit across his face, disbelief, wonder, excitement, awe. Slowly the revolver lowered and the commander stared at the boy with an expression of reverence and adoration.

'Holiness,' he whispered in a hoarse voice.

Without a word, he dropped to his knees and bent forward, kissing the front of the boy's boots.

Puzzled, the other militiamen moved closer, keeping their rifles trained on the line of prisoners. The boy turned, displaying the rosary clearly in the sunlight. The tiny jewels sparkled as they caught the dappled rays piercing the branches above. Grunts of astonishment and incredulity emerged from the soldiers' lips. Their rifles thudded to the ground as one by one they dropped to their knees, bowing deeply.

Relief flooded Losang's body. He filled his lungs with the chill mountain air and nodded to the boy who looped the rosary back over his neck and zipped up the front of his Duvet. Losang waved to the waiting monks, and leaving the militiamen still prostrate on the forest floor, they set off again across the ragged pine-cluttered hillside.

CHAPTER NINE

Tracey had never felt so tired in her life. Her hips ached, her thigh muscles trembled, and the valley they were following seemed to twist and turn endlessly. Each time they rounded a bend, she expected to see a change on the skyline, but always the vista remained the same, weaving and dipping on a tortuous route to nowhere.

'How far does this valley stretch?' she moaned. 'We've been walking for hours.'

'Beats going uphill,' Ramdon grunted. 'One thing you've got to understand about the Himalayas, they're unlike mountains any place else in the world. In the Alps, you can watch the country change bit by bit. Here, you spend all week wandering along the same damned ridge.'

Tracey was silent for a moment, catching her breath. Ramdon was right in that respect, she thought. She had never seen country like it, not in her entire life. Miles were meaningless here. Journeys were measured in days, hours and minutes. In ups and downs. It was beautiful. Awe-inspiring even. But it certainly took an awful lot of puff to walk through.

'Supposing we get lost?' she said. 'I've never seen you even glance at a compass.'

'What's the point? Only one way we can go.'

She was about to speak again when suddenly one of the Sherpas called something in a breathless voice, and frowning,

Ramdon stopped to shade his eyes from the sun.

'What is it?' Tracey asked.

'Somebody's coming.'

She felt a jolt of alarm. 'Khampas?'

'I don't think so. They're moving too fast.'

Tracey followed Ramdon's gaze, squinting into the morning glare. The valley floor undulated gently, and between the boulders she detected a flicker of movement. As her eyes slowly focused, her mouth nearly dropped open in surprise. Mounted on low Mongolian ponies, a group of horsemen came galloping toward them dressed in black breeches, dark blue tunics and white cowboy style hats. The sunlight glinted on their automatic rifles, and dust rose in a heavy cloud from their ponies' hooves. A sense of unreality filled her. 'Who on earth are they?' she whispered.

'Tibetan cavalry.'

'You're joking.'

'No. They work in conjunction with the Chinese. You find them all over the country.'

Dry-mouthed, Tracey watched the horsemen approaching. As they drew closer, she saw cartridge bandoliers criss-crossing their chests and white scarves fluttering from their throats. It was like watching a scene from a distant age.

'Hadn't we better hide?'

'Too late. They've already spotted us.'

The riders swung toward them, guiding their beasts with the natural elegance of men born to the saddle. They made a handsome sight all right. In spite of the danger, she couldn't help admiring the way the sun fell across their elaborate hats, glinted on their rifles, cast dappled shadows across the muscles and sinews on their horses' flanks.

Galloping up, the riders reined to a halt, patting their snorting mounts. Tracey watched their leader, a flat-featured young man wearing a green tunic and black hat to distinguish him from his companions, slowly dismount and stride toward them, his short legs moving with a curious disjointed motion as if he found any manoeuvre out of the saddle a novel activity. There was something about the man's face, the flat Mongolian implacability of it that frightened her. You couldn't talk to a face like that. She could see at a glance such a man would never listen. He belonged to a tight little world shut in by high mountain peaks, and his brain reflected that world, refusing to acknowledge anything which lay beyond the limits of his insular experience.

'Maybe we can bluff it out,' Ramdon whispered. 'Got your Nepalese trekking pass?'

'It's in my pocket.'

'We'll tell him we're a trekking party from Nepal. We wandered over the frontier by mistake after being attacked by Khampas.'

'He'll never believe it,' she said.

'At least let's give it a try.'

The cavalryman stopped in front of Ramdon and said something in his own language. Ramdon answered in the same tongue, pointing to Tracey, then at the Sherpas behind. The cavalry commander listened in silence. When Ramdon had finished, he spoke again, his voice sharp and guttural, and turning brusquely, strode back to his mount. Ramdon gave a rueful shrug.

'What happened?' Tracey whispered.

'He wants us to accompany him to the militia post. He says there's a Chinese officer there.'

'Oh Christ.'

'Better put a brave face on it. Damn all else we can do.'

Tracey was silent as they set off along the valley, walking in front of the horses. Facing the Tibetan cavalry was one thing, but she knew the Chinese officer would never believe her story. She could scarcely believe the succession of bad luck she had suffered since leaving Katmandu. Everything had gone wrong, from the very beginning.

You damned fool, Tracey Morrill, she thought, you knew it was crazy to get involved in this thing. When will you learn to stop being so impetuous?

The valley deepened, and after a mile or so led into the mouth of a second valley, much larger than the first. The walls were thousands of feet high, and the lower slopes had been terraced into grain fields and rice paddies which led to the river floor in a series of intricately-carved steps. Buildings clung to the hillside, and Tracey saw goatherds driving their flocks across the carefully-tiered pastures. The goats were shaggy and sturdy, and carried water bottles strapped to their backs.

The trail passed through a tiny village, the dwellings

ramshackle and primitive. Rough-hewn terraces and wooden balconies adorned the housefronts. At the top of the single street, a large whitewashed building with a flag fluttering from its roof sat like a sentinel towering above the valley floor. Behind it, Tracey spotted a complex of dry-stone pens, and horses grazing on the terrraced fields beyond.

The cavalrymen came to a halt and began to unbridle their animals. The commander walked toward them, patting dust from his blue-black riding breeches. He said something to Ramdon in a curt voice.

'He wants us to step inside,' Ramdon said.

Tracey followed him over the threshold. The interior was dark, musty, filled with the pungent odour of woodsmoke. It was sparsely-furnished but, by Himalayan standards, surprisingly clean. There were a number of chairs arranged along the opposite wall. Filing cabinets dominated the corner, and on one of them Tracey saw an old-fashioned photograph. The walls were covered with maps of the area.

Three militiamen squatted on the floor, playing *sbag*, a game similar to dominoes. When Tracey and Ramdon entered, they rose hastily to their feet and one of them picked up his carbine and stood at attention in the approximate position of a guardsman on duty. Another tapped lightly on a door leading to an inner room. None of them displayed the slightest evidence of surprise.

'I can't help feeling we're expected,' Tracey said uneasily.

The soldier opened the door and waved Tracey and Ramdon inside. With her heart thumping, Tracey stepped past him into the inner office. It was actually larger than the outer one, but just as primitively furnished. Two desks, one holding a typewriter, occupied the centre of the floor. An ancient bookcase had been propped against the far wall to serve as a filing cabinet. On its crooked shelves, cardboard folders were stacked in uneven lines.

Standing by the window staring out across the mountain peaks, was a Chinese officer in a khaki-green uniform. He was young, Tracey thought, then realised instantly the impression was a false one. In reality, the officer was in his middle forties, but his skin was so smooth, his hair so glossy, his limbs so slender that he carried an air of perpetual puberty.

'Come in, Mrs Morrill,' he said in faultless English, 'I have been waiting for you.'

Tracey glanced quickly at Ramdon. For a moment, the officer went on staring into the sunlight, the bright rays casting a flush across his delicate cheeks, then he turned to look at her and she noticed his eyes were very dark and chillingly penetrating. They contrasted strangely with the boyish quality of his features.

'You had quite a dramatic arrival, I hear,' he said. 'We were almost afraid we had lost you.'

'Our plane crashed near Tangpoche La pass,' Tracey muttered nervously. 'We were attacked by Khampa bandits. They forced us over the border.'

The Chinese officer smiled. 'You have a persuasive manner, Mrs Morrill. Under different circumstances, I might have been willing to believe you. But you must understand I already know why you are here. You have come to find your husband, Harold Morrill.'

Tracey felt a cold clamminess settle on her throat. The officer looked terrifyingly assured. He reached down, his fingers toying with a paperweight on the desktop. 'As it happens, our interests coincide in that respect. We too are looking for Harold Morrill. We have been looking for him for some considerable time. Long before the American State Department, believe me. Which is why I have been waiting here to welcome you for several days now.'

He chuckled as he observed Tracey's start of astonishment.

'How could you possibly . . .?' Tracey breathed.

'Know so much? We have our sources.'

'But nobody knew. Only Jenkins at the British Embassy.'

The officer had a way of widening his eyes to lend emphasis to his expression. Tracey felt the shock like a palpable force. She glared up at Ramdon in anger and disbelief. 'And you,' she whispered, not daring to believe it. 'You knew.'

Ramdon refused to meet her gaze. He was staring past the officer's shoulder and through the open window, his face calm and relaxed. There was no trace of guilt on his features. He might have been admiring the view.

My God, had she really been so stupid, so pitifully trusting and childlike? She'd known what he was from the beginning. A crook. An unscrupulous shifty-eyed crook. And in spite of that, she had trusted him. Confided in him. Leaned on him. What a fool she had been.

'You bloody Judas,' she hissed, 'I should have known, the way you talked about the Chinese. You're obviously a communist yourself.'

The officer laughed shortly. 'Hardly a communist, Mrs Morrill. Ramdon here is an inevitable product of the capitalist society, an opportunist. He saw you as a marketable commodity. We pay him well for such services, and being a man of infinite greed, his first and only concern was what price you would fetch. He radioed us almost immediately after your arrival in Nepal.'

Ramdon seemed unmoved by this disclosure. He was still staring out through the open window, his eyes calm and untroubled. His lips had pursed, and his cheeks were vibrating gently as if he was whistling some silent, indefinable refrain.

'You must understand, Mrs Morrill,' the Chinese officer said, 'money is the principal motivating force in Ramdon's life. When a society builds its foundations on such material values, the emergence of men like Ramdon becomes as natural as snow on a winter evening. He is dependable always, as long as the price is right.'

To Ramdon, he said coolly: 'Leave us. I will talk to you later.'

Ramdon showed no emotion as he left the room. Tracey watched him go, tears welling up inside her. She wanted to cry at the awfulness of it. I might have loved him, she thought. God knows I was pretty damned close already.

With a quaking heart, she turned back to face the Chinese officer.

'What happens to me now?' she asked, trying to keep her voice steady.

He shrugged. 'You will be taken at once to Lhasa and from there to Peking. You are the first tangible proof we have of American mischief within our frontiers, and naturally my superiors will wish to exploit that. First however, it is necessary that I interrogate you.'

He pulled up a chair and placed it in front of the desk.

'Please make yourself comfortable, Mrs Morrill,' he told her, 'I have a feeling it is going to be a very long day.'

Morrill was bathing in the river when he spotted Chamdo standing on the bluffs above. Chamdo's clothes were ragged and threadbare and his knees, peeking through the front of his tattered breeches, were crusted with dried blood. Chamdo's hair was almost as long as Morrill's. It hung to his shoulders in an unruly tangle. His cheeks were unshaven, and there were circles of dirt beneath his eyes and in the hollows at the corners of his mouth.

For a moment, Chamdo stood quite still, outlined against the distant glacier. The sun caught his profile, casting a pale sheen across the glossy skin. There was a look in his eyes Morrill instantly recognised, and glimpsing it, he felt his pulses quicken. Without changing expression, he eased out of the river and began to dry himself on his ragged shirt.

'Something's wrong,' he said.

Chamdo nodded. He shifted his stance, lowering his rifle butt to the ground, holding the muzzle gently in his fingertips like a man balancing a walking cane.

'We have news from the village of Amja,' he said.

'What news?'

Goosepimples showed on Morrill's hairless skin and moisture ran down his legs, spreading a circle of dampness on the crusted earth.

'The militia have picked up a woman claiming to be your wife.'

Morrill stopped pummelling and stared at Chamdo gravely, his eyes glowing like dark coals. 'Baima?' he whispered, his voice barely a croak.

Chamdo gave a a gesture of impatience. 'How can it be Baima? Baima is dead. This woman is European.'

Morrill pursed his lips as a strange feeling swept through him. 'Tracey?' he breathed.

It had to be Tracey. There could be no other explanation. And yet the idea seemed preposterous. Tracey here in the Ghyankhala? Impossible.

He felt no sense of warmth or husbandly response. The life they had spent together, those few short months, seemed meaningless to him now. It was like waking after a long sleep and finding the dreams of night intruding into reality. Still, her presence would be impossible to ignore. It raised questions which needed to be answered. A man could not turn his back completely on things which had once been important to him.

Leaning forward, he picked up his clothes and began hurriedly to pull them on. Chamdo studied him in silence, his face calm and thoughtful. 'It is a trap, of course,' he stated in a mild voice.

Morrill did not answer. He was concentrating on pulling up his trousers. Chamdo watched as he fastened the belt around his waist.

'They are trying to draw us out,' Chamdo said. 'They are using this woman as a bait.'

'I cannot leave her,' Morrill told him.

He tugged on his boots and reached for his shirt, drawing it over his head.

'If we respond as they expect us to respond,' Chamdo said, 'we will place ourselves at very great risk.'

'She is my wife,' Morrill insisted stubbornly, 'I cannot leave her.'

He picked up the last of his clothing and scrambled up the hillside, his eyes filled with a strange feverish intensity above the heavy beard.

For a long moment, Chamdo stood staring after him, his features dark and thoughtful. Then, with a sigh, he picked up the rifle, tucked it under his arm, and moving with a light fluid grace, began to clamber in Morrill's wake.

Tracey was lying on the bed when she heard the door softly open. They had placed her in an adjacent room which evidently doubled as a prison cell. It had no windows and was as small and cramped as a railroad compartment. The only light came through the thin slivers between the rooftiles, casting an eerie sheen through the cobwebs clustering the rafters above.

Her interrogation had been less protracted than she had feared. She had talked freely and without restraint. If Ramdon had delivered her to the Chinese, there seemed little point in concealing the truth. They already knew most of it anyway.

The Chinese commander had been pleased at her candour. 'We will talk later,' he'd promised. 'In the meantime, get some rest.'

Now, lifting her head from the pillow, she expected to see him framed between the doorposts. Instead, her senses quickened as she realised it was Ramdon. He was standing just inside the threshold, a wooden bowl in his hand. The thin slivers of light caught his sunbaked cheeks, picking out the hollows and lines. There was no sign of remorse on his features. He looked as calm and as sure of himself as ever. 'Better eat,' he advised, offering the bowl tentatively.

She felt anger welling up inside her. 'You've got a hell of a nerve,' she snapped.

'Shout at me all you want, but at least get this food down. You're going to need all your strength.'

Mildly, he closed the door and shuffled forward, feeling in the darkness for the bunk. His eyes had not yet adjusted to the diffracted light.

Without a word, Tracey took the bowl from his grasp. Ramdon was right. However much she hated him, starving herself for no purpose made no sense at all.

The bowl was filled with rice and boiled vegetables, and she began to eat ravenously, picking at the food with her fingers. Ramdon settled on the bunk beside her. She felt the touch of his body and moved quickly away.

'I don't blame you for being angry,' he muttered.

'You're damned right I'm angry, you treacherous bastard.'

'Try to look at it from my position,' he said reasonably. 'I live by my wits. All right, I'll admit I decided to pick up a bit on the side from the Chinese. But if you'll stop to consider for a moment, instead of flying off the handle the way you're doing, you'll realise I had your interests in mind as well as my own.'

She stared at him blankly. '*My* interests?' she echoed.

'You want to find your husband, don't you? For God's sake, you could go blundering around these mountains for years without catching a smell of him. This way, he's bound to hear about your arrest. The guerrillas monitor every move the militia make.'

She peered at him through the darkness, licking the rice from her fingers.

'Are you putting that forward as a serious justification?'

'Of course,' he said helplessly, 'how else do you expect to find Harold Morrill?'

'I thought the plan was to let the word pass around the villages?'

'Take too long. This way's quicker, more effective, and – let's face it – from my point of view, a damn sight more profitable.'

'The money being only a secondary consideration, I suppose?'

'Of course.'

'What you really had at heart was my welfare?'

'That's right

'I don't know how you have the effrontery to sit here and talk to me like this!'

'I'm only trying to do my best for everyone concerned,' he protested.

'What about the Sherpas? Have you considered what happens to them?'

'Nothing will happen. Sherpas are allowed to cross the frontier at will. They'll be ticked off by the commander and sent back where they came from. If your friend Jenkins is feeling benevolent, he can pay them their wages back in Katmandu.'

'And me? They're planning to take me to Peking.'

Ramdon snorted impatiently. 'It'll never come to that. Morrill will have you out of here before they can organise an escort.'

'But supposing he doesn't? Supposing Harry is already dead, have you considered that? We've only the Chinese reports to go on, after all. This whole thing could be a monumental hoax.'

'Then you'll be nothing more than an ordinary British tourist who crossed the border by mistake. No, if he's really alive, Morrill will come, I'm sure of it. And if he doesn't . . .' Ramdon patted her leg reassuringly, '. . . I'll find a way of getting you out of here myself,' he promised.

The man was incorrigible, she told herself. Having been paid by one side, he was already working out ways to help the other. She might have laughed at the absurdity of it all if the situation hadn't been so damned serious.

Ramdon left her after she had finished the food, and some hours later she woke from a light sleep to hear voices arguing in the office outside. She lay for a moment blinking, peering up at the shafts of sunlight illuminating the cobwebs above. Then the door creaked open and she lifted her head. It was Ramdon again. His face looked tense and troubled.

'What's going on?' she asked.

'Bloody Chinese have turned up. Somehow the word reached the command post at Nutsi. They've sent a deputation to take you back there at once.'

Tracey sat up on the bunk with alarm. 'Can't you stop them?'

'What do you think all the arguing's been about? The militia commander's not happy about it at all. He regards you as his personal prisoner. He was looking forward to escorting you back to Lhasa in triumph. But there's a major out here who outranks him. It looks as though we'll have to go along with the bastards.'

'For God's sake, now see what you've done.'

'Easy, take it easy,' Ramdon said soothingly. 'I won't let them harm you.'

'And how do you propose to stop them? By lulling them to sleep with your fiddle?'

'Listen,' Ramdon said earnestly, 'your husband's probably waiting in the hills at this very minute. You'll be easier to get at, once you're away from the militia post. This place is too heavily guarded.'

Tracey felt the anger coursing through her veins again. Damn Ramdon. He had ruined everything with his stupid greed.

Rising, she shook her head to clear it and ran her fingers swiftly through her hair. Stepping through the doorway, she blinked as she moved into the glare of the outer room. The office was full of Chinese soldiers. They stood staring at her intently, their uniforms creased and worn from travelling in the high mountains. And yet, she realised, although the place seemed crowded, there were no more than half-a-dozen at the outside, a small detail indeed to be escorting a valuable hostage.

The militia commander was perched in front of the window, his absurdly young face dark as thunder. His arms were folded and he was clearly sulking. In front of the desk stood a man in the uniform of an army major. He snapped something at Tracey she did not understand, and waved toward the outer door. She glanced at Ramdon, then still blinking, crossed the reception room and moved on to the verandah.

A line of yaks stood tethered along the wooden rail. The village inhabitants had gathered in the narrow street and she saw them studying her through dark solemn eyes. One of the Chinese came up behind her and bundled her roughly toward a waiting animal. There was a crude wooden saddle strapped across its shaggy hide. She realised she was meant to mount, and gripping its mane for support, swung her leg over the bulky flanks, settling back into position. The soldier seized her wrists and clipped on a pair of handcuffs. Tracey felt the chill steel biting into her flesh as the man looped a cord around the chain and tied it securely to the beast's massive horns. Perched in the saddle, with her wrists firmly shackled, Tracey struggled to maintain an air of dignity in the face of the watching populace.

The militia commander came out of the building still arguing heatedly with the army major. The major barked something in a curt voice and the commander blushed. Stepping back, he bowed his head in a gesture of subservience and stood with lips compressed, his spine against the doorpost.

Ramdon too was arguing with the army major. Apparently the Chinese did not want to take him along, but Ramdon was insisting. In the end, the major shrugged irritably and waved the Engishman to one of the waiting yaks. Tracey felt relieved. Ramdon was exasperating, unreliable, infuriating. But he was the only friend she had.

They set off in convoy, the major in front, Tracey and Ramdon following close behind. The rolling movement of her animal felt strangely soothing and she swayed gently to the rhythm of its gait. The bell on its throat tinkled in her eardrums.

For a while, the village children trotted along excitedly at their side, but soon the trail grew steeper and they fell back, returning at last to their homes far behind.

'How long will this journey take?' Tracey asked Ramdon.

'Christ knows. The command post at Nutsi can't be far. The bastards got here fast enough when they heard the cavalry had grabbed you.'

The Chinese had confiscated Ramdon's rifle, but he carried his violin case strapped to his narrow spine. Tracey's anger had not subsided, but the realisation that Ramdon did not intend to desert her mollified her feelings toward him. Despite her fury, she felt soothed by his presence.

The trail narrowed, hugging the contours of the hillside. She watched it dip around the shoulder of a narrow bend and then, as they turned the corner, felt her senses jump at the sight of a man perched directly in their path. He looked like a scarecrow, his lean frame huddled in tattered animal skins. His features were gaunt and haggard, his chin obscured by a heavy beard which sprouted profusely above a vicious scar encircling his throat. His hair tumbled raggedly to his shoulders, and in his fists he clutched a submachine gun which he pointed menacingly in their direction.

As she stared into the man's face, Tracey felt a tremor pass through her body. Something inside her began to throb. Memories, vague and distorted, flooded into her brain.

Neither the Chinese major nor any of his soldiers displayed the slightest hint of surprise at the newcomer's presence, but Ramdon, startled, cursed savagely and raised his arms in a gesture of surrender.

'Stop behaving like the Lone Ranger,' she told him mildly. 'This man is my husband, Harold Morrill.'

At the cave, Chamdo and the guerrillas changed out of their Chinese uniforms. The khaki battledresses had provided a useful camouflage over the years, and their own Mongolian features had made the deception easy to carry out, but constant wear and the inevitable ravages of age had caused the outfits to deteriorate, and soon he knew they would become unusable.

For some reason, Chamdo felt restless and uneasy. Since rescuing the woman he had been filled with a sense of deep foreboding. He could see Morrill and his wife talking animatedly by the cave-mouth, and the sight of Morrill's face, flushed and intense, worried him. Not since the old days had Morrill displayed such fervour. Chamdo remembered with increasing wariness the way he had changed after meeting the girl Baima. He hoped history was not about to repeat itself. This new woman might arouse in Morrill memories and emotions he would not be able to control. The thought troubled Chamdo. He did not want to lose Morrill again.

Thirty feet away, sitting on the chill ground, Tracey studied her husband wonderingly. He had changed almost beyond recognition. Gone was the healthy glow of civilised living she remembered so well, gone was the air of nervous intelligence. This man was like a hunted animal. His face was haunted, his eyes demented. His lank hair was caked with dirt, his features as chipped and savage as the rocks surrounding them.

It was hard for Tracey to grasp the fact that this grotesque figure was the man who had once shared her most intimate moments, harder still to accept that in the middle of this desolate wilderness she had found him alive after all these years.

'It was good of you to come,' she said.

He grunted, his eyes studying her balefully. 'I had to find out if the story was true.'

'Still, I know you were taking a risk. They meant to trap you.'

'They've been trying to trap me for years. They haven't managed it yet.'

She stared about her, marvelling. The guerrillas were drifting into the cave to rest. On the pastures below, the yaks were grazing peacefully.

'How on earth do you manage to survive? So few of you.'

'Fourteen,' he told her. 'Once there was more than a hundred, but some got killed, some fell sick, others lost the will to fight and drifted back to their villages. Now only the strong remain.'

'Do you really hate the Chinese so much?'

He hesitated, and for a moment she glimpsed in his eyes a look so anguished, so ridden with suffering and human loss, her stomach twisted in sympathy. He had always been a sensitive man, she recalled that well; too sensitive, her mother used to say. Never trust a man who thinks too deeply, that was her mother's point of view. But then Harry and her mother had never hit it off, from the beginning. She wondered what the old lady would say if she could see him now.

'Look at these people,' Morrill murmured, waving at the guerrillas behind them. 'For centuries, they closed their borders to foreigners and intruders. Not through truculence or churlishness, you understand. The Tibetans are the warmest race on earth. But they're simple souls who live according to the Buddhist scriptures, who despise the taking of life and fear man's predatory nature. In their naive way, they really believed they could protect their way of life simply by shutting themselves in. Well, it didn't work. The Chinese invaded and destroyed everything the Tibetans held dear. They vandalised their monasteries, executed their holy men, forced the populace to relinquish its most cherished and ancient beliefs. Try to understand that if you can. All these people ever asked from life was the right to be left alone.'

'You've told me their reasons for hating,' she said evenly. 'What's yours?'

'I'm one of them now. I think as they do, feel as they do.'

'No,' she insisted quietly. 'With you it's something else. Something . . . personal.'

A cloud seemed to pass over Morrill's face. He looked down at the ground, tracing his finger through the dust. She sensed a wall of stubborn resistance.

It was hard to sit here and pretend there was some kind of bond between them, harder still to recall that bond without feeling at least a semblance of personal indignation. After all, it was she who had been the injured party.

'You think you were right?' she demanded. 'Leaving me the way you did, without a word?'

He shrugged. 'I had no choice.'

'Did you ever spare a thought for my feelings while you were acting out your schoolboy fantasies? They told me you were dead. They said you'd fallen down a crevasse.'

'It was the agency who put up the cover story.'

'Couldn't they at least have told me the truth? I was your wife, Harry.'

Morrill studied her in silence for a moment. Beneath the thatch of unkempt hair, his face in some ways looked younger than ever. There was a pleasing evenness to the bone structure. The nose was straight and perfectly proportioned. The lips were full, the teeth white and even. Only the eyes spoiled the illusion. Dark and fathomless, they held an air of torment that made Tracey instinctively shudder.

'Wife?' he echoed. 'Come on, Tracey. We had a relationship, an interlude, a transitory involvement nothing more. We didn't even realise the step we were taking.'

'And that gave you the right to opt out at will, is that it?'

'I didn't mean to hurt you. It was my job, that's all.'

'You could have divorced me, Harry. I could have taken that. It's the lies which really stick in my throat.'

He shifted uncomfortably on his haunches, his face dark and sullen. 'You had no right to come here.'

'Why not? Wasn't that *my* job? Speaking as a wife, I mean. After all, I like to know what my status is. Widow? Abandoned spouse? Unwilling accomplice? What?'

'If you felt so bad about it, why didn't you have the marriage dissolved?'

'I thought you were dead, can't you understand that?'

'Who told you otherwise? The agency?'

Tracey nodded, looking down at the ground, and Morrill pulled a face.

'I thought it was too unreal to be a coincidence. They sent you here to contact me?'

'Yes,' she whispered.

'Okay, you've contacted. Now get it off your chest.'

Tracey took a deep breath. 'You're going about this all wrong, Harry. You're undoing all the things you think you are fighting for.'

Briefly, she told him about her meeting with the State Department representative, Waldo Friedman. She sketched in the details of the US/Chinese science and technology agreement and explained how his actions were jeopardising the relationship between the two countries. Morrill listened in silence until she had finished, then he started to laugh.

She stared at him blankly. 'What are you laughing at?'

'You. You're so naive, Tracey. Do you imagine I give a damn about the State Department and their stupid technological agreement?'

'But you must. They're the people who employ you.'

'Nobody employs me. I'm my own man. I've been my own man for years now. What I do here has nothing to do with Washington DC. It's for me. For these people who've become part of me.'

She hesitated, choosing her words with care. 'Harry, you've got to come back. You're fighting against the interests of your own nation.'

'I have no nation,' he stated. 'Look at me, Tracey. How much do you recognise in my face, in my eyes, in the texture of my skin? I'm a stranger, isn't that true? I'm not the man you married, Tracey. I'm not the man you lived with. That man died. I've been born again.'

'What are you talking about?'

'I'll tell you if you really want to hear it. You might find it difficult to believe, but I'll tell you anyhow.'

She nodded.

And yet, strangely, she felt reluctant for him to proceed, as if once he embarked on his confession, the barrier between them would be complete. He wasn't a bit like the Harry Morrill she'd expected to find. Harry had always been something of an enigma, but this man was beyond her comprehension.

Slowly, hesitantly, he began his story. Fascinated, she studied the scar on his throat as he described how he was strangled at the hands of Jerry Schonfield. He explained how Chamdo had found him and taken him to the monastery, how the high lama had blown *prana* into his body, restoring his life. He described his meeting with Baima and the emotions it had aroused. She felt no jealousy, no feeling of resentment. That part of their relationship was long over. He told her how he had gone to live with Baima at Lamringyhana, how he had escorted the lamas to the frontier, how the Chinese had come and destroyed the village. When he reached the part where he had discovered the bodies of Baima and her family, his voice choked into a sob.

She waited in silence, filled with a sudden sympathy. 'You loved her?' she asked in a quiet voice.

He nodded. The recounting had hurt him, she could tell. He seemed to withdraw within himself, as if the pain of exposure was almost too much to bear.

'I'm beginning to understand,' she said. 'You see this war as a personal vendetta between you and the Chinese. But you're wrong, Harry. You're not helping Baima's memory. You're simply destroying yourself.'

'Who cares?' he muttered dully.

'I care. Because it's so pointless. What do you hope to gain by this ridiculous charade? Don't you see, Harry? As long as you remain in the Ghyankhala, your memories of Baima will haunt you for ever. What you need are new influences, new ideas. Come back with me. Return to your old world. It's your only chance.'

'This is my world,' he said stubbornly. 'It's where I belong.'

She shook her head. 'You're an American, not a Tibetan. You wanted revenge, and you've hurt the Chinese badly for what they did at Lamringyhana. But enough is enough, Harry. The violence can't go on for ever. You don't wipe out a crime by simply committing another. Withdraw while there's still time. There's no need for you to die here.'

'Dying or living,' he said, 'it makes no difference.'

Tracey was silent. There was nothing left to say. He needed comfort, he needed solace, he needed something to make him whole again. But she thought sadly: I was wrong to imagine I could bring any influence to bear. We took our separate roads years ago.

Slowly, he unfolded his legs and rose to his feet. 'Come, you must be tired,' he said. 'You can get some rest inside the cave.'

'What will happen to us now?'

'We'll escort you to the Nepalese border. There's a monastery a few miles on the other side, at Cho Mangpai. You'll be able to pick up porters there, provisions. After that, it's a month's trek to Katmandu.'

She let him lead her inside the cave. The floor was crowded with sleeping figures, among them Ramdon wrapped in a grimy blanket, stretched out next to the wall. She settled down at his side, pulling her borrowed bedding around her. She was filled with a curious emptiness, the simple knowledge that she had failed. There had been no emotion between them, no sense of his being aware of her as a woman, and without that she knew she could never hope to take him back.

Ramdon watched Morrill's retreating spine, blinking in the misty darkness.

'So that's your old man,' he whispered. 'Bit of a rum character, isn't he?'

She nodded.

'Is he coming back with us?'

'No,' she said. 'He's staying here. He wants to carry on the fight.'

Ramdon grinned, his teeth gleaming against the sun-baked skin.

'What are you smiling at?' she said.

'I'm glad, that's all.'

'Glad, why?'

'Because I've decided to grab you for myself.'

It was impossible to tell if Ramdon was joking or not, and suddenly she didn't care. All she wanted was to rest.

'Go to sleep, Silas,' she said wearily. 'For God's sake, just go to sleep.'

CHAPTER TEN

In the early hours of Wednesday morning, 23 February, Waldo Friedman, special envoy for the US State Department in Washington, was summoned from his Georgetown apartment and taken by military escort to Degermark Lecture Chamber on the second floor of the White House. The chamber had once served as a reception room for Eleanor Roosevelt and successive presidents had used it for a variety of purposes over the years. Its walls were lined with photographs from the early part of the twentieth century, and above its mantelpiece hung Rembrandt Peale's famous portrait of George Washington. A plastic screen had been erected in front of a line of chairs and, when Waldo arrived, he found the Secretary of State and Jack Hirsch, his department chief, already waiting.

'Glad you could get here, Waldo,' the Secretary said.

Waldo had dressed hurriedly, and in his confusion had omitted to put on a necktie. Being a fastidious man by nature, he was uncomfortably conscious of the fact that his clothes were rumpled, his face unshaven. 'What's happened?' he asked.

Jack Hirsch laughed dryly. 'Relax. We're not in a state of war yet. But there's something we'd like you to take a look at.'

At the Secretary's invitation, Waldo sat down in one of the empty chairs. Jack Hirsch walked across the floor until he was standing beside the cinema screen. He turned and looked once at the Secretary of State, and Waldo thought he detected a flicker of uneasiness in Hirsch's manner. The purpose of the unexpected meeting intrigued him. It was not often he was summoned so dramatically, especially in the middle of the night.

'Dowse the lights,' Jack Hirsch called to the chamber usher.

The room faded into darkness and Waldo heard the whirr of a cinema projector from the cubbyhole behind, then a beam of light shot across the chamber and a series of pictures flickered on to the silver screen. Waldo saw a vast mounain range, a land of rugged peaks, scarred glaciers and deep valleys with rivers running through them like silken threads. The significance of the pictures baffled him. He could see no connection between the tundra-like wilderness he was watching and himself.

'What is this?' he asked, puzzled.

'Satellite pictures,' Jack Hirsch explained. 'This film was

taken from a satellite called PS3/400, unofficially known as Old Sagamore. The country you're studying is the Ghyankhala region of western Tibet, which runs along the Nepalese border. It's wild, rugged and practically unpopulated.'

Mystified, Waldo watched the images flickering by. This, he realised, was where the American Harold Morrill was reputed to be harrassing the Chinese occupation forces. When the film ended, a tiny cue dot flashed across the screen and the sheet went blank. Neither Jack Hirsch nor the Secretary of State said anything. Waldo's first sense of confusion had given way to a feeling of bewilderment. 'That's all?' he muttered.

'That's the end of the moving pictures,' Jack Hirsch said. 'Now we'd like you to take a look at one or two blow-ups.'

A photograph flashed on to the screen. It showed an indeterminate section of mountainside, scarred by fissures, cracks and defiles. Because the sky was blotted out, the features were difficult to discern.

'This is one of those same shots magnified a hundred times,' Jack Hirsh said. 'We do that automatically every thousand frames or so. Notice anything curious about it?'

Waldo frowned. 'No.'

'See this little blob in the top lefthand corner?'

Hirsch pointed to a smudge high on the mountain's left flank. Waldo studied it in silence for a moment. 'Looks like a fold in the ground,' he said.

'No, it's too even for that. Colour's all wrong. Something about it doesn't quite fit. Here's the same section enlarged another hundred times. What do you make of it now?'

The second picture was much more detailed than the first, but the images were blurred and indistinct. Narrowing his eyes, Waldo was able to make out a series of tiny blobs spread across the hillside. 'People,' he declared.

Hirsch nodded. 'Right. People on the move. Picture quality's beginning to deteriorate, but here's the same section blow-up. Now you can clearly see the outline. No doubt about it, we've got people there.'

Waldo stared at the figures on the cinema screen. They were heavily smudged and miniscule in size, but he had to agree that they appeared human. Between them was a denser patch of shadow which momentarily confused him. It looked like a stain on the camera lens, an elongated blob, solid and compact.

154

'They appear to be carrying something,' he muttered. 'Some kind of chest.'

'Not a chest,' Jack Hirsch said. 'We don't think it's a chest. Let's take a look at the next enlargement.'

A third photograph flashed across the screen. It was heavily magnified and showed little more than a series of shapeless blotches.

'What do you make of that, Waldo?'

'Hard to say,' Waldo answered.

'It's a sedan chair. See these lines along the bottom here? They're the support posts.'

Waldo studied the strange object intently. 'Well ... it's possible, I guess.'

'Now take a look at the roof, Waldo,' said the Secretary sitting beside him.

'The roof, sir?'

'What do you make of those curious markings there?'

The still's quality had now faded to such an extent that accurate identification was difficult to assess, but by narrowing his eyes, Waldo was able to detect a series of odd shapes set against the oblong blur. 'How do you know they *are* markings, Mr Secretary? They could be anything. Shadows, distortions on the print. You've got this thing blown up to maximum range, remember.'

'We know they're markings,' Jack Hirsch said, 'because we've had them authenticated by an expert. They're the sacred symbols of the Dalai Lama.'

Waldo hesitated. Fumbling in his pocket, he was about to bring out a cigarette when the Secretary of State offered him one of his own.

'Do you understand, Waldo, what the Dalai Lama means to the Tibetan people?'

'Yes sir,' Waldo said, leaning forward to accept the Secretary's proffered light, 'he was their leader until he quit the country in 1959.'

'More than their leader, he was also their god. They really believed that . . . that he was some kind of immortal presence.'

'Well, he's not immortal any more,' Waldo grunted. 'He's dead.'

'All Dalai Lamas die, Waldo,' Jack Hirsch put in, 'but the Tibetans believe in the process of reincarnation. And since the

Dalai Lama is considered a god, it stands to reason that in Tibetan eyes his spirit continues to live on. We were wrong to imagine that the Tibetan royal succession ended with the Dalai Lama's funeral.'

Waldo frowned. 'But he had no children surely?'

'Waldo, when a Dalai Lama passes away, the Tibetans believe his soul enters the body of a young boy. The monks who form his immediate entourage carry out extensive tests to discover which boy has assumed their ruler's identity.'

The Secretary continued: 'When they're satisfied they've found the right boy, he's taken to the Jokhang, the holiest shrine in Lhasa, for consecration. In theory, he assumes control of the country at the age of eighteen.'

Waldo shook his head in bewilderment. 'What is all this leading up to?'

The Secretary nodded to the chamber usher and the lights were switched back on. Waldo blinked in the unexpected glare.

The Secretary said softly: 'We've received an intelligence report from the British who maintain an office in New Delhi that a new Dalai Lama has been chosen among the Tibetans in exile there. The belief is, the monks are trying to smuggle him through to Lhasa for consecration.'

'And you think our satellite photographs have picked up their procession?'

'It makes sense,' Jack Hirsch said. 'The Ghyankhala is the least inhabited section of the entire country. If you were trying to sneak somebody in there, it's the obvious route to choose. And those chair markings seem to confirm it.'

The Secretary rose to his feet and pushed one hand into his jacket pocket. Standing there, dapper, intense, the cigarette dangling loosely from the fingers of his free hand, he looked somehow dated and theatrical.

'Have you any idea, Waldo, what would happen if the word leaked out that a new Dalai Lama had entered Tibet?'

Waldo considered the thought for a moment. 'There would be an uprising,' he declared.

'Our assessment exactly.'

'My God,' Waldo grunted, whistling softly, 'we could be witnessing the beginning of a whole new Tibet.'

'Waldo, they won't get through to Lhasa,' the Secretary told him, 'because we can't afford it.'

156

'I . . . I don't understand.'

'Waldo, nobody criticised the Chinese invasion of Tibet more than the United States. Ultimately, we want to see them out of there. We want to see a unified Tibet with its own autonomous government again. Nothing can alter that.'

'I understand, Mr Secretary.'

'But this isn't the time, Waldo. Ten years from now, we'll give them all the support we can. But right at this moment, a Tibetan uprising would be disastrous to the interests of this country.'

Waldo was silent for a moment. The Secretary looked like a parson delivering a sermon.

'How do you figure that, sir?' Waldo asked, shifting uneasily.

'Nothing is as important as that science and technology agreement, Waldo. We must have that monitoring station covering the Sakhalin and Kuril islands. Our relationship with China is delicate to say the least. If there was some kind of explosion in Tibet, the US would find itself in an impossible position.'

'But Mr Secretary, at the risk of sounding pedantic, the science and technology agreement is a separate issue. What we're discussing here is the right of a nation to determine its own future. That's part of the basic fabric of our own Constitution.'

The Secretary looked at Jack Hirsch helplessly.

'Waldo,' Jack said, 'nobody's arguing about the right of the Tibetan people to self-government. All we're saying is, in view of our own interests, this isn't the time.'

'Not the time?' Waldo exclaimed. 'What does that mean, for Christ's sake, not the time?'

Leaning forward, the Secretary rested his hand on the nape of Waldo's neck, gently massaging his skin. The touch of his fingers was soothing.

'Waldo, I understand how you feel, believe me,' the Secretary told him in a gentle tone. 'The intricacies of diplomacy are never easy to follow. In many ways, it's not unlike a card game. Signs, body signals have to be observed and analysed to produce an assessment of the grand design. Sometimes it's necessary to do things we don't fundamentally approve of, in order to achieve things we actually do. In this instance, we have been forced, very much against our will, to curtail a course of action which, in different circumstances, we might well support.'

'Curtail?' Waldo echoed.

The Secretary's face grew more serious still. He seemed to have different levels of expression which he switched and altered as the occasion demanded.

'Through certain channels,' he stated, 'we have informed the Chinese about our satellite film. The information was passed delicately of course, and cannot be attributed to this government. It was also offered on the direct understanding that the science and technology talks will be immediately resumed.'

Suddenly, Waldo understood. He leaned back in his chair, staring at the two men facing him. 'I can't believe this is happening,' he muttered.

'We had no choice, Waldo,' Jack Hirsch put in. 'We've got to have that monitoring station. It's a question of priorities, can't you see that?'

'I know what you're thinking, Waldo,' the Secretary said, patting Waldo's knee and smiling like a sage old uncle. 'If we can turn our backs on our own Constitution, what's the point in diplomacy at all? But it's not strictly true, Waldo. We've simply frozen the issue for the moment. We'll return to the subject of Tibetan independence, believe me, as soon as the moment is right, and think what a better position we'll be in to influence the authorities in Peking if we've managed to narrow the gap between our two governments. At the same time, we'll have given ourselves a major toe-hold in the Soviet Union's Far East Theater. That's what diplomacy all comes down to in the end, Waldo. Judging which action will best serve your country's interests at the time.'

Waldo said nothing. He had never accepted the premise that the end justified the means.

He watched the Secretary's smile broaden. 'Now what I want you to do is fly out to Paris in the morning and await the arrival of the Chinese delegation. I want you to pick up those talks where you left off, Waldo. I want that entire package signed, sealed and delivered by the end of the month. Think you can do that?'

Waldo knew he had no choice, whatever his personal feelings. Secretly, he believed the Secretary's action was immoral. But as a State Department employee, his compliance was taken as a matter of course. Sighing, he nodded his head. 'I'll do my best, sir,' he promised.

Lhasa, Tibet

The sound of footsteps echoing in the corridor outside woke Lin Hua from a dreamless sleep. The night was dark and very cold. In the slivers of starlight from the open window he could see his breath steaming on the pre-dawn air.

The footsteps grew louder, their clatter reverberating through the hollow emptiness of the Potala Palace. Lin Hua sat in bed, shivering a little in the chill, and reached for his spectacles. His heart was thumping. He knew the major, Tang A-hsi, would not disturb him without good reason. Their association was a difficult one at the best of times and by mutual consent they kept personal contact to a minimum.

There was a heavy knocking on the bedroom door. Clearing his throat, Lin Hua said loudly: 'Enter.'

The soldier who stood there was small and reedlike, his upper lip displaying the beginnings of a thin moustache. His uniform was baggy around the knees, and his body slouched in a posture of nervousness and uncertainty. 'You are to accompany me at once,' he announced in a high, boyish voice.

'Is something wrong?' Lin Hua asked.

The soldier shook his head. 'I know nothing,' he admitted. 'Only that I am to bring you with all possible speed.'

His brain in a turmoil, Lin Hua dressed quickly and followed the young soldier along the endless maze of corridors into the open air. Even inside his padded combat jacket, he felt himself shivering as the piercing cold of the early morning bit into his flesh. His teeth chattered as he trotted lightly down the broad, stone staircase. At the foot of the steps, a camouflaged army vehicle waited in the darkness, its engine softly purring. Lin Hua clambered into the passenger seat, and with the soldier taking the driving wheel, they set off through the deserted streets of the Tibetan capital. A few dogs howled at them from the shadows, but there was no sign of any human presence.

They left the outskirts of the town behind and took the road to Gonggar. Lin Hua's sense of anxiety steadily deepened. He could not imagine what this extraordinary summons was all about. Numerous possibilities popped into his brain, but he dismissed them instantly. Then, after nearly an hour, he spotted floodlights on the valley floor ahead, and as they drew closer, watched the grotesque outlines of three massive helicopters gradually loom into view. They were standing in the approximate shape of a triangle, their engines humming on the crisp pre-dawn air. Their hulls were light green, their noses bulbous, and Lin Hua could see the pilots' cockpits raised high above the bulging fuselages, giving the craft a curiously unwieldy look. Soldiers were running to and fro in noisy confusion, carrying packs of supplies toward the waiting aircraft. The sound of barked orders echoed harshly in Lin Hua's eardrums.

As his driver drew to a halt, Lin Hua glimpsed Major Tang A-hsi striding toward him across the frozen earth. Tang A-hsi was dressed in a quilted cloak, his face masked by a pair of rubberised snow-goggles. His cheeks looked flushed and elated, and in the blinding glare of the floodlamps, Lin Hua watched his lips twist into an enigmatic sneer.

'You're late,' Tang A-hsi said, his voice haughty, tinged with contempt.

'We came as quickly as we could,' Lin Hua stated. 'What is happening here?'

'We have news at last. The Dalai Lama's procession has been sighted in the Ghyankhala.'

'The Ghyankhala?' Lin Hua echoed dubiously. 'That wilderness?'

'Exactly. Where else would a fugitive choose to cross the frontier? We are leaving at once. You will join me in the leading aircraft. When we have deposited our men, our helicopters will ferry in provisions and fuel supplies in relays.'

'And then?'

The major smiled thinly. 'The Dalai Lama's journey is about to come to an abrupt end,' he said. 'Our orders are precise. Whatever happens, he must never be allowed to leave the Ghyankhala.'

Tracey heard the roar of the helicopters in the first flush of early morning. She opened her eyes, peering around the cave's interior. The place was deserted. A few cooking pots, a disordered scattering of blankets and bedding were all she could discern. For a moment she was puzzled. Then she realised the guerrillas had scrambled outside to investigate the noise.

She joined them at the entrance, pushing her way through

the throng of excitedly babbling men. She could see the helicopters spread out in loose formation scanning the valley below. They looked immense, their giant rotor blades thrashing the air like the wings of grotesque insects. She counted three machines hovering, and as she watched, the first helicopter put down on the valley floor and miniscule men scrambled from its fuselage into the open. She watched them spread out, running hard, moving with the curious frenzied motion of soldiers on exercise. But this was no exercise, Tracey knew. They were here to do what soldiers did the world over. Kill.

She watched the two remaining aircraft land and disgorge their cargoes, then the troops formed a ragged line, spanning the entire width of the valley floor. Slowly, they began to move toward its head, checking the scrub and the patches of stunted woodland.

Tracey looked around for Morrill. He was standing with Ramdon, his beard fluttering in the wind, his eyes glittering with hate as he watched the miniature figures below. Tracey pushed her way to his side. 'Where did they come from?' she muttered.

He glanced down at her, shrugging. 'Christ knows. Lhasa probably.'

'Are they searching for us?'

'Maybe. They're looking for somebody. And if they keep coming, they're bound to find the cave. No way they can miss it.'

Tracey glanced behind her, looking for a way of escape. The mountainside was steep, but not unscalable. They could still run if they scrambled upwards. But they would be out in the open.

'They'll spot us if we move,' she said.

'I know, but we can't stay here. We'll get the things together and head toward the summit. If we can gain enough altitude, maybe those choppers won't be able to follow in the thin air. They must be operating at their maximum level now.'

He barked out a series of commands and the guerrillas began assembling their weapons and provisions. They worked briskly and with a minimum of fuss. Tracey could see they were used to handling such emergencies. Within ten minutes, they had gathered everything at the cave mouth. Equipment which could not be carried was abandoned on the rocky floor. The yaks were left grazing on the lower pastures.

Tracey studied the approaching figures below. They were closer now, but not alarmingly so. She realised the soldiers were moving more slowly than she had imagined, and felt reassured.

Turning, she again studied the hillslope above. It looked steep and inhospitable. 'How high is it?' she asked Morrill.

'Twenty-one thousand feet.'

'What happens when we get to the top?'

'We run for the frontier. It's our only chance.'

She glanced at the troops in the valley. The helicopters had risen again and were zig-zagging from ridge to ridge, acting as the searchers' eyes and ears.

'Think we can stay ahead?'

Morrill's face was grim as he picked up his machine-gun and slung it over his shoulder. 'We've got to,' he told her softly. 'Either we stay ahead or we die.'

At Morrill's command, they left the cave and began to clamber up the steep fractured hillslope. The guerrillas spread out in a ragged line, the sound of their laboured breathing harsh and discordant in the frozen stillness.

Tracey's boots slipped and stumbled on the loose moraine, and in what seemed no time at all, she was gasping desperately for air. She tried to turn her mind from that, focusing her energy into the simple process of moving upward. There was no sound from the valley, no shouts of discovery, no clatter of rifle shots or roar of approaching helicopters. Good start, she thought. So far, they had not been spotted.

Doggedly, she pushed on, following the line of panting men. And then, just as they were approaching the summit, she heard the thunderous echo of rotor blades and realised with a sinking heart their flight had been detected. The helicopter came out of nowhere, a grotesque shape, impossibly ugly, swaying in the air currents. They backed against the hillside, sheltering their faces from the buffeting downdraught. Dust spiralled into the air. Tracey could see the pilot and navigator clearly through the plexiglass windshield.

Panic rose in her breast. They were trapped. It mattered little how hard they climbed. The helicopter could follow them every foot of the way. She saw the features of the guerrillas tense with alarm, their hair blowing wildly in the slipstream. Morrill's beard fluttered around his cheeks and his mouth worked furiously, voicing meaningless oaths which were lost in the stunning clatter of the rotor blades.

With a start of fear, Tracey heard a new sound rising above the clamour. Machine-gun fire. She saw bullets kicking at the earth around their feet and glimpsed the navigator leaning out of the 'copter's door, strapped in place by a canvas harness; as she watched, he swung his machine gun in a deadly arc, spraying the mountainslope below.

Tracey wanted to run, but somehow she couldn't move. She felt her heart thumping against her ribcage. The pilot was hovering almost level with her face, struggling to keep his machine steady as his companion carefully adjusted his aim. At such close range, she realised he couldn't miss. Terror, wild and debilitating, clutched at her throat. Her legs seemed to wobble under her.

And then, in one breathless moment, Morrill and Chamdo, operating independently, began to fire back in frenzied bursts. Tracey felt the hot flame from their muzzles searing her cheek. She jumped as the rhythmic stutter of their machine-guns hammered at her eardrums. She saw the navigator leap and jerk convulsively in his canvas harness. Something splashed across the plexiglass shield, a grotesque welter of blood, brain and bone fragments. Desperately, the pilot revved his machine in a frantic effort to get away. Morrill switched aim, firing wildly, ripping the windshield to shreds. The helicopter dipped, tilting over on its side, and dry-mouthed, Tracey watched in horrified fascination as the massive rotors caught the rocks, sending the machine crazily spinning, rolling over and over like a stricken starling. It plummeted into the hillside, erupting outwards in a monstrous pumpkin of smoke and flame. A wave of white-hot air washed her face, and pieces of fuselage and twisted metal showered upon them from the buffeting air currents. She ducked back, holding her arms across her head, and only when the torrent of wreckage had finally stopped did she slowly straighten and stare in silence at the blackened remains. The framework was twisted beyond recognition and smoking in the morning sunlight. Relief flooded through her. They had destroyed it, thank God.

Tracey was about to turn when, with a start of alarm, she spotted Ramdon sprawled on the ground, his features creased with pain. A sob burst from her throat as she stumbled toward him. 'Harry,' she yelled, 'Silas is hit.'

They reached Ramdon at almost the same instant, turning him over on to his back. There was blood on Ramdon's shirt, just above the left hip.

'What happened?' Tracey gasped.

Ramdon's face had paled, but he grinned up at her in his curious crooked way. 'I must have stuck my arse out. It's an old habit of mine.'

'Is it bad?'

'Don't know. Hurts like hell.'

Morrill pulled up Ramdon's shirt and examined the blue-rimmed hole in Ramdon's flesh. Blood was gushing out in what seemed bucketfuls.

'That looks serious,' she whispered.

Morrill grunted. 'Shrapnel tear. Fatty substance above the hip. You're a lucky man, Ramdon. It looks a damn sight worse than it actually is. Soon as we can stop I'll put some stitches in, but first we've got to reach the summit before those choppers start ferrying troops up here.'

The surviving helicopters made no attempt to follow their companion. Instead, they sped back to the valley floor and began picking up the detachment of soldiers. Tracey saw the danger immediately. If they could drop the troops somewhere nearby, Morrill's little band of followers would be easily surrounded and cut to ribbons.

Together, they hoisted Ramdon to his feet, and supporting him on each side, began to stumble frantically in the wake of the retreating guerrillas. The thinness of the atmosphere drained Tracey's strength, but she struggled gamely upwards, feeling the hard line of Ramdon's body pressed against hers, blood from his side dripping down her wrist.

She was filled with surprise and wonder. For one blinding panic-stricken moment she'd thought she had lost him, and the feeling inside her, the awful brain-numbing stomach-curdling sense of despair had been like nothing she had ever experienced before. This man, this impossible man had affected her more deeply than she could possibly imagine. She found it strange caring for someone more than she cared for herself.

They heard the helicopters roaring loudly, but no pursuit followed. Tracey had expected to come under immediate fire.

She decided the speed of their flight had left the soldiers too far behind to effectively follow.

Two of the guerrillas turned back and relieved Tracey and Morrill at Ramdon's side, and though she was reluctant to leave him, she knew her strength was fading rapidly and felt a sense of relief as she stepped back, sliding Ramdon's arm around the guerrilla's shoulders.

All day, they pushed steadily southwards, watching the country change bit by bit, stopping only for an occasional rest or to gobble down mouthfuls of indigestible food. There was no sign of the pursuing Chinese, and soon it became evident that they had been effectively outstripped. Tracey was too exhausted to feel grateful.

As evening approached, Morrill called a halt in a narrow gully flanked on two sides by overhanging buttresses. The guerrillas holding Ramdon lowered him gently to the ground. His eyes were closed and he was shivering violently. Alarmed, Tracey touched his forehead. It felt icy against her fingers.

'Harry,' she yelled.

Morrill ran toward her, and kneeling at Ramdon's side, gently felt his cheek.

'Hypothermia,' he said softly. 'The shock of the injury must have drained his body heat.'

Tracey's senses lurched. Ramdon couldn't die now, not after all they had gone through. He couldn't just die when she'd realised for the first time how much she needed him.

'He's shaking like a jelly, Harry. For God's sake, you've got to do something.'

Morrill was staring at her, his eyes curiously intense. Suddenly, she realised she was crying. She just couldn't help herself. Tears streamed down her cheeks. It wasn't fair. At the very moment she had found Ramdon, here she was on the point of losing him. She couldn't go back to that other life, not now. She needed him alive, she needed him beside her.

As if he understood what was going through her mind, Morrill slowly nodded.

'Bring some blankets,' he ordered. 'Wrap him up good from head to foot.'

Still sobbing, she opened up the bundles of bedding and tucked the coarse material around Ramdon's body. Morrill sat crosslegged at his head.

'What are you going to do?' she whispered.

Instead of answering, he closed his eyes and grew very still. Tracey frowned, watching him lean forward and press his fingertips against Ramdon's temples. He appeared to be sinking into a trance. His bearded cheeks tensed and hardened, the muscles assuming a curious rigidity. His entire body became solid and immobile, every sinew, every nerve end frozen into place. He was like a statue carved out of stone.

Baffled, Tracey studied him in silence. She had no idea what was going on. Morrill's cheeks grew visibly paler, as if his spirit, or whatever lifeforce existed within his scarecrow frame, was being slowly drained through his helpless pores.

Wonderingly, Tracey glanced down at Ramdon and a gasp burst from her lips. Ramdon's trembling had stopped. He was lying on his back, his chest rising and falling evenly like a man in the throes of a deep dreamless sleep.

Still Morrill did not move. The pallor in his cheeks became more marked with every passing second. On impulse, Tracey put out her hand and touched Ramdon's forehead. Despite the coldness of the mountain air, his skin felt warm to the touch. In amazement, she let her fingers trail over her husband's wrist and jerked back her hand in astonishment. Heat was radiating fiercely out of Morrill's pores.

Her exclamation of surprise woke him from his reverie. Glancing down, he studied Ramdon in silence for a moment, then looked at her. 'How is he?' he asked.

'The shivering's stopped,' she said. 'He's sleeping.'

'Good.'

She went on staring, keeping her eyes fixed on his face as the colour slowly returned to his cheeks. 'How did you do that?' she whispered.

He shrugged. 'Every human being has the capacity to harness powers within himself he may not be aware of. In the western world, such powers are regarded with suspicion and awe. Here, they have always been recognised as part of the essential nature of things.'

Morrill's look disturbed her strangely. His eyes seemed gentle and sad. It was not the sadness of yesterday. This was something deeper and more complex. A sadness blurred and undefined.

'You cried,' he said softly. 'You cried when you thought he was going to die. Ramdon must have meant a great deal to you.'

She nodded. 'I like him,' she muttered.

She thought for a moment, then added fiercely: 'I like him a lot.'

He was silent as she rose from her knees and began to spread out her bedding. Strange feelings rose inside him. Emotions he had almost forgotten flooded through his chest. He felt baffled, bewildered. The new sensation was startling in its intensity. With a sense of simple disbelief, he realised what it was.

He was jealous.

When morning came, they continued their journey southward. Morrill pushed the pace as hard as he dared, conscious of Ramdon's weakened state and their own depleted reserves of energy. They saw no sign of the Chinese. Morrill began to feel a cautious sense of optimism. With luck, it looked as though he and his men had lost them.

They pressed on steadily through the pale light of morning, leaving the mountaintops behind and following a winding trail which led gently downwards along the flank of a shallow valley. Morrill's brain was in a turmoil. He felt bewildered by what was happening to him. Finding he had emotions again seemed a novel experience. He had believed himself dead for so long now, it seemed strange to discover he could still feel pain, loss, envy.

Too much of him had died with Baima. Now, seeing Tracey again had revived some fractional spark within him. He wanted her, he realised, wanted her badly. He studied her furtively through the long day's flight, admiring the clean sweep of her limbs, the marvellous symmetry of her cheekbones, the dark tangle of her hair. She was beautiful, he thought, but she had something else, something which, if the truth had known, had attracted him from the very beginning. It was an aura of strength pervading her like a palpable force, a quiet strength, serene in its purity. He had been too young to appreciate it in his early youth. Now the worrying thought came to him that he might already be too late. He watched her with Ramdon, saw the way her face lit up whenever the Englishman drew near, and felt rancour rising inside his chest. The feeling persisted, strengthening steadily throughout the day until by the time evening fell, he hated Ramdon with a blind, unreasoning passion.

He called a halt in a defile high on the mountainside, concealed from both the air and the valley below, and they made camp wearily, spreading their blankets on the frost-ridden ground. It was their second night on cold rations. Tomorrow, with luck, they would reach the safety of the frontier.

Morrill sat on his own in the darkness, watching Tracey and Ramdon with an air of moody resentment. Ramdon, after his experience the previous day, appeared to have completely recovered. Morrill had dressed and stitched the wound with materials from the surgical kit, and Ramdon seemed as jaunty as ever, laughing boisterously at things Tracey whispered in his ear. Morrill felt his jealousy mounting. Damn the man. Strictly speaking, in the context of the law, Tracey was still Morrill's wife. He had behaved badly toward her, true, but he was ready for atonement. Ramdon had no right to interfere.

As the night lengthened, Ramdon slowly drifted into sleep. Morrill waited until he heard him gently snoring, then gathering his blanket tightly around him, he moved over to Tracey's side. She blinked, her breath steaming on the icebound air.

'Still awake?' he whispered.

She nodded as Morrill settled on the ground, spreading his legs in front of him.

'I know how you feel. It's the altitude. Stops most people from sleeping until they get used to it.'

Her lips were slightly open and he could see her teeth gleaming in the starlight. 'How's Ramdon?' he asked.

'He's making a remarkable recovery, thanks to you.' •

'That was nothing.'

'You think so? It gave me the shivers.'

'Just a simple transference of body heat, that's all. A useful talent to have when you live at these altitudes.'

'I'm really very grateful, Harry.'

'That's okay.'

He hooked his arms around his knees, hugging them close to his chest. Through the darkness, he could see the solitary sentry, a young Gokoho boy called Chuhu, leaning watchfully against a rock.

Trying to keep his voice casual, he said: 'To tell the truth, I'm kind of regretting it myself.'

She looked puzzled. 'Why?'

'Well, I know this sounds ridiculous, but I don't like the way you look at Ramdon.'

Her eyes widened in surprise and disbelief, then she gave a short clipped laugh. 'Harry, you're jealous?'

He shrugged again, keeping his face averted. Inside, his heart was thumping wildly.

'Now who's affected by the altitude? You walked out on me, remember?'

'I know. It was churlish and irresponsible. I couldn't blame you if you hated me for that.'

'I don't hate you, Harry.'

'I've spent so long fighting the Chinese, I guess I've forgotten there's another world out there. Seeing you again reminded me. I feel kind of strange tonight. Like I've just recovered from a long illness.'

'I'm glad, Harry.'

'It's a funny sensation coming back to life again. It's like somebody pulling a curtain away from in front of your eyes. Suddenly you see things clearly for the first time in years.'

'Will you come back to Washington?' she asked.

He frowned. 'I can't do that,' he muttered.

'Why not?'

'It's over, that other life. You can't turn the clock back, Tracey.'

She was silent, staring into the night, and he rested his head against the rocks, drawing the blanket more tightly around him. What the hell am I talking about? he thought. Who says it's over? A man can be born again, can't he? Can learn to think and feel anew. All it takes is the right incentive, the right motivation. Wanting to. Needing to.

He was filled with a sudden sense of uncertainty. The idea had startled him. 'Tracey?' he whispered.

'Yes?'

'Supposing I did go back?'

She blinked at him through the darkness.

He added hastily: 'I'm not saying I will, mind you, but supposing ... just supposing I figured it all out and decided – okay, it's time to go home? What happens with Ramdon?'

She moistened her lips with the tip of her tongue. His

bluntness had startled her. 'I don't know. That's up to Silas, I imagine.'

'You're still my wife, Tracey.'

'Harry, that was over long ago.'

'Supposing I don't want it to be over? Supposing I say let's give it another try?'

'You're crazy, Harry.'

'I want you back, Tracey.'

There, it was out. He had told her and he felt better now. 'Listen, I'm not asking you to make promises you won't be able to keep. All I'm saying is, let's consider it. Maybe the idea will grow on me, I don't know. Maybe all I need is a little breathing space. But if I do say "yes", I want you to give me a second chance. We're older now, we understand things better. This time, we might be able to make it work. It's worth salvaging, Tracey.'

She looked bewildered. Fear flickered momentarily in her eyes. 'Harry, I don't know what to say.'

'Then don't say anything. Think it over. We'll reach the border tomorrow night. Let's talk about it then.'

He clambered to his feet, moving back to his own place as Tracey lay staring at the stars, troubled and confused.

Thirty feet away, Chamdo watched her through the darkness. His features were impassive but, deep inside him, a gnawing uneasiness had begun to grow.

CHAPTER ELEVEN

Losang Gyatso lay among the trees and stared at the helicopters above. They were motionless now, their bulbous bodies perched on the lip of a small plateau, the massive rotors sprouting from their roofs like clumps of bizarre foliage. Tiny figures moved around their base. Losang could see tents flapping in the wind, and the dark cluster of oil-drums framed against the dawn sky. From his position of concealment, he counted twenty to thirty Chinese soldiers, and felt his spirits sink. It was the sound of their helicopters which had woken him in the early morning. He had been sleeping with the others in a deserted hut deep in the woodland on the valley floor and, drawn by the strange whirring noise, had crept out to investigate. Now, watching the massive machines being refuelled, he realised for the first time the difficulty of their position. The valley narrowed at this point, its sides drawing together to form a distinct bottleneck. The plateau, or knoll, lay at its mouth like a natural cork. The Chinese had come in the night, or at least as dusk was falling, and had set up their camp on the knoll's rim, commanding an excellent view of the valley below. Though the narrow bed was cluttered with scrub and offered a perfect refuge for Losang and his group, the walls were so bare and precipitous he realised it would be impossible to leave without being detected by the watchers above. He could, of course, attempt to escape under cover of darkness, but one glance at the jagged overhanging rocks convinced him that such a move would be reckless in the extreme.

For himself, he cared little about personal safety. He had always been a devoutly religious man and, to Losang's mind, death was simply another step in the endless process of reincarnation. But for the young god king in his care, such a climb would be out of the question. Losang Gyatso's mission was sacred. He had to transport the god king to the Jokhang in Lhasa. Losing him would be unpardonable.

Losang was at a loss what to do. The Chinese, from their elevated vantage point, commanded the access and exit points to the valley interior. Moreover, once their troops began a systematic search of the woodlands, they would be bound to discover the deserted shepherd's hut in which Losang and his party had taken refuge. The dilemma was a bewildering one and Losang's mind was in a quandary. If they moved, they would be discovered. If they remained where they were, they would also be discovered. In the end, he took the step he always took in such circumstances. He consulted the State Oracle.

In this respect, Losang was most fortunate, for in his exiled home in Dharmsala, one of Losang's functions was to act as the Oracle's mouthpiece. On such occasions, the god of the temple was summoned by much chanting, clashing of cymbals, blowing of trumpets and burning of incense, but in the absence of these accessories, Losang merely settled himself against a treetrunk and sank into a deep trance. He looked like a statue, perched crosslegged among the knarled and twisted tree-roots. The sun gradually rose, casting fingers of dappled gold across his stony features. A bird flutterd to the ground at his feet and hopped about curiously, but Losang seemed oblivious to its presence. When he awoke, nearly an hour later, he felt considerably better. The Oracle's advise had been reassuring. Though their position was precarious, Losang was happy to discover it was not without hope, and his heart was jaunty as he made his way back to the shepherd's hut.

The others were waiting anxiously when he arrived. They crouched beneath the ceiling rafters, their breath steaming on the chill dawn air, their faces tense and nervous. Bowls of holy water stood on the ground in front of them. Barley cakes, shaped like bee-hives, lay at the bowls' sides, waiting to be eaten. In the corner, by the crumbling remains of an ancient stove, Wangdui was busily brewing their morning tea. The young god king was sitting in his sedan chair, which they had manoeuvred with difficulty through the narrow doorway the evening before. Losang approached him and bowed. 'Holiness, the Chinese occupy a high mound at the valley mouth. It will be impossible for us to leave as long as they remain in position.'

The boy's eyes flickered worriedly. He passed his fingers, heavily encrusted with rings, along the line of his upper lip. 'Can we wait until nightfall?'

'The valley walls are steep and treacherous,' Losang told him gravely. 'If we attempt to scale them in the dark, we run the risk of falling to our deaths.'

'But we cannot expect to remain concealed for ever.'

'No,' Losang answered calmly, 'we must wait.'

'Wait?' the boy echoed. 'Wait for what?'

Losang lowered his head. Standing in front of the sedan chair, shoulders bowed, hands folded lightly over his stomach, he looked like a man in a position of prayer.

'For something to happen,' he said.

Ramdon woke with a start. It was broad daylight, and though ice glittered among the rocks and coated the grass-clumps on which they lay, the warmth of the lifting sun was rapidly dispersing the post-dawn chill.

172

Around him, the guerrillas were up and moving, and Ramdon sensed an air of urgency and excitement which made his senses quiver. Something was wrong.

He scrambled to his feet, wincing as a stab of pain shot upwards from his damaged side. He saw Morrill standing at the edge of the narrow defile, delivering orders in a fevered undertone. Morrill's haversack was already on his back, his machinegun dangling from his shoulder.

'What the hell's going on?' Ramdon demanded.

Morrill glared at him, and there was no mistaking the hostility in his face. Ramdon could feel Morrill's dislike like a physical force.

'Tracey's gone,' Morrill said.

Ramdon frowned. He looked down at the place Tracey had lain. Her blankets lay spread among the boulders, but there was no sign of her boots or haversack.

'What do you mean, she's gone?' he muttered uneasily.

'Gone, for Christ's sake. Disappeared. Vanished. Pouf.'

Ramdon felt panic rising inside him. She couldn't have, he thought. People didn't vanish into thin air.

'Where the hell could she go in this emptiness?'

'Back into Tibet. We've picked up her trail.'

'But that doesn't make sense. Why?'

Morrill hesitated. He was making no attempt to hide his jealousy. Ramdon guessed at once what was causing it. The bastard wanted Tracey for himself.

Some of the fury settled in Morrill's eyes and he shrugged. 'She's not alone,' he grunted. 'Chamdo's with her.'

'Chamdo?'

'My guess is, Tracey is his prisoner.'

Ramdon was feeling more confused by the minute. 'Why on earth would Chamdo take Tracey prisoner?'

'To stop me crossing the border, I guess. He probably sees Tracey as some kind of threat. He's scared I'll pull out and leave him, go back to Washington.'

Ramdon felt his muscles tense. 'What gave him that idea? For Christ's sake, two nights ago you wanted nothing to do with her.'

'Well, maybe I've changed my mind.'

Ramdon felt his own anger rising, but with a conscious effort focused his brain on the problem in hand. Damn it, he had no intention of letting Morrill take Tracey, but he would worry about that when he knew Tracey was safe and free.

Quickly, he considered the situation. 'If Chamdo's heading back into Tibet, surely he'll run straight into the Chinese?'

'Not Chamdo. He's too damned clever. He'll detour around and keep on going. My guess is, he's hoping I'll follow. He wants to lead me back where we came from. Well, I'm sending the others on over the border. No sense risking everyone's lives over this. I'm going after Chamdo alone.'

Ramdon hitched up his trousers, running his thumbs around the inside of his belt. 'We'll go together,' he declared.

Morrill glared at him. 'You're wounded.'

'I can still walk, can't I?'

'You'll only slow me up. I'll have to move fast if I want to catch him.'

'Don't worry about me. Worry about yourself.'

'You're crazy, I tell you. If that bleeding starts, I'll have to leave you behind.'

'Listen, I'm not asking you to take me along,' Ramdon said. 'I'm telling you I'm coming. If Tracey's in some kind of danger, I intend to be there. Now we can go separately, or we can go together. Make up your mind.'

Morrill stared at him with a look of guarded wariness in his face, as if he was mentally identifying and evaluating a potential threat.

At length, he nodded slowly. 'Okay,' he agreed, 'come if you want.'

'I'll get my fiddle,' Ramdon said.

Tracey scrambled breathlessly through the thin warmth of the early morning. The trail bobbed and dipped around rocky fissures, steeply rolling hillslopes and clumps of colourful rhododendron trees. Chamdo had left the main trail behind, following a tributary track which wound steadily downwards toward the valley floor. He spoke little, but followed relentlessly in her wake, prodding her shoulders with the blunt nozzle of his submachine-gun.

In the cold stillness of the pre-dawn morning, he had woken her with his fingers on her lips. Opening her eyes, she had felt the gun's chillness on the skin beneath her left ear. Silently, he had guided her over the cluster of sleeping forms and into the glow of the early dawn. He had offered no explanation for this extraordinary behaviour, and when she tried to question him, he had merely grunted and ordered her to be silent.

For nearly two hours, he had forced her along the trail with the remorseless vehemence of an animal drover. The look in his eyes frightened her. It was not the depth of emotion she saw there, but the sheer lack of it. Chamdo felt nothing toward her at all, neither pity, nor anger, nor hate. In Chamdo's mind, she did not exist as a human being. She was an instrument, nothing more. She realised he would kill her, if he had to, with the same lack of feeling or compassion.

There was no time to speculate on Chamdo's motives. She had to concentrate on escape. Alone in such wilderness, she knew her chances would be slim, but one glance at that impassive face convinced her that to remain in Chamdo's charge would be tantamount to death. He meant to kill her, she felt sure of it.

All morning, they pushed hurriedly forward, crossing one valley and moving into the next. She wondered if Silas would follow her. Probably, she realised. But Silas was hurt, his strength depleted. He would never catch Chamdo, the pace they were setting.

Toward noon, Chamdo called a halt at last. Breathlessly, Tracey flopped against a boulder. The thin air had exhausted her stamina, and her limbs were trembling from exertion.

Chamdo gave her some *tsempo* from his haversack. 'Eat,' he commanded in a guttural tone.

Scarcely realising what she was doing, Tracey pushed the food into her mouth and started to chew. She watched Chamdo warily as he settled on the ground, the machine-gun resting across his knees. His eyes were flat and incurious, indifferent to her fear, indifferent to her interests. She had to pull herself together, she thought. She had to force her brain to think. She had to forget the paralysing fatigue which crept remorselessly through her body and find a means of escape.

'They left the main track just about here,' Morrill said, pausing to examine the ground.

Ramdon knelt at his side, feeling the sun's warmth striking his face and shoulders. His wound pained from scrambling frenziedly at Morrill's side, but he was careful to allow no murmur of protest to issue from his lips.

175

He studied the earth wonderingly. 'How can you tell?' he asked.

'See this scuff mark? That's Chamdo's boot. He's got a patch on the rim.'

'For Christ's sake,' Ramdon exclaimed, 'his prints are facing the other way.'

'Right. He walked backwards just to fool us.'

'You're crazy!'

Morrill shook his head. 'See how this toe-mark is deeper than the heel? That's because the toe came down first. It's an old trick, but it only works if your pursuer is too slow to spot it.'

Ramdon glared at him with rising irritation. 'Who the hell do you think you are, Davy Crockett?'

Morrill rose without speaking, and easing the machine-gun across his shoulders, pressed rapidly on. Ramdon scurried to keep up, clutching his side with his free hand. His violin case jostled and bounced against his spine. The bastard was going fast on purpose, Ramdon thought. The need for haste was plain enough, but Morrill was stampeding along like a lunatic. Ramdon guessed why. Morrill was hoping Ramdon's side would open up so he would have an excuse to leave the Englishman behind.

Well, to hell with that. To hell with you, Harry Morrill, Ramdon thought. Tracey's in trouble, and I intend to be there, no matter what. I'll keep going even if my spine splits in two.

'What is it with you, Morrill? Yesterday, you couldn't wait to get rid of us. Now suddenly you're busting a gut to get Tracey back. I don't understand that.'

'She's my wife,' Morrill muttered.

'Was your wife, you mean. For Christ's sake, man, as far as Tracey's concerned, you've been dead for years. You're no more married to her than I am.'

Morrill spat on the ground. 'She's my wife,' he repeated sullenly.

'You've been stuck in these mountains too bloody long, my old son. First piece of ass you see, suddenly it's love's sweet song all over again. Why don't you ask Tracey what she thinks?'

'I intend to, soon as this is over.'

'If she's got any sense, she'll send you packing.'

Morrill glanced at him, his bearded face flushing hotly. 'I

know what you're after, Ramdon. I'm not blind. You want her for yourself.'

'Right. Damn right I want her. What's wrong with that? She's a free agent, isn't she?'

'Back off, Ramdon. I told you, she's still my wife.'

'I'll bet she won't come near you with a bargepole.'

Morrill sighed. 'I know what you're thinking. I walked out on her once, maybe I'll do it again. Well, I don't blame you for believing that, but I'm older now, I've grown up a lot. This time I intend to make it work. I think we'll be good together.'

'Morrill,' Ramdon told him wearily, 'you won't ever be good together, because when this is over, Tracey's coming back with me.'

'Not if I can help it, coach.'

'That's just it. You can't. You're out, understand? Out.'

Morrill's lips compressed tightly beneath his beard. He paused to check a broken rhododendron twig, running his fingers lightly down the stalk. Dabbing at the tip with his thumb, he examined the skin for traces of moisture. Then he eased the machine-gun into a more comfortable position and began to hurry on.

'You don't know her, Ramdon,' he muttered. 'How long have you been together, a few days? You've never lived with her the way I have.'

'I know just how long you lived with her, you bastard. Five months. Five bloody months. Jesus, you make it sound like a lifetime.'

'In a funny sort of way, it *was* a lifetime. I was happy then. I didn't realise it, but I was happy, and I want her back.'

He stopped suddenly, jerking to a halt. 'Listen, this isn't helping any, is it? We'll never find Tracey if we spend all our time quarrelling.'

'You started it, you son of a bitch.'

'Let's call a truce. First we find her, then we start worrying about who gets to keep her.'

Ramdon hefted his violin case against his spine. He realised the American made sense. His own temper was already so frayed, his powers of concentration were completely shattered.

'Okay,' he nodded, 'we'll do it your way. But sooner or later, we'll have to thrash this out.'

At that moment, from high on the crags above them, they

heard the thunderous roar of an engine split the air. The noise continued for several seconds, echoing eerily along the valley. Then as quickly as it had begun, it faded into silence. Startled, Morrill fumbled in his haversack and slid his field-glasses from their leather case. Silently, he swivelled the lens into focus, concentrating on a jagged knoll which rose like a sentinel, blocking the valley mouth. The rocks merged, solidified. He spotted clusters of dark fuel drums, covered with camouflaged netting. Tents dotted the craggy windswept ground, and Morrill could see the outline of two helicopters where the earth levelled into a small plateau. Miniscule figures were moving around the machines, carrying fuel-drums to and from the main supply dump.

'Chinese,' Morrill hissed without lowering the glasses. 'They've got the choppers up there. They're servicing and refuelling them.'

'What about troops?'

'They're up there too.'

'What the hell?' Ramdon muttered in a puzzled voice. 'I thought they were right on our tail.'

'So did I,' Morrill whispered.

He pushed the glasses back into their leather case. 'We were wrong all along,' he said. 'They must have happened on our valley purely by chance. They weren't after us at all. The bastards are looking for somebody else.'

Tracey stopped so suddenly Chamdo almost bumped into her.

'You'll have to excuse me,' she told him, moving sideways off the edge of the track.

He swung the machine-gun into alignment, cocking it audibly. Pausing, she peered back at him with a look of studied patience on her face. 'Some things a lady has to do alone,' she said. 'I have no intention of allowing you to accompany me.'

Chamdo hesitated, looking uncertain. He made a guttural sound deep in his throat and gently uncocked the machine-gun. With her heart pounding, Tracey slipped off the trail and slid down the dusty bank. The land dropped in a series of undulating slopes to thick clusters of rhododendron bushes which lined the rim of a jagged cliff. Tracey's senses were racing. She had fooled Chamdo for the moment, but it might be the only chance she'd get. She had to escape now, whatever the consequences.

178

She slithered to the rhododendrons and pausing, studied the cliff below. A distinct flake ran across the rock-face, sliding diagonally toward the valley floor. It looked narrow and dangerous, but not entirely unscalable. She had managed worse, far worse. At the time, of course, she had been doing it for fun. Her nerves had been calm, her responses sharp. Now she was scared out of her wits.

Easing her feet forward, she began to slither down the flake, keeping her seat pressed hard against the rock. Below her boots, the valley swayed alarmingly. She hated descending face-outwards at the best of times. The sense of exposure was too great. But it was the only expedient way. She needed to see where she was going.

Rocks clattered into the empty air and she tried not to watch their ponderous descent, tried not to count the seconds before they hit the rubble below, concentrated instead on edging a few more inches downwards, holding her breath as she fumbled for tiny footholds.

One slip and it would all be over, she thought. She would tumble into the void like a crippled swan. There would be no Silas Ramdon then to dominate her senses. No Harry Morrill to confuse her. No decisions to reach, no pledges to make. Only oblivion.

Foot by foot, Tracey continued her tortuous descent, and she was almost at the bottom when the flake suddenly crumbled beneath her and she felt her body tumbling as she crashed the last few feet on to the bank of flinty moraine, grazing her elbow.

Anxiously, she scanned the clifftop above, looking for signs of Chamdo. The noise of her fall had been loud and echoing. He must have heard it.

As if in confirmation, Chamdo suddenly appeared on the cliff-rim, the machine-gun clutched in both hands. Desperately, Tracey jammed herself flat against the rocky wall. At such an angle, she knew she was safely concealed from the heights above, but if Chamdo decided to ease down the flake, he would spot her immediately.

Chamdo however, seemed reluctant to attempt such a hazardous manoeuvre. Instead, he loosed off a burst with his machine-gun, and Tracey started violently as the rhythmic *rat-tat-tat-tat* reverberated on the chill evening air. She heard Chamdo curse, and begin to thrash at the rhododendron bushes, tearing the branches aside.

Terrified, she eased herself up from the wall and, sucking in her breath, plunged madly into the thicket. She scrambled through the thickly-clustered treetrunks, caught by a strange bout of hysteria. Branches slashed into her face and tugged at her hair, but she sprinted frenziedly on, driven by some inner fever.

She scarcely knew how long she scurried across the valley floor. The seconds stretched into minutes, and the clumps of woodland gave way to boulder-studded meadows where a river, its current milky with sediment brought down from the high glaciers, twisted snakelike toward the valley mouth. Several times she stumbled and fell, but remorselessly dragged herself up and battled on. Soon, the grey shades of night began to rise from the hollows and fissures.

She spotted a hut nestling at the water's edge. It was large but primitive, its sloping roof emitting thin clouds of smoke through the narrow tiles. Gasping, she stopped and studied it warily, her eyes narrowing. Clearly it was occupied, but by whom?

She shook herself. What difference did it make? Here in the open, she would surely die. She needed help, she needed shelter. Sobbing, she stumbled wearily toward the door, her hair tangled across her dirt-smeared face. She hammered on the rough-hewn panel with her fists, and without waiting for an answer, swung it slowly open.

Smoke wafted into her face, and dimly through the darkness, she saw butter lamps burning on the bare earth floor. The interior was filled with people, their forms smudged and distorted as they stared curiously back at her. In the centre of the room, she noticed a sedan chair, intricately-carved, and sitting upon it, the figure of a young boy. He was, she estimated, thirteen or fourteen years old. Around his neck hung a rosary of brightly-coloured beads. His face was gentle, his bearing regal, and as she looked, he smiled at her welcomingly, and raising one bangled hand, beckoned her in.

Morrill and Ramdon heard the stutter of machine-gun fire at precisely the same moment.

'It's him,' Morrill exclaimed.

Without waiting for Ramdon to follow, he left the trail, sprinting wildly through the trees, peeling the machine-gun from his shoulder as he ran. Wincing, Ramdon struggled to catch up, fiery lances of pain darting into the flesh beneath his ribcage. Hobbling and stumbling, he brushed aside the branches lashing into his face, squinting into the dusk for Morrill's retreating form.

The machine-gun burst had lasted barely a moment, a solitary clatter, rapid and abrupt. Had Chamdo, realising Morrill and Ramdon were close, decided to finish Tracey off, Ramdon wondered? The thought sent a shiver down his neck. He couldn't bear to contemplate that, Tracey dead or dying. If that bastard had harmed a hair on her head, he'd make him curse his mother for giving him birth.

Ahead, the ground dipped steeply, falling in a series of gentle slopes to a great burst of foliage tracing the rim of a ragged cliff. Morrill had come to a halt and was standing with feet spread apart, the machine-gun cradled against his right hip, its canvas strap taut around his neck as his fingers lightly caressed the trigger. Barely ten feet below, framed against the rhododendron clumps, Chamdo was peering up at him, startled, his own weapon held loosely in his fingers.

Ramdon slithered to a halt, gasping hard, and peered desperately around. There was no sign of Tracey.

Morrill kept his machine-gun fixed on the Tibetan's chest. The two men seemed frozen into a silent tableau, Morrill's face inscrutable beneath the bristling beard, Chamdo's sullen, defiant, gauging distance, light and the prospect of raising his weapon in time.

'Drop it,' Morrill ordered curtly.

For a moment, Chamdo seemed about to refuse, then the light died in his eyes and without a word, he tossed the machine-gun into the dust. Morrill stepped forward, keeping his gaze fixed on Chamdo's face, and reaching out with one foot, kicked the weapon into the nearby shrub. 'Where is she?' he demanded in a soft voice.

Chamdo nodded behind him at the precipice. 'She went down the cliff.'

Morrill's cheeks blanched. 'You son-of-a-bitch.'

'Don't worry. She's still alive. I watched her dart into the thicket while I was checking the bushes here.'

'Thank Christ,' Ramdon breathed, feeling a blessed wave of relief flood through him.

Morrill studied Chamdo, his lean face taut and expressionless in the gathering dusk. 'Why did you do it?' he whispered.

Chamdo looked sullen and resentful. 'She was going to take you away.'

'Who said so?'

'I heard. I was listening last night when you promised to return to Washington.'

'Well, supposing it's true? Surely that decision is mine?'

'You have no right to leave us. You think you can turn your back on everything we have fought for? You brought us hope, you brought us leadership. How can you desert us now?'

'It's not a question of desertion, Chamdo. I go where my duty takes me, and my work here is finished. What we do no longer serves my people's interests. We are weary and dispirited, our souls sickened by war and death. It's over, can't you see that? You must cross the border and join your countrymen in Nepal.'

'I will not live in exile,' Chamdo stated bluntly.

Sighing, Morrill lowered the machine-gun until its muzzle pointed at the earth. 'You hate too much,' he said. 'It has destroyed all the human things inside you.'

Chamdo sneered. 'What do you know about hate? You never understood the nature of hate.'

Morrill's lips twisted wryly. 'Oh, I understand it all right. I hated too, but I was wrong. There's no future in it, Chamdo, no sense or logic to it.'

'It was I who taught you how to hate,' Chamdo said softly.

'You?'

'Yes, me. At the monastery of Cho Mangpai, you sent me away. You sought the path of completeness, you said.'

'I remember,' Morrill murmured.

'It was a madness that afflicted you. I cured you then, just as I shall cure you now.'

Morrill frowned. 'Chamdo, what are you talking about?'

'Your body had been invaded by evil forces. I destroyed them, exorcised your spirit, made you whole again.'

A terrible suspicion took root in Morrill's mind. He wanted to turn his back on it, bury it away for ever in that corner of his brain he reserved for the unthinkable, but no matter how he tried, the thought kept nudging upwards, stubbornly, inexorably. He felt his legs go weak and watched the trees swaying in his vision.

'Baima,' he whispered.

Chamdo nodded, a fierce exultation in his face. 'Baima,' he said.

And now in Morrill's mind he saw the trail dipping downwards, the mist over the valley obscuring the village from the ridge above, he felt the first stomach-chilling spasm of fear as he glimpsed the blackened ruins of Lamringyhana, the shapeless heaps of rubble, the charred rafters tilting obscenely in the sky.

'No,' he croaked.

Ramdon stared at him in puzzlement. He understood little of what was being said, but he saw that Morrill's face, beneath his beard, had gone chalk-white.

'How could you?' Morrill breathed. 'They were your own people.'

Chamdo shrugged. 'You were our only hope. We needed your knowledge, your expertise. What was a life or two by comparison?'

'And the soldiers?'

'There were no soldiers,' Chamdo told him patiently. 'We used the uniforms taken from the men we had killed.'

In a daze, Morrill held the machine-gun at arm's length and moved back, leaning against a tree. Nausea swept upwards from his stomach. It wasn't easy for a man to accept the realisation that everything he had fought for, everything he had believed in had shown itself, in that final moment, to be counterfeit and worthless.

And again he remembered the gnawing anguish clutching at his heart as he clawed demented at the shifting smoke-blackened rubble, tearing aside window-frames, pieces of battered furniture, discovering in the pale mist of early evening the bones of the dismembered corpses. He heard his voice as he crouched among the debris howling like a wolf into the gathering darkness.

There were things a man knew in his heart were deeper and more terrible than anything he could put a name to, yet still, ostrichlike, he might turn his eyes from them, begrudging the pain, fearing the soul-searing horror of the truth. He had lacked that, the ultimate grace of clarity, vision, awareness. The suspicion in his mind had funnelled inward from behind his head, and he had ignored it as he might turn his back on an unacceptable weakness.

There were tears in his eyes and he was thinking back to Baima, remembering the gentle softness of her features, the

183

warmth of her body, the way he had loved her in that calm placid period of hope and fulfilment.

'You murderous bastard,' he whispered. 'Do you realise what you've done?'

'I have given you purpose and direction,' Chamdo said.

'You've destroyed the only thing in my life I ever really cared about.'

Chamdo shrugged. 'It was for your own good, Morrill.'

'All these years, I took you for my friend. But you're a monster. You and the rest of them, Jigma, Tuseng and the others. You murdered innocent people, your own people, just to provide a focal point for my hate.'

'You needed something to make you see sense again. We did not enjoy what had to be done. We did it with sorrow in our hearts because it was necessary.'

'All these years we have lived together, you let me go on hating the Chinese when the ones I should have hated were sitting there at my side, sharing my food, sharing my thoughts, hiding the truth of what they had done in a monstrous, unspeakable lie.'

Chamdo's face looked calm. 'It was you, Morrill, who taught us the nature of expediency.'

'Chamdo,' Morrill said softly, 'I am going to kill you.'

Ramdon watching, puzzled, was about to interrupt when the sudden roar of a helicopter reached them for the second time that evening. It was only a momentary burst – the Chinese on the plateau above were clearly testing their engines – but just for a second it diverted their attention and Chamdo seized the opportunity to make his bid for freedom. He ducked backwards, dodging between the rhododendron clumps and sprinted along the rim of the crumbling cliff.

Morrill seemed to jerk back to reality. With a startled murmur of protest, he straightened upwards from the tree and swung the machine-gun into alignment. 'Stop,' he shouted, 'stop, or I'll cut you in two!'

But Chamdo kept running.

Still Morrill made no move to fire.

'Shoot,' Ramdon yelled. 'Shoot, for Christ's sake! If he gets to Tracey before we do, he'll bloody well kill her.'

Morrill turned to him, his features slack with indecision. 'I can't,' he croaked, 'he saved my life.'

With a savage curse, Ramdon tore the weapon from his grasp. He switched the lever to 'fire' and, cradling the butt against his damaged side, lightly squeezed the trigger. The gun purred in his fists. He felt the deep satisfying shudder of the metal frame lurching against his hipbone and watched the line of tracer bullets arcing into the gathering night. But the burst missed completely, the shots ripping splinters out of the nearby trees.

Chamdo heard the deadly rattle and tried to duck. His foot slipped on the precipice lip and he tumbled over, grabbing at a rhododendron branch. Suddenly he was dangling in space, his fists clutching the slender twig, his knuckles gleaming white through the skin. They saw his face staring up at them, the eyes wide with alarm. They saw his legs wildly thrashing as he fought to gain a foothold on the contourless slab. There was a harsh tearing sound as the branch ripped from the treetrunk, and Chamdo yelled in terror, his hands clawing upwards, lunging for the foliage above. Then, in one breathless second, the branch gave way and they watched him plummet earthwards, his body turning slowly, gracefully, like a swimmer executing a complex dive. The thud as he hit the ground was like the crack of a rifle shot.

Ramdon eased to the clifftop and peered over the edge. He could see Chamdo sprawled on the scree below, his face turned upwards, his eyes lifeless, staring at the sky. His skull had been crushed into a pulpy mass of flesh and splintered bone.

Sighing, Ramdon turned and walked back. Morrill was still standing motionless, his eyes glazed and heavy with shock. Ramdon thrust the machine-gun into his hand and gently took his arm. 'Come on,' he said in a gentle voice, 'let's go find Tracey.'

CHAPTER TWELVE

Tracey saw them coming from the cabin door, Morrill stumbling along like a man in a trance, Ramdon guiding him by the elbow. A sob of joy and relief burst from Tracey's throat, and she darted into the open, running toward them. She fell into Ramdon's arms, clinging to him blindly.

He pulled back, studying her anxiously. 'Are you all right?' he hissed.

She nodded, laughing and crying in turns. 'I'm fine, fine. How did you get here?'

'We came down the cliff-face.'

'In the dark?'

'We had to. It was the only way.'

Suddenly, she noticed Morrill's stony silence. He was staring blankly at them both, his eyes dull and confused. She eased out of Ramdon's arms.

'What's wrong with Harry?' she muttered.

'Shock. Something Chamdo said. It didn't make sense to me.'

'You saw Chamdo?'

Ramdon nodded. 'We had a little . . . discussion.'

'You know he tried to kill me? If I hadn't managed to scramble down the cliff, God knows what might have happened.'

Ramdon slid his free arm around her shoulder, squeezing her hard against his chest. 'Well, he won't harm you any more. Chamdo's dead. He went over the edge.'

Looking back, Tracey saw Losang Gyatso emerge from the doorway of the shepherd's hut and move toward them through the darkness. He was still wearing his padded jacket, but his shaved head gleamed in the starlight.

As he approached, Ramdon muttered: 'Who the hell is this?'

'His name is Losang Gyatso. He gave me shelter for the night. He and his friends are on their way to Lhasa.'

Losang drew to a halt and bowed politely, his hands folded across his stomach. 'These are your companions?' he asked Tracey.

She nodded. 'This is Silas,' she said, 'and the gentleman with the beard is my husband, Harry Morrill.'

'Mr Morrill appears to be experiencing some kind of distress,'

Losang observed, noting the glassy look in the American's eyes.

Ramdon studied Losang curiously. Losang was a lama, Ramdon could tell. The eyes gave him away. Small, quick and deeply brown, they carried a curious ethereal quality. He looked like a man who had turned his back on the pleasures of the world.

'Is your friend in need of attention?' Losang inquired.

'Well, he's had a bit of a jolt,' Ramdon said. 'We're not quite sure what it's all about, but I'd like to bet a bowl of hot tea would pick him up marvellously.'

Losang inclined his head. 'We have tea and food freely available. We have, in fact, been expecting you. Please follow me into the hut.'

They stepped through the doorway, and Ramdon blinked as he realised the room was full of people. Faces peered back at him, reflecting eerily the flickering lamp-light. He recognised the familiar odour of melting butter, burnt incense and unwashed clothing. 'What is this?' he muttered. 'Napoleon's retreat from Moscow?'

He spotted the young boy sitting alone on a sedan chair. Like Losang Gyatso, the boy's face was gentle and withdrawn, and he wore an elaborate cap trimmed with strips of brilliant gold.

Losang stopped in front of him and respectfully bowed his head. 'Holiness,' he said, 'these gentlemen are the friends of the English lady.'

The boy's eyes swept over Morrill and Ramdon and raising one hand, he beckoned them forward. Ramdon noticed the air of reverence which descended upon the room's occupants. It was like being in church, for Christ's sake.

'What the hell is this?' he muttered under his breath.

'Bow,' Tracey told him. 'You must bow your head.'

'What for?'

'Because it's customary. It's a matter of respect. This is the new Dalai Lama.'

Ramdon saw Morrill suddenly start, and a gleam of awareness entered the American's eyes. He turned, peering around the packed, smoky room. Then he looked at Losang Gyatso and the boy sitting in front of him.

'What did you say?' he whispered to Tracey in a strangled voice.

'It's the new Dalai Lama. They're taking him to Lhasa to have him blessed at some kind of sacred shrine.'

Morrill's head tilted back and colour flooded into his cheeks. His gaze seemed to swivel into focus. All the anguish of Baima's death, the revelation of his friends' treachery, flooded out of him in a single moment.

Seizing Ramdon's arm, he bundled him forward. 'Bow, you bastard,' he hissed.

Blinking in confusion, Ramdon ducked his head. Standing beside him, Morrill did the same.

The boy addressed them in English. 'You are the one who makes war against the Chinese,' he said, speaking to Morrill. 'Your wife has been sent by your government to take you home again.'

Morrill nodded silently. The boy looked at Ramdon. 'And you are the pilot from Katmandu. The one who plays the violin.'

'That's right,' Ramdon admitted, easing the instrument case across his shoulder.

'You are welcome to stay with us and share what we have,' the boy went on, 'but I fear we find ourselves in a difficult dilemma. We are unable to proceed on our journey because the Chinese control the entry point to the valley. However, we believe you have been sent to deliver us. Your coming was foretold by the Oracle.'

'Oracle?' Ramdon echoed uncertainly.

Morrill frowned in puzzlement. 'What is it you expect us to do?'

'Every hour we remain here makes discovery more possible,' Losang told him. 'We know you have come to help us. It has already been prophesied.'

'But you can't hope to travel all the way to Lhasa without the Chinese knowing. Once you leave the mountains and reach the high plain, they'll be no place to hide.'

'You are quite right, Mr Morrill. But by then, we expect our people will have heard of our coming. We believe they will travel in their thousands to greet their god king.'

Morrill felt his pulses beginning to race. 'By God, the man was right. A new Dalai Lama in Tibet would blow the country sky-high.'

Losang Gyatso was staring at him the way a child might stare at its father, filled with an innate faith in his benevolence and goodness, knowing deep in its heart that this individual, above all others, would never let it down. In the face of such confidence and trust, Morrill felt strangely subdued.

'You could knock out those choppers,' he suggested. 'Without their aircraft, the Chinese would be grounded. Even if they saw you go by, you could be half-a-day's march away by the time they climbed down from that plateau.'

'Alas, such a thing is not possible,' Losang told him with regret.

'Why not? There are only two machines. You must have nearly twenty or thirty men here.'

'You don't understand, Mr Morrill. We are monks of the Tsedrung foundation. We live our lives according to the Buddhist scriptures. It would be unthinkable for us to harm or kill another human being.'

'Even for the survival of your own god king?'

Losang's dark eyes looked deep and sad. 'Even for that,' he admitted.

Morrill sighed. He understood Losang Gyatso's reasoning. He had lived in Tibet long enough to know the complexities of the Buddhist mind.

He turned to Ramdon and Tracey. 'We've got to help,' he said.

'Why?' Ramdon asked.

'It's our duty. If these people can break through that bottleneck at the valley mouth, if they can make their way to Lhasa, the whole country will rise in revolt.'

'Well, that doesn't make a lot of sense to me,' Ramdon said. 'Why should we start another uprising?'

'Because it's their one chance to win back their freedom, that's why.'

'Is that so? Well, remember what happened the last time they tried it? The Chinese whipped them to a standstill. Is that what you want? Death and destruction all over the place?'

'For Christ's sake,' Morrill snapped fiercely, 'things have changed since the old days. The Chinese can't act in secret any more. Too many satellites about, too many high-powered sensor devices and telescopic cameras. If they really care about world opinion, they'll have to bow to a unified demand for Tibet autonomy.'

'And you think we can fix all that?'

'We can if we get them out of here.'

'You're nuts,' Ramdon said bluntly.

'Listen, you son-of-a-bitch, everything I've been fighting for all these years is suddenly within my grasp. All I've got to do is wipe out those helicopters and render the Chinese immobile. Stuck on top of that mesa, it'll take them hours to find their way down.'

'Haven't you forgotten something? This is your war, not mine. I'm a neutral, remember.'

'Goddamn you, I can't knock those helicopters out alone.'

'I'll come with you,' Tracey told him quietly, her cheeks pale, her eyes deep and sombre.

Morrill looked startled. 'You?'

'Somebody must. If the monks won't do it, then it's up to us. After all, we're trapped here as well.'

Ramdon stared down at her with an expression of exasperation. Wasn't that just like a woman, stabbing a man in the back? He hadn't come here to fight the bloody Chinese army. He hadn't come to fight anybody. The only thing he truly cared about was getting himself and Tracey safely back to Katmandu.

'I think we owe these people something,' Tracey whispered. 'I don't know about you, Silas, but I'd hate to spend the rest of my life knowing I might have changed world history, and didn't even try.'

'We're asking to get ourselves killed,' Ramdon muttered.

'If we stay here, the bastards'll probably kill us anyhow,' Morrill put in. 'Wouldn't you prefer to think there was some kind of reason behind it?'

'Speaking personally,' Ramdon said, 'I'd rather be a coward and not die at all.'

'Supposing you don't have any choice.'

'That's just it. I don't have any choice. If your mind's made up and I can't talk you out of it, then God help me, you might as well count me in.'

Morrill laughed out loud with triumph. He turned back to Losang Gyatso who had been watching their exchange with a placid expression on his face.

'Give us food and refreshment,' Morrill said. 'We'll rest here for one hour, then make our way to the plateau. When dawn comes, keep watch from the cover of the woods. As soon as the helicopters go up in flames, then you must make your escape.'

Losang Gyatso smiled benignly and bowed his head. He looked like a man to whom the vagaries of the world were part of a constant and closely-ordered pattern.

'It is exactly as the Oracle foretold,' he said.

Lin Hua stepped out of the tent in the pale glow of the early morning. A thin wind whipped at his cheeks, chilling his facial muscles. Frost coated the ground, and beyond the plateau, he could see a faint dusting of fresh snow on the hillside above.

He had slept badly in spite of his padded sleeping bag. It was not the cold that had kept him awake, but the memory of Major Tang A-hsi's savage behaviour the night before. From the beginning, Lin Hua's relationship with the major had been a difficult one. Tang A-hsi was a member of 'the new class' forged by the Cultural Revolution. He had many friends in the Culture and Propaganda Department, and regarded Lin Hua as a *zhishifenzi*, an intellectual, the ninth category of political undesirable. During the reign of Chairman Mao, Chinese intellectuals had suffered continual persecution, and though they had at last risen to a new level of prestige and status, men like Tang A-hsi continued to view them with hostility and suspicion. This, Lin Hua knew, had strongly coloured Tang A-hsi's feelings toward him, for as a member of the armed forces, the major belonged to an important élite. But there was also another reason for Tang A-hsi's contempt. Major Tang A-hsi was Han Chinese, one of the thousand million who made up the bulk of the Chinese people. Lin Hua on the other hand was a non-Han, and though he subscribed to the Han language and culture, he had been born a Tanka, a relative of the Yao tribe. The Tanka referred to themselves as the *shui-mian-ren*, meaning 'water-folk', and so integrated had they become with their neighbours that there was little in dress, appearance or tradition to choose between them, but Major Tang A-hsi, with the inflexible contentiousness of his nature, continued to regard Lin Hua as a part of a subhuman species, unworthy of consideration or interest.

Tang A-hsi had a rigid contempt for those people he regarded as inferior, and his brutality toward them went almost beyond reason. Last night, they had picked up a party of shepherds, three men in faded animal skins driving their flocks to the lower pastures. Though obvious from the beginning that the luckless captives knew nothing of the Dalai Lama's approach, Tang A-hsi had insisted on questioning them into the early hours of the morning and Lin Hua had been forced to sit in on the interrogation as interpreter.

The poor Tibetans, their innocence showing plainly on their faces, had been baffled by the major's examination and, infuriated by their lack of response, Tang A-hsi had beaten them with his pistol butt, then with a vicious ornamental riding crop, pounding their skulls and faces until the weals glowed red across their tortured flesh.

Sickened by the senselessness of it all, Lin Hua had protested vigorously, but Major Tang A-hsi had refused to listen. When his frenzied whipping failed to produce any effect, he ordered his men to batter the unfortunate prisoners with their rifles, and only after they had fallen to the ground unconscious did Tang A-hsi bring the proceedings at last to a halt. Now, in the chill glow of the early dawn, he had sent an orderly to awaken Lin Hua so he could witness the prisoners' execution.

All his life, Lin Hua had despised men like Tang A-hsi. Their lack of compassion, of simple common charity, had always baffled him. They followed the dictates of the state with an absence of emotion which made Lin Hua despair for the future of the human race.

He felt his spirits sinking as he watched the three prisoners being dragged into the centre of the plateau. After the beating, they had been tied to rocks and left outside in the biting cold. Now they were scarcely able to move. Lin Hua saw frost coating their hair and the ragged remnants of their clothing. In places, their flesh looked blackened, though whether from frostbite or the results of Tang A-hsi's beating, Lin Hua was unable to determine.

The troops clustered around the open area, their thin bodies shivering in the chill. Behind them, the morning sunlight glistened on the windows of the two massive helicopters. Lin Hua recalled grimly what had happened to the third. By an astonishing twist of fortune, they had stumbled on a party of guerrillas in an isolated valley, and the pilot, imprudently tackling them singlehanded, had been shot from the sky. Lin Hua suspected that was largely responsible for Major Tang A-hsi's excessive display of zeal. The loss of a helicopter would take some explaining to the military authorities in Peking, and Lin Hua guessed that Tang A-hsi needed a success to lessen his degree of liability. He was clearly ready to do anything to halt the Dalai Lama's approach.

Each prisoner was forced to kneel in line at the centre of the plateau, his hands tied behind him, ropes from his neck leading to soldiers standing with rifles ready and loaded at his rear. In the biting cold of the early morning, they waited in silence for Tang A-hsi to make his appearance.

A tentflap was thrust back and the major stepped into the sunlight, pausing for a moment as he breathed deeply in the thin air and rubbed his cheeks with his fingertips. He strode toward Lin Hua, his eyes blazing with a curious excitement. 'Good,' he said, 'I am glad to see you have decided to honour us with your presence. It is important, I think, for everyone to witness affairs of this nature.'

'Major Tang A-hsi,' Lin Hua said patiently, 'you are executing these men for no reason. They had done nothing. They know nothing. They are simple shepherds who did not deserve the beating you gave them last night.'

'You are such a fool, Lin Hua. I could tell the prisoners were lying by the way they evaded my questions. I am not an animal. Unnecessary pain distresses me deeply. But I never shrink from my duty. They must pay the penalty, that is the law.'

'You have already hurt them enough. All night, they have been left outside in this terrible cold. It is unlikely their damaged bodies will ever be the same again. At least let them live. What can be gained from such senseless slaughter?'

Tang A-hsi glared at him. 'I knew you were a weakling the first moment I looked at you,' he snapped. 'Your lack of resolve is an insult to the aims and struggles of the People's Revolution. Do not speak to me of these men again. Their execution will commence at once.'

With a sinking heart, Lin Hua stood in the icy stillness and listened to the rattle of the rifles being cocked.

Tracey, Ramdon and Morrill witnessed the killings from the scrub at the plateau's edge. They had climbed up through the darkness hours, reaching the rim in the first gleam of morning to discover the thin lines of troops shivering in their khaki uniforms, the squat outline of the army major waving and gesticulating angrily, the pathetic figures of the three shepherds kneeling dejectedly on the plateau floor. Then the rifles cracked on the thin dawn air, and the prisoners tumbled into the dust. The affair was chilling in its simplicity. It was hard to believe life could be dispatched with such casual lack of concern. When it was over, there was no ceremony. The corpses were dragged by their feet and dumped over the rim of the adjacent cliff. Then at a word of command, the troops began to disperse.

'My God,' Tracey breathed.

Morrill's face looked inscrutable. 'You've just witnessed the benevolent hand of the Chinese liberators. I'm glad you still have the capacity to feel shocked. I guess I've seen it too many times before.'

'What had those poor men done?' Tracey whispered.

'Probably nothing. Now we know the kind of people we're up against.'

He took out his binoculars and focused them on the helicopters ahead. Their green flanks seemed to glisten in the sunlight. Dappled fingers of frost showed plainly on their windshields. Armed guards stood beneath the overhanging rotors, their faces pinched and miserable in the bitter cold.

'We've got us a problem,' Morrill muttered. 'Those choppers are perched right out in the open. If we attempt to approach, even from the other side, they'll spot us easy.'

Ramdon rubbed his nose with his thumb. 'Why don't we use the fuel dump as cover? There's only about thirty feet between those oil-drums and the first machine.'

'Not enough. They're too well-guarded. We'll stand out like firecrackers in this sunlight.'

Morrill pushed the binoculars back into their leather case. His memories of Baima were totally forgotten. Everything that had happened was lost now in the sudden urgent need to destroy the Chinese vantage point at the head of the pass. 'What we need is a diversion,' he said. 'Something that'll grab those Chinks' attention while we get across the open ground.'

'You mean, like an explosion?'

'Right.'

Tracey peered about her. The plateau at this point was rather like a saucer resting on its side. She, Morrill and Ramdon were lying at its uppermost tip. Beneath them, the ground sloped downwards in a steep clay bank to the level area where the tents were pitched. Here, thick brush cluttered the stony earth.

'We could always build a fire,' she suggested. 'We've plenty of wood to use as fuel.'

Morrill stared at her for a moment. 'Tracey,' he said, 'that diversion is the only chance we've got of sneaking in there.'

She nodded, puzzled. 'I realise that.'

'I need Ramdon to help me handle those guards.'

Tracey felt her senses quicken as she realised what Morrill was getting at.

'Think you can gather some of the scrub together and build a good blaze behind that rock over there?'

She swallowed back her panic, nodding quickly. 'I can do it,' she promised.

'It's got to be big enough to absorb their interest. I mean all their interest, understand?'

'I tell you I can do it,' she whispered.

Morrill patted her lightly on the wrist. 'We'll circle around to the other side. As soon as you get the fire going, pull back down the slope to the valley floor. We'll meet you later at the shepherd's hut. Good luck.'

She nodded silently, her throat tight and constricted. Ramdon bent forward and she felt his lips lightly brushed her cheek. Then, with her nerves quivering, she watched them slither away.

As Lin Hua strode back to his tent, he felt his anger rising. He was not an excitable man, had never been prone to fits of temperament, but Tang A-hsi's treatment of his Tibetan prisoners had aroused Lin Hua's deepest emotions. Tang A-hsi used his power with a reckless disregard for the people around him, and it was Lin Hua's sacred duty to see that his behaviour was curtailed.

Inside the tent, Lin Hua rummaged among his things until he found what he was looking for, a scroll of writing paper and a fountain pen. He sat at the tiny camping table and began to compose his letter to the military authorities in Peking. He was halfway through the second page when the tentflap was thrust rudely aside and he glanced up to see Tang A-hsi himself standing there. The major's bulky frame shut off the sunlight, casting a shroud of shadow across his features and the bulging protuberance of his upper chest.

'What are you doing?' he demanded.

Lin Hua looked at him impassively, unintimidated by the major's harsh tone. 'My duty,' he answered.

The major ducked beneath the canvas roof, letting the tentflap fall behind him. 'What is this? A letter?'

Lin Hua nodded. 'To your superiors in Peking.'

Without a word, Tang A-hsi picked up the sheet on which Lin Hua had been writing and read it through in silence, his thick lips carefully moulding the syllables. No expression showed on his brutish face as, finishing, he tore the paper into a number of different pieces and scattered them contemptuously on the ground.

Lin Hua stared at him calmly. 'That was a pointless gesture. I shall merely write another.'

'You will write nothing,' Tang A-hsi told him in a taut voice. 'I am the officer in command here. You are my subordinate, nothing more. Decisions on what is necessary to complete my appointed task lie essentially with me.'

'Your methods are barbarous,' Lin Hua said. 'You defile the name of communism throughout the world.'

Tang A-hsi's features settled into a humourless smile. 'Are you objections political, or personal?'

'They are both,' Lin Hua answered evenly. 'I despise you as a man because you lack the qualities which distinguish man from the predatory creatures which surround him. I despise you also as a communist because your savage conduct destroys the principles of our great movement.'

Tang A-hsi's smile tightened into a grotesque grimace. 'And this you intend telling the military authorities in Peking?'

Lin Hua nodded calmly. 'Now, or later, I will tell them.'

Tang A-hsi turned and gently ran his fingertips along the ridge-pole, his face thoughtful, his lips pursed. He looked like a man in a deep introspective study.

Flicking at an imaginary fly, he said: 'You are a foolish man, Lin Hua. You are a long way from Peking. The mountains are high, the landscape desolate. Write your letter, if you will. I have a feeling you will never live to deliver it.'

*   *   *

Breathlessly, Tracey scrambled about the underbrush, selecting the driest twigs, dragging them out by the roots and piling them in an untidy heap against the leeward side of the massive boulder. She worked in a frenzy, conscious that time was vital. By now, Harry and Silas would have reached the edge of the fuel dump. The fire, she had to start the fire.

Her fingers were torn and bleeding as she ripped at the tangled branches, scarcely noticing the discomfort, conscious only of the need to hurry. Her absorption with the task in hand somehow alleviated her fear. She forgot the panic bubbling inside her and concentrated instead on building up her fuel pile. It was four feet high already. Another few inches, then she would set it ablaze and discreetly make her escape.

Tracey scarcely knew why she was doing this. As Silas said, it was not their war. Harry's maybe. He had committed himself years ago. But she and Ramdon were neutrals. And yet, the implicit faith on the faces of the young boy king and his band of lamas had moved her deeply. She had to help. She did not know why. It was something inside her. An emotion so basic, so profound, she found it impossible to ignore.

In personal terms, she had been conscious of a commitment so vague she could scarcely put a name to it, but real and tangible in its own peculiar way, drawing her toward Harry her husband, forcing her to consider the possibility of turning back, assuming again a life which even now seemed so distant in her memory it might have happened to another person. But the indecision had gone now. Seeing Ramdon again, feeling him touch her in that transitory moment of meeting outside the shepherd's hut had convinced her beyond any reasonable doubt that the allegiance she felt toward Harry was a counterfeit thing fashioned by some ill-conceived sense of ethics and duty. It was Silas she wanted. When this was over, they would escape together. She'd done her bit, everything they'd asked her. But God knew she was not about to sacrifice her future with a man she did not love. If she loved anyone at all, she loved Silas, if it were possible to love a creature so mercurial and remote. He had good points, she thought. Everyone had, even Silas, though she had to admit she'd seen precious little of them yet. Silas was a maddening contradiction of a man, impossible to pin down, impossible to ignore, but when it came to the important things, the basic things, she felt sure his heart was in the right place.

Her eyes caught a clump of brushwood which had dried in the sun and she was reaching for it, panting gently, when suddenly the earth gave way without warning beneath her. She felt the soil crumble and her foot slip, and then, before she'd had a chance to grab at something solid, she had tumbled into the open and was rolling helplessly down the steep clay bank, her arms and legs thrashing wildly. She saw the camp spring into view and an involuntary cry burst from her lips as she plunged full-length into a cluster of prickly thorn bushes. Lying on her back limbs, outspread, cheeks scratched and bleeding, she stared in horrified fascination at the troops in front of her. She was still obscured from their line of vision, but the noise of her fall had attracted their attention and the nearest soldiers were already strolling forward to investigate.

I mustn't panic, she told herself. The worst thing I can do is panic.

But she couldn't help herself. Terror, wild and paralysing, seemed to erupt inside her head, and she struggled desperately to tear herself loose from the prickly tendrils. She heard the sound of her clothing tearing, but the wicked thorn-points held stubbornly fast. With a sickening sense of dismay, she lay back and watched the Chinese slowly approaching.

Morrill and Ramdon heard the crash of Tracey's fall at almost the same moment. Ramdon caught the blur of her clothing as she plunged down the hill and vanished into the prickly shrubbery. He watched the soldiers freeze in their tracks, their heads turning toward the sound of the disturbance. Oh Christ, he thought, they'll spot her in a minute or two. She's out of sight, tucked among those bloody thorns, but if they wander over there, they'll see her easy.

Several of the Chinese had already begun to stroll in her direction and Ramdon was conscious of a strange numbness starting up inside him as if some indefinable force had threatened the most precious thing in his life.

Behind the oil-drums, the two men looked at each other. 'We've got to do something,' Ramdon hissed.

Morrill's face was drawn and tense. 'We can't distract their attention without pulling it to ourselves. If we do that, we'll have to forget the helicopters.'

'To hell with the helicopters. What about Tracey?'

Ramdon peered around the oil-drums. The nearest Chinese still had thirty or forty yards to go. A daring plan entered his mind. Maybe they could rescue Tracey and destroy the helicopters at the same time.

'Listen,' he said, 'think you can handle those guards by yourself?'

Morrill looked confused. 'Why?' he asked.

Ramdon didn't answer. Unslinging the instrument case from his shoulder, he opened it and took out the violin. Morrill watched in puzzlement as Ramdon reached down and picked up the bow.

'What are you going to do?'

Ramdon winked, his dark eyes blazing with excitement. 'I'm going to give the performance of my life,' he said.

And turning quickly, he began to scramble for the trees.

CHAPTER THIRTEEN

The noise rose on the wind and drifted across the crowded campsite, blotting out the murmur of soldiers' voices, the clatter of accoutrements, the cackle of birdsong. Inside the tent, Tang A-hsi froze as the weird strains reached his eardrums. He looked down at Lin Hua, frowning deeply. The sound was like nothing Tang A-hsi had ever heard before. He felt a coldness on his neck and a shiver run through his diaphragm. Despite his rank, Tang A-hsi was a primitive man who still experienced fear when faced with the unnatural or the unexplained.

Lin Hua had risen to his feet and was staring at him in silence, his thin cheeks suddenly pale. 'What is it?' he whispered after a moment.

Tang A-hsi shook his head. The wailing noise went on, rising and falling like the lament of some demented demon. Tang A-hsi threw back the tentflap. The entire camp had come to a halt. Everywhere, soldiers had frozen in their movements and were standing in silence, staring at the trees.

Tang A-hsi strode into the sunlight, Lin Hua scurrying along at his heels. Tang A-hsi's eyes narrowed as he scanned the bristling thicket. The sound seemed to be rising from the bushes directly in front of him. He barked an order and troops hurried forward, tearing the branches aside.

Crouched on the ground, Ramdon was playing blissfully away. His eyes were closed, his lips twisted into an enigmatic smile. He looked like a man in a state of aesthetic ecstacy, the violin clutched to his chin, his fingers dancing as the bow slid lightly over the tuneless strings.

For a moment, Tang A-hsi could only stand and stare in bewilderment. Then, with an effort, he recovered himself and bellowed a savage command. A soldier stepped forward and slapped the instrument from Ramdon's grasp. He was hauled to his feet and dragged across the plateau to where Tang A-hsi and Lin Hua were standing.

This is it, he thought grimly. It's up to you now, Silas boy. You'd better act like the whole world depended upon it.

He feigned an air of innocent surprise as he looked down at the squat Chinese major who was studying him with an expression of astonishment and rage. The major's cheeks were covered with purple blotches and Ramdon could see his facial muscles quivering as he struggled to control his temper. Beside him stood a small man in a civilian Duvet. He too was peering at Ramdon with puzzlement and amazement, but his features were gentler, and Ramdon was relieved to detect a glimmer of sympathy in his small dark eyes.

The major bellowed at him in a harsh voice. Smiling, Ramdon shook his head, shrugging his shoulders to indicate that he did not understand. The major yelled again, and flecks of saliva flew from his lips into Ramdon's face. Somebody should tell this man his breath stinks, Ramdon thought.

He could see the man was controlling his anger with a monumental effort. The soldiers crowded around them, fascinated by Ramdon's unexpected appearance. The major turned to the civilian beside him and said something in a low voice. The civilian inclined his head respectfully and addressed himself to Ramdon.

'Do you speak English?' he asked.

'I do,' Ramdon said.

'My comrade, Major Tang A-hsi, would like to know what you are doing here.'

'Playing the violin,' Ramdon answered reasonably.

A glint of humour entered Lin Hua's eyes. 'My dear friend,' he said, 'I fear if I tell him that, your chances of survival will be exceedingly slim. Major Tang A-hsi is a man of violent temper and the most barbarous disposition. He delights in ill-treating his prisoners. For your sake, I urge you most sincerely to speak as freely as you can.'

'I've witnessed some of your major's handiwork,' Ramdon said. 'He seems to enjoy killing people.'

The civilian deftly moved his eyebrows, an elegant gesture, ambiguous in meaning. 'Yes, this is what we have fashioned with our Cultural Revolution. A human tank. Under Chairman Mao, it was men like Tang A-hsi who spread chaos and strife across the length and breadth of China, preaching the glories of world revolution, burning down embassies, parading unbelievers before howling mobs of Red Guards, sweeping the country into a frenzy of panic and hatred. Emotion is as foreign to him as sympathy or compassion. He understands only two things. Fear and pain.'

'Then why don't you stop the bastard?'

'I would like to. Indeed, if I ever return to my homeland, I intend to. But I fear he plans to kill me.'

The major, who had been watching this exchange with mounting impatience, snapped something in a curt voice and the civilian, sighing, said: 'He is demanding an answer. What do you wish me to tell him?'

'Tell him exactly what I said.'

'That is most unwise, my friend.'

'Let's try and see, shall we?'

The tiny civilian translated Ramdon's statement and Ramdon watched the colour heighten in the major's cheeks. With an exclamation of fury, the major slapped Ramdon hard across the face. The blow was heavy and unexpected, and Ramdon felt pain lance into his skull as his head jerked viciously to one side.

You little yellow bastard, thought, I'll make you pay for that.

But inside, his spirits was sinking. The major was clearly not to be trifled with. The next few minutes looked like being unpleasant indeed.

Thrusting forward his chin, the major yelled at him again and Ramdon wrinkled his nostrils as he caught the rank odour

201

of the major's breath. His lips felt swollen, and the salty taste of blood trickled into his mouth.

'My dear sir,' he heard the civilian say earnestly, 'I urge you to co-operate with the utmost speed. Have no doubt that the major here intends to kill you. He is a dangerous man and completely without principle. He will beat you to death on the merest whim. At least spare yourself unnecessary pain.'

Ramdon grinned crookedly. The swelling on his mouth made his face seem distorted. None of my friends will ever believe this, he thought, Silas Ramdon playing the bloody hero. That's what women do for you. Screw up the convictions of an entire lifetime.

He was just beginning to re-focus his vision when the major, with a grunt, hit him hard in the stomach. Ramdon doubled forward, retching, and seizing his head with both hands, the major brought up his knee and smashed it into the Englishman's face. Ramdon heard the nose shatter with an audible crack. His eyes flooded with water. The front of his skull seemed to turn numb.

He tumbled to the ground and began to vomit on to the stony earth. The major stared down at him for a moment, then nodded to a waiting soldier. The man stepped forward, and raising his rifle, brought the butt down on the base of Ramdon's spine. Ramdon shrieked with pain, arching his back, clawing frantically at the hollow above his buttocks. His body felt paralysed from his hips to his knees. Dimly, he saw the soldier raising his rifle again. Jesus God, he thought, if Morrill doesn't do something soon, there won't be enough left of me to scrape off the plateau floor.

Tracey plucked desperately at the thorn branches holding her in place. She heard a tearing sound as she dragged one arm free. Panting hard, she rolled on to her side and began to loosen her hair. The wicked prickles were digging into everything. She tugged loose her shoulder and sat up, easing her hips away from the clinging tendrils. She could see the camp clearly now, the soldiers gathered in a cluster at its centre. Ramdon was on the ground, coughing and spitting into the dust. As she watched, a soldier raised his rifle and brought it down hard on Ramdon's spine. Tracey shuddered.

With a deep breath, she gave one final tug and dragged

herself free, then scrambling sideways, she ducked behind the thorn bush and flattened herself against the earth. Her position was only marginally better. She was concealed from the camp but she still could not move. There was no cover within scrambling distance, and any attempt to climb the bank behind her would be suicidal. As she lay speculating, she heard a series of dull thudding noises drifting toward her from the central encampment. With a chill of horror, she realised what the noises were. The soldiers were beating Ramdon.

Tears sprang to her eyes and she felt the muscles knotting in her chest. My God, they're killing him, she thought. Why doesn't Harry do something?

Fifty yards away, Harry Morrill heard the beating too. His shrewd eyes studied the knot of soldiers intently. Their entire attention was absorbed by Ramdon crouching foetus-like on the dusty earth, the blows raining savagely down on him from the men above. Even the helicopter guards were drawn by the spectacle. Now, only one sentry stood between Morrill and the nearest aircraft.

Morrill's features hardened. He reached down and undid the nylon cord at his waist. Wrapping it around his fists, he stretched it taut in front of him in the manner of the classic garrotte, then rising from his crouch, he left the fuel dump and began to scramble across the open ground. He was, he knew, fully exposed, and if one of the Chinese had chosen that moment to glance casually in his direction, he would have been instantly discovered. But the soldiers were too engrossed with Ramdon to notice what was happening elsewhere.

Morrill's moment of enlightenment with Chamdo had wrought in him a strange diffusion of purpose; the revelation had been startling in its import, and for a brief period he had been like a man whose emotional structure had been irreparably fractured, but the madness had passed. His meeting with the Dalai Lama had produced a new focal point, giving him a strength and resolution he had seldom experienced before. Even the memory of Baima was forgotten. His brain was cool, his senses sharp as, breathlessly, he watched the sentry's slender frame swaying steadily closer. Fifteen feet, ten, five. He waited until he was directly behind the man's back, then in one vicious motion, looped the cord around the soldier's throat and jerked it tight, feeling a sudden twitching as his victim's musculature went into a defensive spasm. He stabbed his knee expertly into the base of the man's spine as he tightened his grip coldly and savagely around the helpless neck. The soldier's rifle clattered to the ground and his hands clawed at the cord biting into his windpipe. Morrill eased him back, increasing his pressure, ignoring the convulsions racking the man's helpless frame.

Thirty seconds later, Morrill undid the cord from the motionless corpse and doubled back the way he had come. He selected a heavy oil-drum and, tipping it on its side, began to roll it toward the nearest helicopter. He was careful not to look at the commotion in the centre of the encampment. He was too exposed, too naked here in the open. If he glimpsed the soldiers, his nerve might go.

The Chinese were still beating Ramdon mercilessly. If the Englishman was still alive, it would be a miracle.

Reaching the first of the helicopters, Morrill unscrewed the oil-drum lid and began to pour its contents beneath the bulbous hull. The fuel soaked into the ground, spreading a rapidly-widening patch across the stony earth. When the drum was half-empty, Morrill lifted it up and splashed some of the fuel across the lower portion of the fuselage. He moved as quickly as he dared, panting with exertion. There were still no shouts of alarm or discovery. The bastards were too preoccupied with what they were doing to Ramdon. And making a bloody good job of it too. Poor bastard, Morrill thought. It didn't matter how he had felt about the man. Their past differences were over and forgotten. Now Ramdon was an ally. They were part of a team.

Morrill satisfied himself the helicopter was well and truly dowsed, and was about to drag the oil-drum across the open ground to the second machine when he realised with a start the Chinese had turned in his direction. Jesus Christ, he thought, what was happening?

He ducked back behind the aircraft wheels, pressing himself against the fuselage, and peered gingerly around the edge. A chill ran through his stomach. They were coming his way. The major, Ramdon, the whole bloody kit-and-caboodle, making for the helicopters.

The realisation chilled him. Crouched behind the fuselage, he knew there was no question of retreating to the fuel dump. If he left the protection of his flimsy cover, he would be spotted instantly.

With a sinking heart, Morrill realised he was trapped.

Ramdon's body was a screaming shell of pain. His left eye was closing fast and his smashed nose had swollen to twice its normal size, making the front of his skull seem curiously out of proportion. A strange dampness chilled his skin and he knew the wound had opened up in his side, sending blood seeping steadily into his lap. Trapped as he was on the flat stony ground, he could do little more than cover the gash with his elbow.

Throughout the battering, he had struggled mightily to protect his groin and kidneys, breathing through his mouth, the iciness of his fear chilling all sensation until the blows which rained upon him seemed strangely remote, almost detached from his consciousness. Only when rough hands seized his shoulders and dragged him to his feet did his senses merge into reality.

I'm dying, he thought. I must be.

Through a hazy blur, he saw the army major and the little civilian arguing heatedly. He guessed he was the subject of their discussion and his lips twisted into a painful grin. Whoever the little man was, Ramdon had found himself a friend.

He tried to stand straight but his legs seemed incapable of bearing his weight and he knew that without the soldiers to support him, he would tumble into the dust.

It had been quite an education, his first taste of Chinese hospitality on the losing side. 'I told you so,' Morrill would say in his sanctimonious way. Well, the major wasn't typical, Ramdon thought. He had met plenty of others, and they weren't the same, not by a long shot. 'A battering ram', the civilian called him. He, Ramdon, could testify to that.

The major gave an angry snarl, and turning his back on his argumentative colleague, barked out a rapid series of instructions. Ramdon felt himself being propelled toward the nearest helicopter. The civilian scrambled along at his side. 'I am sorry,' the man said. 'I warned you about the major. He refuses to listen to reason.'

Ramdon struggled to speak, but his swollen lips refused to form the words. He tried again, and in a hoarse, curiously unreal voice, stuttered: 'What's the bastard got in mind for me?'

'Decapitation,' the small man said. 'It amuses him to devise novel methods of killing. It is his version of finesse.'

The soldiers drew to a halt at the helicopter door and Ramdon felt his arms being strapped tightly behind him. The movement hurt, and pain lanced through his battered body. For a moment, he thought he was going to pass out, but with a conscious effort of will forced himself to remain awake. Baffled, he watched the helicopter pilot clamber through the fuselage hatch.

With a roar, the engines started. Ramdon waited with the others, blinking uncertainly. Nothing seemed real any more. The whole world had split into a series of fractured images. He saw the helicopter's side vibrating fiercely, he saw the major's face flushed and bloated, he saw the diminutive civilian, pale with disgust, watching anxiously from the sidelines.

Ramdon wanted to vomit, but he knew there was nothing left in his stomach. He'd done all that, back at the parade ground. They'd kicked it out of him, reduced him to a skulking bundle of fear and pain.

Well, he hadn't shown them how he felt, he thought. They'd got no satisfaction on that score. He'd hidden it well, bottled it up inside his skull. Spat in their eye, in the happy proverbial phrase. Trouble was, he knew he couldn't keep it up much longer.

Above his head, the massive rotors began to revolve. Numbly, Ramdon watched them gather speed. Soon they were spinning around in a dizzy blur. The civilian seized his arm, his face tense and earnest. 'This is your last chance, my friend. I beg you to relent. Tell the major what he wishes to know. At least it may gain you a brief respite.'

Ramdon struggled to smile, but the result was not entirely successful. His face had swollen to such an extent, he was no longer capable of controlling his own expressions. He did not trouble to reply. He could think of nothing to say.

At a signal from the major, he felt the soldiers slowly raising him upward and, in that blinding moment of awareness, he suddenly guessed their intention. Bastards. They were going to lift him inch by inch until the massive rotor blades sliced his skull cleanly from his body. It seemed a messy and undignified way to go. Not the way he would have chosen, he thought. He had never expected a peaceful death – a plane-crash maybe, a desperate dive into some snowstorm – but losing his head in such a ludicrous fashion carried an element of vulgarity and farce.

Surprisingly, he felt no sense of terror or alarm. The beating had created a curious soporific effort within him, until he was like a man on the brink of a coma. Only his pain was real.

He could feel the downblast from the rotors pounding the top of his skull and his hair danced crazily in the wind. The slipstream scoured his face and cheeks, making it difficult to breathe. He was almost level with the blades now, an inch or two from obliteration. He closed his eyes, gritting his teeth, waiting with a curious and fatalistic detachment for the final moment.

And then, at the very point of contact, the remaining helicopter burst into flame with a thunderous roar.

Tracey saw the soldiers drop Ramdon to the ground, and a sob of relief emerged from her throat. They had almost killed him, probably would have if Harry hadn't acted so promptly.

The Chinese were milling about in confusion, their frenzied faces flickering in the glow of the fire. The helicopter was blazing fiercely now, tongues of crimson and black licking out of its porthole windows. A thick pall of heavy smoke drifted across the campsite, blotting out the onlookers, swirling over the rows of fluttering tents.

With wild cries, soldiers ran to fetch water from the nearby spring. Others tried to smother the flames with handfuls of scooped-up dust.

Tracey rose from behind the thorn-bush and darted in through the eddying smoke. Men were scrambling everywhere, jostling and bumping each other drunkenly. She dodged and twisted through their ranks, tears streaming down her cheeks. Reaching Ramdon's side, she fell to her knees. His battered face peered up at her, the eyes glittering fiercely. He tried to grin, but his mouth was so swollen the smile looked grotesque.

'Undo my arms,' he croaked, rolling on to his hip.

Sobbing Tracey tore at the bonds binding his wrists. 'What have they done to you?' she choked.

'Never mind that. Just get me untied.'

'Where's Harry?'

'Up there in the smoke someplace.'

'Oh Silas, I was sure they'd killed you.'

Ramdon grunted. 'Don't celebrate too early. I'm not at all sure they haven't.'

She could scarcely see the knots, the way the tears were flooding her eyes. Desperately, she fumbled with the tight, ungiving bonds, and at that moment a figure materialised through the smoke above her. With a start of horror, she realised it was the Chinese major. His plump cheeks were blackened and dishevelled, his eyes dazed. For a moment, he stood peering down at her, then his lips began to writhe like angry snakes as he tore at the pistol on his belt.

My God, he's going to shoot me, she thought.

'Run,' Silas snapped. 'Run, you fool!'

But Tracey couldn't move. Her brain seemed paralysed. The major pulled the revolver free and pointed it at her forehead, gripping his firing wrist with his free hand. She crouched back on her knees, terror flooding her chest. Then, through the billowing smoke, a second figure emerged.

Harry.

She saw his beard fluttering fiercely in the wind, his lean face glistening in the glow from the blazing fuselage.

In one deft motion, she watched him whip a strip of cord across the major's throat, jerking it tight. A terrible gurgling sound emerged from the major's lips, and the revolver dropped from his grasp as he clawed frenziedly at the deadly noose around his neck, his boots drumming the earth in a desperate tattoo.

'Hurry,' Ramdon gasped, 'for Christ's sake, hurry.'

Whimpering, Tracey tore at the last of Ramdon's bonds, tugging them free. He sat up, rubbing his wrists ruefully, stretching his fingers.

'How does it feel?' she asked.

'Pins and needles,' he told her.

He squinted through the eddying smoke. 'Help me into the helicopter, quick.'

She hesitated. 'You know how to fly that thing?'

'Bloody right. It's the Chinese equivalent of the Sikorsky S55. I used to fly the rice run out of New Delhi.'

She took Ramdon's arm, hooking it over her neck, feeling his weight sag heavily against her as they ducked beneath the spinning rotors and stumbled toward the fuselage hatch. Ramdon was wincing with pain. When they reached the opening, he seemed unable to clamber inside. She tried to help him, wrapping her arms around his hips, but he doubled forward, coughing helplessly, blood from his face streaming down the neck of his open shirt.

Someone bundled her aside and she saw Morrill, his eyes watering from the smoke, grip Ramdon around the top of his thighs and shove him bodily across the flight deck. He followed swiftly, leaving Tracey to help herself.

The pilot was still sitting in the cockpit. He stared up at Morrill with terrified disbelief as the American appeared behind his seat. Without a word, Morrill hit him hard between the eyes. The man jerked back against the plexiglass windshield, blood streaming from his nostrils. His eyes looked dazed and strangely out-of-focus.

Seizing him by the shirtfront, Morrill dragged him from the cockpit and hurled him bodily through the open hatch. Painfully, Ramdon squeezed into the pilot's seat, checking the controls.

'Can we get this airborne?' Morrill yelled at him.

'Sure we can. Just hang on.'

Tracey felt the machine vibrating beneath her feet. Pipes ran along the interior of the metal shell and she hooked one arm around them, gasping desperately at the air. Everything seemed to be happening at once. She was wheezing badly, her lungs choked with fumes.

A shot rang out, and the bullet chipped the outer fuselage. Through the swirling fog, Tracey saw the soldiers running toward them. 'They've spotted us,' she yelled.

'Christ,' Morrill snapped.

He slung the machine-gun from his shoulder and switched the lever to 'fire'. He squeezed the trigger, but nothing happened. The ammunition clip was empty. She heard him curse again.

The machine lifted gently, hovering above the ground. Two of the troops leapt upwards, hooking their arms across the flight deck rim, tilting the massive craft over to the side. Ramdon, at the controls, struggled to keep them upright, but the machine weaved backwards and forwards alarmingly.

With a roar, Morrill left his stance and brought the butt of his machine gun down on the knuckles of the nearest man. Tracey watched in horror as the soldier lost his grip and plummetted earthwards, turning a graceful somersault before thudding like a sack of sand into the grass on the plateau summit.

'Give me a hand here,' Morrill yelled.

Tracey scuttled across to join him, her senses reeling. Morrill was trying to prise open the fingers of the second man. She leaned through the hatch, holding on to the rim, driving her heel downwards on the soldier's unprotected wrist. At the last second, he shifted his grip and she felt his fingers clutching her ankle.

'Harry,' she screamed as in one breathless motion she was dragged bodily through the open doorway. Morrill dropped his machine-gun and grabbed her wrists, jamming his shoulder against the fuselage wall.

A shuddering jar ran through Tracey's entire body and panic seemed to explode inside her as she realised she was dangling helplessly, Morrill gripping her from above, the solider hanging to her ankle below. The helicopter bucked and lurched like a wild thing. She could see Morrill's face, his lips stretched tight in a grimace of strain and exertion. He'll never hang on, she thought. He'll never hold the two of us up here. Sooner or later, he'll have to let go, then we'll tumble earthwards like a pair of graceless vultures.

The weight on her ankle seemed immense. She felt the entire leg was being ripped from its socket. For some reason, she dared not look down, but kept her gaze fixed firmly on the undercarriage above her, as if only the glimpse of that tiny platform could offer any semblance of stability and succour.

'Kick ... the bastard ... free,' she heard Morrill hiss through taut lips.

Numbly, she jabbed at the Chinaman's hands with her other foot, but he held on grimly and she knew he was just as terrified as she was.

The helicopter was careering drunkenly from side to side and she heard the crackle of shots from the ground below, the thin silk-like swish of incoming bullets streaking the air above her head.

'What the hell is going on back there?' Ramdon screamed from the cockpit.

'It's Tracey,' Morrill yelled, 'they've pulled her through the hatchway!'

'Is she okay?'

'There's some bastard hanging on to her ankle.'

Ramdon's lips worked furiously as he swore. He could scarcely see through his swollen eyes, and his fists, gripping the controls, vibrated rhythmically as he battled to keep the helicopter aloft.

'Think you can hold her if I try to prise him loose?' he shouted.

'Won't that be dangerous?'

'Not half as dangerous as carrying on the way we're doing. Any minute now, those Chinese are going to blast us out of the sky.'

'Okay,' Morrill bellowed, 'do what you can.'

To Tracey, he called: 'Hold on tight. Ramdon's going to try and shake him off.'

She felt her senses freeze as Ramdon dipped the machine, tilting it earthwards in a crazy arc. 'Make sure he doesn't take me with him,' she hollered.

'Just hang on. Here we go.'

The helicopter swooped and Tracey felt her body tilt with the sudden shift in momentum, felt the soldier below tighten his grip, his fingers digging into the hard gristle around her ankle bone, felt the air battering her face, bringing the tears to her eyes as she struggled desperately to breathe in the buffeting slipstream, and then, with a start of horror and disbelief, she glimpsed the tip of a solitary tree zooming swiftly up to meet them.

'Harry,' she yelled, 'Harry!'

'Shut up,' he gritted. 'Save your wind.'

'Harry . . .'

But Harry wasn't listening, nobody was listening, not even the soldier clinging so miserably to her ankle, because he had seen it too, he had felt the same blinding explosion of terror and alarm watching the treetop rising, expanding, thickening, taking on form and substance, its branches reaching toward them, and then, at the last possible second, just as she'd closed her eyes unable to watch any longer, Ramdon lifted the helicopter in a delicate arc, skimming the very tip of the leafy foliage, and she heard a massive thud as the Chinese soldier drove headlong into the knarled trunk, felt his grip loosen on her ankle, felt her body swinging wildly, uncontrollably as, gasping, Morrill dragged her over the rim and on to the flight-deck floor.

The helicopter lifted and for a fractional moment seemed to bob gently on the air currents, then with a thunderous roar, it soared into the sky and she watched the troops, the tents, the blazing inferno of the second aircraft diminishing rapidly beneath them.

'Thank God,' she breathed as she sprawled, drained and exhausted, on the metal floor. 'Thank God.'

Her arms were aching where Morrill had held her and her leg felt numb from the hip down. Scarlet weals showed on her wrists, the mark of Morrill's fingers. She remembered the force of the tree's impact, tearing the soldier from his grasp. It had been a miracle. She felt the tears coming again and choked them back, peering at the others. They looked like creatures from a different universe, their clothes tattered, their faces blackened with smoke, their hair wild and unkempt. Above the roar of the rotor blades, Tracey could hear Ramdon singing. His words sounded cracked and distorted as they issued between his swollen lips.

'Look,' he said suddenly, pointing downwards through the plexiglass windshield.

They stared out over the twisting labyrinth of valleys and ridges. The mountains glimmered in the sun. Tracey saw snow-capped peaks, silver rivers, craggy hillslopes glowing with a pinkish sheen on the early morning. She felt a sudden tightening in her stomach. There were people down there, *hundreds* of people. From every corner, long columns of shifting humanity followed the tracks over the high-altitude passes. It was like watching ants on the move. The hills seemed alive with tiny figures, all converging on the valley mouth.

'The people of the mountains,' Morrill said. 'They're going to meet the Dalai Lama.'

'But how could they possibly know?'

Morrill's blackened lips tightened into a grin. 'They know,' he told her. 'Don't ask me how, but they know all right.'

'That's an army down there,' Ramdon yelled. 'The Chinese will never stop him now.'

Morrill nodded thoughtfully. The smile had left his lips. He looked not sad exactly, but oddly reflective.

'What does it mean?' Tracey whispered.

'War. What you see here is only the beginning. When the Dalai Lama reaches the high plain, the people will flock to him in their thousands.'

'But the Chinese . . .'

'I have a feeling the Chinese are already too late. Look at those figures down there. The word is out. Either the Chinese let the Dalai Lama through, or they'll have a revolution on their hands.'

Tracey stared fascinated at the converging columns of people. It was as if the mountains themselves had suddenly taken life.

She felt Morrill's hand close upon her own, gently squeezing her fingers. To Ramdon, he said: 'You've got to put me down.'

'What for, squire?'

'If there's fighting, I'll be needed.'

'I thought you were all set to go back to Washington?'

'I was wrong. Put me down, for Christ's sake.'

'Okay, hold on to your hat. I'll find a suitable landing spot.'

Morrill turned to Tracey, his face pale and serious. It was not the face she remembered as a girl. He had changed a lot since then. She liked him better now, she decided. He was stronger, cooler. In different circumstances, she might even have loved him, but she doubted it, for beneath that outer aura of intimacy, he was still a stranger.

'This is where I belong,' he told her. 'You understand that, don't you?'

She nodded in silence. His eyes looked extraordinarily gentle. Strange, she had never noticed before now how long his lashes were. She saw the gleam of his teeth between his parted lips.

'Those things I said, I mean them all. But I realise now that isn't enough. Wanting something doesn't mean that it's yours by right. I'm not a fool, I've seen the way you look at Ramdon. If you went back with me now, you'd regret if for the rest of your life. For Christ's sake, I'd regret it myself. I'd never be able to forget that I'd run out, deserted these people in their moment of need. I've got to stay. I've fought too long, dreamed too hard. We may be on the brink of a new Tibet. My place is here.'

Ramdon found a level place on the valley floor and gently lowered the shuddering aircraft. He hovered for a moment several feet above the ground as he carefully checked the area around them, then he settled the wheels gently down on the stony earth.

Morrill stepped forward and kissed Tracey lightly on the mouth. She felt his body pressing against her, then he let her go. Turning, he patted Ramdon on the shoulder. 'So long, Englishman. Be good to her, you hear?'

Ramdon grinned up at him, his swollen face bloody and grotesque.

'Good luck, squire. We'll be listening for you on the newscasts.'

Shouldering his machine-gun, Morrill leapt to the ground and ducked under the whirring rotor blades. Ramdon worked the controls and, gracefully, the helicopter rose into the air. Staring through the hatchway, Tracey watched Morrill's slender figure diminishing rapidly on the earth below. In less than a minute, she could see him no more. She felt no sense of pain or loss. He belonged here in a way she never could. It was his world, and though she had shared with him that brief coalescence of the sexes, it had been too perfunctory, too distant, too casual and remote to have any meaning for her now.

It was Ramdon she cared about. Poor bruised battered Ramdon. She looked at him fondly as he swung the 'copter southward, curving high above the valley mouth.

'How are we for fuel?' she shouted.

'We've got enough to get us as far as the monastery. After that, we'll have to hoof it out, I'm afraid. Not in any particular hurry, are you?'

She shook her head, smiling. He was hardly everyone's idea of a dream man, particularly now with his face smashed and swollen. But that was the strangest thing about human emotions. You could go through life making all the right moves, and at the moment you least expected it, somebody like Silas Ramdon would come along and knock your perspective all askew.

'Tracey,' he said, 'can I ask you something?'

'Go ahead.'

He leaned forward, checking the row of dials in front of him. She watched his fists tighten on the controls, his knuckles showing white through the skin. He seemed nervous and ill-at-ease.

'What's wrong?' she muttered.

214

'I guess I'm not terribly good at this sort of thing.'

'Try,' she prompted.

He hesitated. 'Well . . . I realise I'm hardly what you might call an elegant man . . . in fact, I know damned well a lot of people regard me as crazy, but . . .'

He broke off, swearing under his breath. 'This isn't going too well, is it?'

Gently, she massaged his shoulders. 'Why don't you just go ahead and ask your question,' she whispered. 'You might be surprised at the answer.'

'You really mean that?'

She smiled at him affectionately. 'Of course I mean it.'

He steeled himself, taking a deep breath. 'Do you think you could get me on television, playing my violin?'

With a cry of exasperation, Tracey grabbed the cushion from the co-pilot's seat, and clutching it in both fists, began pounding him furiously over the head.

It was raining as Waldo Friedman, special envoy for the US State Department, entered the courtyard of the Chaumont Palace in Paris. The gendarmes' capes glistened wetly, and the turreted roofs looked strangely dour in the morning downpour.

Waldo's spirits were low, and had been ever since his arrival at Charles de Gaulle airport the evening before. He had spent his entire life working for the US government in Washington and had been called upon, at various times, to carry out tasks he would not voluntarily have chosen, but never in his recollection had his duty weighed so heavily on his conscience.

He knew the Secretary had been wrong to leak the Tibetan satellite pictures to the Chinese authorities in Peking, terribly wrong. Such a move had been in direct conflict with the principles of the Constitution. The Tibetan people wanted nothing more than their freedom, and in the interests of expediency – the science and technology agreement – the US had denied them that. It was unjust, immoral, and he wished to God he'd had no part of it. But he was an instrument, nothing more. The major decisions belonged with other people. Like everyone else, Waldo simply followed orders.

He felt strangely subdued as he registered at the Palace security desk, climbed the marble staircase and made his way toward the conference room. He had almost reached it when

Emile Le Gras, the Palace supervisor, called him into his office. For a moment, Waldo had the wild idea the Chinese once again had failed to materialise, but Le Gras' first words dashed his hopes immediately.

'They're waiting for you,' he said. 'The translators are miked up and ready.'

'Well, I guess we'd better get started,' Waldo sighed.

'One moment please. We have a phone call from your office in Washington. I thought you might like to take it in here.'

Waldo nodded dumbly. He reached out, accepting the receiver from Le Gras' hand. 'Hello?' he said.

There was a burst of static, then the voice of Jack Hirsch, Waldo's department head, broke through loud and clear. 'That you, Waldo?'

Waldo's senses came instantly alert. Hirsch's voice was at least an octave higher than usual, its timbre tense and strained.

'Is something wrong, Jack?'

'Waldo, I want you to turn around and walk right out of there. Check out of your hotel and catch the next plane back to Washington, is that understood?'

Waldo frowned. 'What's up, Jack? I'm just about to meet the Chinese delegation now.'

'Stay out,' Hirsch snapped. 'You hear me, Waldo? I don't want you having any contact with those people. The agreement is off, got that? Off.'

'Jack, you're not making any sense.'

There was a pause at the end of the line, then Hirsch said: 'We've just had word the new Dalai Lama has broken through to the high Tibetan plain. The people are thronging to meet him in their thousands. It looks like exploding into a full-scale revolution.'

'Christ,' Waldo murmured.

'We can't afford to be seen signing co-operation treaties with the Chinese at this particular moment, Waldo. The Secretary is about to make a fresh call for Tibetan autonomy at the United Nations. He'll be demanding the Chinese withdraw to the original frontier and leave the Tibetan people to conduct their affairs in peace. We believe the Chinese will capitulate. Naturally, we don't want anything getting in the way of that.'

Waldo was silent for a long moment. He took a deep breath. 'I understand,' he said softly. 'I'll catch the next flight out.'

Gently, he replaced the receiver and looked at Le Gras. 'Better tell our Chinese friends I shan't be joining them this morning, Emile.'

'What?' Le Gras stammered. 'What are you saying, M'sieur Friedman?'

'Instructions from my government. I am to return to Washington immediately. I'm afraid the authorities in Peking are about to learn that boycotting negotiations is not an exclusively eastern pastime.'

Leaving Le Gras spluttering helplessly, Waldo tugged on his coat and made his way down the broad marble staircase.

He was whistling jauntily as he hailed a taxi at the courtyard door.

His latest bestseller…

CYCLOPS

CLIVE CUSSLER

Dirk Pitt didn't go looking for adventure. It found him easily enough. His chance witnessing of an airship disaster and gruesome discovery of the fate of the crew set in motion the most nail-biting chain of events of his career.

But it was when he found his trail leading towards a fabulous treasure hidden fathoms deep in the murky depths of the ocean that he realised he was onto something very special indeed. For somewhere in the raging waters lay the legendary lost lady of El Dorado, the golden prize that had already lured thousands to their graves…

0 7221 2756 1   ADVENTURE THRILLER   £3.50

Also by Clive Cussler in Sphere Books:
Mayday!
Vixen 03
Iceberg
Night Probe!
Raise the Titanic!
Pacific Vortex!
Deep Six

CONQUISTADORES

BOB LANGLEY

MAN OF LEGEND . . .

Killing meant little to Segunda. As a boy he had hunted the predators that roamed his father's *estancia* in the Argentine: as a man he hunted people.

With the outbreak of war in the South Atlantic, Segunda's skills became invaluable, for even against the best-trained army in the world, a lot of damage could be done with fourteen inches of razor-sharp steel . . .

ADVENTURE THRILLER   0 7221 5379 1   £2.50

A selection of bestsellers from Sphere

FICTION

BIRTHRIGHT	Joseph Amiel	£3.50 ☐
TALES OF THE WOLF	Lawrence Sanders	£2.50 ☐
MALIBU SUMMER	Stuart Buchan	£2.95 ☐
THE SECRETS OF HARRY BRIGHT	Joseph Wambaugh	£2.95 ☐
CYCLOPS	Clive Cussler	£3.50 ☐

FILM AND TV TIE-IN

INTIMATE CONTACT	Jacqueline Osborne	£2.50 ☐
BEST OF BRITISH	Maurice Sellar	£8.95 ☐
SEX WITH PAULA YATES	Paula Yates	£2.95 ☐
RAW DEAL	Walter Wager	£2.50 ☐

NON-FICTION

SOLDIERS	John Keegan & Richard Holmes	£5.95 ☐
URI GELLER'S FORTUNE SECRETS	Uri Geller	£2.50 ☐
A TASTE OF LIFE	Julie Stafford	£3.50 ☐
HOLLYWOOD A' GO-GO	Andrew Yule	£3.50 ☐
THE OXFORD CHILDREN'S THESAURUS		£3.95 ☐

All Sphere books are available at your local bookshop or newsagent, or can be ordered direct from the publisher. Just tick the titles you want and fill in the form below.

Name _____

Address _____

_____

Write to Sphere Books, Cash Sales Department, P.O. Box 11, Falmouth, Cornwall TR10 9EN

Please enclose a cheque or postal order to the value of the cover price plus:

UK: 60p for the first book, 25p for the second book and 15p for each additional book ordered to a maximum chrge of £1.90.

OVERSEAS & EIRE: £1.25 for the first book, 75p for the second book and 28p for each subsequent title ordered.

BFPO: 60p for the first book, 25p for the second book plus 15p per copy for the next 7 books, thereafter 9p per book.

Sphere Books reserve the right to show new retail prices on covers which may differ from those previously advertised in the text elsewhere, and to increase postal rates in accordance with the P.O.